## *"Are you going*

The little boy's whispered question jolted Nina, then settled like a knife in her heart. For so long she'd wanted to be a mother, to love and be loved unconditionally. A few more years, and the possibility would fade—like so many other dreams.

How should she answer him? It would be cruel to hold out a promise and then snatch it away when it was time for her to leave.

"I'm just visiting," she said, trying to sound upbeat. She waited for a response. He merely stared at her. "Your father asked me to come and help you learn English. Would you like that?"

Longing filled his sad blue eyes. *"Da Pozhaluista."* Yes, please.

With her heart pounding, she knelt beside Sasha and squeezed his shoulder. Then she looked at the boy's father.

"I'll take the job," she said in English.

# Available in October 2006
# from Silhouette Superromance

# Family at Last

## KN CASPER

SILHOUETTE®
*Super*ROMANCE™

First published in Great Britain 2006
Silhouette Books, Eton House, 18-24 Paradise Road,
Richmond, Surrey TW9 1SR

© Kenneth Casper 2005

Standard ISBN: 0 373 78037 0
Promotional ISBN: 0 373 60495 5

38-1006

Printed and bound in Spain
by Litografia Rosés S.A., Barcelona

Dear Reader,

We all like stories about heroes, about brave acts that result in happily-ever-after outcomes, about those bigger-than-life characters out to save the world. Sometimes we forget that ordinary people can be heroes, too, and that ordinary actions can be heroic.

Take, for instance, people who adopt children. They extend compassion and hope to the most precious and most vulnerable members of our society. Ordinary people with an extraordinary capacity to love.

The story that follows is about one of those heroes, an aging bachelor who has security and comfort but wants more. He tells the heroine that adopting a young orphan is the best thing he's ever done. And it's true—for him and for the millions of people who adopt neglected and unwanted children.

I hope you find inspiration in this story of love and challenge. I certainly enjoyed writing it. Maybe because I have this tremendous admiration for genuine heroes.

I enjoy hearing from readers. You can write to me at PO Box 61511, San Angelo, TX 76906. USA. Please also visit my website at www.kncasper.com

*KN Casper*

This is for Pavel Soika.
May the wind be always at your back,
and the horizon always bright.

My special thanks to Helmut Soika,
who generously shared his inspirational
story and inspired me.

My sincere appreciation to Laurie White and
Nina Gettler, for their invaluable assistance with
the Russian elements of this book.
Any errors are solely mine.

And a very warm tribute to Vera Koth,
my first critique partner and a continuing
source of inspiration. She's been a part of
every story I write, and she always will be.

## *PROLOGUE*

"IT'S SASHA AGAIN. THIS time he's curled up in a fetal position under his desk and won't come out."

"Is he hurt?"

"Physically he's fine," the woman assured him. "Mr. Morrison, we've discussed this before. These constant disruptions in the classroom—"

"I'll be right there."

He didn't want to hear another appeal from the principal that he remove his son from the public school and enroll him in a private institution for kids with special needs. Her advice might be sound, but transferring him wasn't that easy.

Six minutes later Jarrod pulled into the parking lot of Misty Hollow Elementary. Mrs. Keller was waiting for him at the door.

"What happened?" he asked, not breaking stride.

"He stole food from the cafeteria."

They arrived at the classroom. Through the wire-gridded window in the upper half of the door Jarrod saw a young teacher he didn't recognize, standing near the whiteboard. She was facing a semicircle of desks, all but one of which were occupied by rosy-cheeked first graders. At the far end of the crescent, curled up on the floor, was his son. Sasha's eyes were closed, his right thumb in his mouth. He lay absolutely motionless, but Jarrod knew he wasn't asleep.

He placed his hand on the door handle.

"Mr. Morrison—" the principal started.

"Not now."

He entered the bright, colorful room. Posters decorated the walls, and a large corkboard was festooned with childish crayon drawings: stick figures, smiling dogs, lopsided flowers and precariously tilted houses.

Sasha looked up warily. Jarrod saw a spark of hope, of relief, as well as a plea for deliverance. This poor little boy that nobody wanted was depending on him to make things better.

He stepped over to the empty desk and murmured the child's name as he extended his hands. Sasha didn't immediately move.

Jarrod wasn't surprised to see that the pale blue eyes staring up at him were completely dry. In the six weeks Sasha had been home, he'd never once cried. Not with joy. Not with sorrow. Not even with anger or frustration, and there had been plenty of provocation.

Taking his time, Jarrod sat on the undersize chair, softly repeated Sasha's name and made a beckoning motion with his hands. Several more seconds passed before the boy removed his thumb from his mouth and crawled silently onto his lap. He didn't put his arms around Jarrod, didn't hug him, just burrowed against him, his small body reverting to the fetal position.

Jarrod stroked the little arm and whispered words of comfort, words he knew the boy understood by tone rather than meaning. *No one will hurt you. I won't let them. You're safe now.* The room around them remained a silent tableau.

Jarrod looked up at the teacher. "Tell me what happened." He kept his tone pleasant, because he didn't want to alarm the child in his arms.

"Sasha…"

The boy tensed.

"Don't use his name. Just say 'he.' I'll know who you're talking about."

She looked puzzled, but finally nodded. After instructing the rest of the class to continue working, she lowered her voice. "We'd just returned from lunch in the cafeteria. He had two rolls tucked under his shirt, and the other children started teasing him."

"What did you do?"

Her amber eyes shied away. "I didn't want him eating in class. I put them on my desk and planned to return them later."

What harm would it have done to let him hang on to a couple of pieces of bread? It took self-control for Jarrod to stay relaxed. He hoped the pounding of his heart didn't scare the boy.

"Did he object?"

"He started to hold back, but then he gave them to me."

Jarrod swallowed the observation that she was bigger than Sasha, that she represented authority and that in his world he was helpless to oppose it. "Go on."

"The children started telling me about other things he'd done, like going through the trash and taking things. I was asked to fill in at the last minute this morning. Mrs. Keller told me he lacked language skills, but not that he was so…socially backward." She glanced at the principal, then quickly averted her eyes. "Everybody wanted to talk about him…"

"You are aware, Ms.—"

"Alicia Peters."

"Ms. Peters. While he doesn't understand English, he is able to recognize his own name?"

"Mr. Morrison—" Mrs. Keller interjected, as if to defend the teacher.

"He comes from a different culture," Jarrod continued, "one where food and other essentials are in short supply. In addition, he's shy and withdrawn. That doesn't make him stupid. He heard everyone repeating his name over and over again, so he knew you were talking about him…making fun of him."

"I'm sorry," Ms. Peters said. "I didn't mean to upset him so…" Jarrod continued to stroke the boy's arm and found doing so strangely relaxing. What these people didn't understand—although he'd told them quite clearly—was that Sasha had been raised in an orphanage that was right out of the nineteenth century.

With murmured encouragement Jarrod gently set the boy on his feet, rose from the chair and clasped his warm hand.

"His learning experience for today is over. I'm taking him home." He turned to the flustered substitute teacher. "He'll be back in the morning."

She and the principal stood by with matching frowns as he led the boy from the room. Sasha held his hand, not tightly, but with enough pressure to let Jarrod know he was grateful for being rescued.

They walked to the car in silence, not because Jarrod didn't have anything to say—he wanted very much to assure his son he'd done nothing wrong and that no one was angry with him. But language was still a major obstacle.

# *CHAPTER ONE*

THE MAN'S DEEP VOICE WAS SOFTENED BY just enough of a Southern drawl to be charming, without making him sound like a hick or a con man. Not much small talk, though. He was eager to get down to business, and that suited Nina just fine. She wasn't looking for a friend, just an employer.

"How fluent are you in Russian?" Jarrod Morrison asked.

"I'm a native speaker. It's my first language." She didn't mention she'd been born and raised in Russia when it was still the Soviet Union. She was proud of the fact that she didn't have an accent in English, even on the phone, where accents were most apparent.

"What are your qualifications as a teacher?"

She switched the receiver to the other ear. "I've taught Russian part-time for seven of the past ten years at the college level. I've also privately tutored business executives and their personnel engaged in international trade."

"I want to be absolutely honest with you, Ms. Lockhart, about what I will be asking of you. I have adopted a seven-year-old Russian orphan, Alexander—Sasha."

She conjured up an image of a tough street kid, the refuse of a system gone corrupt and soulless.

"Sasha knows no English," Jarrod continued, "and I don't speak or understand a word of Russian."

"How do you communicate?"

"By pointing mostly, and a few words he's managed to pick up from me and television. His lack of English is seriously handicapping him, though. He was given a nonverbal intelligence test when I enrolled him for school. His IQ was rated at sixty-five, which they categorize as low cognitive ability. That's the politically correct way of saying he's mentally retarded. I don't believe he is."

*Or you're not willing to?* she thought. What parent wanted to admit his child was deficient? She sympathized, but denial didn't solve problems; it perpetuated them.

"Those tests are based on cultural values Sasha doesn't share," the man at the other end continued. "That's why he needs an experienced tutor, someone who can teach him the skills necessary to bring up his test scores."

"Intelligence cannot be taught, Mr. Morrison."

"I'm aware of that." Impatience and frustration hardened his tone. "Sasha may be developmentally delayed, but that doesn't mean he's stupid. He simply lacks the tools to express himself and absorb new information. Learning English is the first step in overcoming those hurdles."

She heard desperation in his voice. Nina didn't consider herself softhearted; the world she came from didn't allow it. But something inside her melted at his determination to give the boy a fighting chance to prove himself. The challenge also intrigued her. It represented an opportunity to save one of the innocent victims of the system her mother had been so enthusiastic about.

"I won't be able to determine if I can help your son, Mr. Morrison, without meeting him."

"Fair enough. Can you come to North Carolina? I'll pay your expenses, of course. The sooner the better."

She mulled it over for only a few seconds. Her contract here in Atlanta was over, her bonds with Lorenzo severed. She was anxious to move on. "Would tomorrow be convenient?"

He let out an audible sigh of relief. "That'll be perfect. I'd like to get this resolved as soon as possible. Shall I make your flight reservations, or do you want to arrange them yourself?"

"I'd just as soon drive."

"It'll take you about five hours from central Atlanta. The plane ride to Asheville is only an hour."

"But there's the two-hour wait at the airport and the constant worry about security delays. Driving is much easier, and I'd like to see the countryside."

"The mountains are beautiful this time of year. One other question," he said. "Do you smoke?"

"No."

"Good."

"And if I'd said yes?"

He paused a moment. "I'd ask you not to around my son. If you couldn't agree to that condition, I wouldn't hire you."

Not an unreasonable request, Nina decided, though his attitude about it seemed a bit arrogant.

"Keep track of your expenses and mileage

and I'll reimburse you. Let me give you directions on how to find our house."

Nina cradled the receiver a few minutes later and wondered if she was doing the right thing. Until now she'd always lived in large cities—New York, Chicago, L.A., Atlanta. This would be her first excursion to a place of less than a million people—considerably less.

She'd checked Misty Hollow, North Carolina, in her road atlas. Population: 2,468. The nearest interstate was in Asheville, thirty miles to the west. Definitely out of the way. She'd enjoyed the constant relocating until now, but recent events had convinced her she was ready to settle down, to find something she could barely remember—stability, a place to call home.

Then there was the matter of her prospective new employer. Jarrod Morrison had told her he was forty-five, and that he'd never been married. Why would a confirmed bachelor adopt a seven-year-old boy? Could he be a pervert, a pedophile? The thought sickened her. If he was… If he planned to use her to get to the boy…

Well, he'd soon find out she was no enabler. If she got any indication, any hint that his intentions were less than honorable, she'd inform the authorities.

She'd have to be careful, though. False accusations could wreak a lot of damage.

If he was involved in anything unsavory, however, merely associating with him might be dangerous. Men of that sort were known to be ruthless.

Maybe she ought to call him back and say she'd reconsidered, that she didn't feel qualified to teach such a young, traumatized child, that she'd gotten another, better offer, that… Surely she could concoct some sort of excuse. Or simply not show up.

But the plea in his voice had sounded so sincere, and the little boy… She knew what it was like to be with strangers, alone and frightened.

He'd said the drive from Atlanta to Misty Hollow would take about five hours. If she left early in the morning and didn't stop to eat along the way, she could be there by lunchtime.

THURSDAY MORNING DAWNED bright and clear. Jarrod woke Sasha at seven. The child washed, brushed his teeth, dressed and combed his hair without being told, then came to the kitchen table, where bacon, eggs, toast and jelly, juice and milk were waiting. The boy always seemed awed by the amount of food, and looked up at Jarrod, as if asking permission to eat it. Breakfast in summer at the orphanage, Jarrod had learned, consisted of a thick slice of coarse brown bread and a piece of fruit—half an apple or pear, maybe a plum—and a small glass of milk. In winter porridge replaced the fruit. No seconds.

This morning, as Jarrod repeatedly encouraged Sasha not to gobble his food, he felt more hope than he had since he'd brought the boy home. He knew better than to draw any conclusions from the mere tone of the woman's voice on the telephone, but he liked her responses to his questions yesterday, the intelligence they implied and the hint of compassion he heard.

Nina I. Lockhart. She'd said the *I* stood for Ivanova, which meant her father's name was Ivan. She'd also said she was a thirty-four-year-old widow with no kids. Sounded sad to him, but he didn't dwell on it. All that really mattered was that she was a native speaker, an experienced teacher.

Rather than put Sasha on the school bus this morning as Jarrod had been doing for the past week, he drove him to school.

Alicia Peters was distributing papers on the miniature desks when he tapped on her open door. She glanced up and was about to speak when she recognized him. Her face clouded, and what would probably have been a friendly greeting lost its enthusiasm.

"I'm sorry for my rudeness yesterday," Jarrod said, as he stepped inside.

She blew a lock of brown hair away from her oval face and made a valiant attempt to relax her features. "I handled the situation poorly," she acknowledged. "I'm the one who should be apologizing."

She'd used poor judgment, but then she'd apparently been ill-informed about Sasha. She didn't strike him as harsh or indifferent.

A bell rang and first graders began storming into the classroom. Sasha stayed close by Jarrod's side. Jarrod crouched down and gently gripped the boy's thin arms. "You'll be alright today," he said, uncertain how much his son comprehended.

Alicia placed a hand lightly on her pupil's shoulder. Sasha's response was to gaze at his father more intently, his eyes begging to be taken away again.

Jarrod swallowed hard. "I'll see you after school." He was torn between wanting to wrap his son in his arms, and not wanting to embarrass him in front of his classmates. He compromised by brushing the cowlick of straight blond hair into place. "Come home on the school bus, okay?"

After a brief pause in which he seemed to understand he couldn't win, Sasha assumed a stony expression. His sad eyes were still dry. Jarrod's heart ached. Why was doing the right thing so hard?

"I'll make sure he gets on the bus, Mr. Morrison," Alicia said. "He'll be fine."

As she led the boy to his desk, Jarrod rose to his feet. After a last glance through the glass door, he quickly turned away before he lost his resolve.

At home he found it difficult to concentrate on the investment accounts he was managing for his clients. His mind kept wandering to his son's forlorn eyes.

Jarrod was collating September's quarterly tax forms as they came out of the printer when the phone rang. He glanced at his watch. Twelve-thirty.

"Mr. Morrison, this is Nina Lockhart. I'm here in Misty Hollow, but I seem to be going around in circles. I drove south on Duchene and turned right onto Franklin like you told me, but it's taken me right back to Duchene."

He apologized for the mix-up. One of the oldest roads in the county, Franklin wove back and forth through the hills, crossing Duchene twice. He thought he'd told her to take the second sign, but maybe he hadn't, or maybe she'd missed that part. He started to give her more detailed instructions to his house, then had another idea.

"Have you had lunch?"

She hesitated a moment. "Not yet."

"Me neither. If you're at South Duchene and Franklin, there's a café on the northeast corner of the intersection."

"I'm so turned around I don't know which way is up, but there's a place called Jessie's across the road."

"That's it. If you like plain cooking, I can meet you there in ten minutes. I'll buy you lunch while we talk."

Jarrod thought he heard relief when she accepted his invitation. Was it because she was hungry, or frustrated at getting lost? Or had she developed a case of nerves about meeting a strange man alone in an isolated house? He hadn't considered that possibility. He should have.

Jarrod arrived at the restaurant in less than the allotted time.

"I'm supposed to meet someone," he told the hostess at the door. "Her name is Nina—"

"Yes, sir." She snatched a menu from a stack and led him across the noisy, tin-ceilinged room.

The woman sitting by herself in a booth at the far corner had the fine Slavic features, the delicate nose, high cheekbones, pale, creamy skin he'd seen so much of in Russia. Her thick honey-blond hair hung in natural waves to her shoulders.

The hostess dropped the menu on the table. "Enjoy your lunch."

Jarrod extended his hand and introduced himself.

They shook. "Sorry to be such a bother," she said in the cultured voice he recognized from the phone call. He slid onto the bench seat across from her.

A waitress appeared almost instantly to take their orders.

"I recommend the stuffed peppers," he said. "It's their specialty.

"How was your drive?" he asked once they'd ordered. She had the most gorgeous blue eyes he'd ever encountered. He'd have to guard against staring, because Nina I. Lockhart was mesmerizing.

"Aside from getting lost? Beautiful. The leaves are just starting to turn. I imagine it'll be breathtaking in a few more weeks."

They continued to exchange small talk until their food arrived.

"Why did you adopt a Russian boy if you don't speak Russian?" she finally asked, once the waitress had gone.

"I didn't adopt him because he was Russian," Jarrod answered, "but because he needed a home." He must sound like a pompous ass. He made a concerted effort to lighten up. "Besides, as I told you, I have absolutely no knack for languages, so any foreign kid would have been a problem communications-wise."

"Why adopt a foreign child at all?"

He split open the green pepper and let the steam rise. "The obstacles for an unmarried man to adopt in North America are virtually insurmountable if the child isn't related. Foreign adoptions aren't a whole lot easier. I had just about given up when I found Sasha."

"Was the adoption legitimate?" she asked.

He was momentarily jarred by her bluntness. But it was a fair question. There was a thriving international black market in children, some of them real orphans, others stolen from their parents.

"Absolutely legal and aboveboard," he said. "I can show you the papers at the house, signed by American and Russian government officials, with all sorts of raised seals and ornate stamps."

She smiled. "Bureaucrats really dig those things, don't they?"

Oh, yes, he decided. He wanted to see a lot more of that smile. It brightened her pretty face and had the potential to turn him into putty.

"Tell me about him," she said, digging into her beef-and-rice-filled bell pepper. "This is excellent, by the way."

"A few more months and he would no longer have been eligible for adoption. The Russian government is more interested in placing the very young. At eight, he would've been taken off the list and sent to another institution. At sixteen he would've been inducted into the army."

She nodded, apparently not surprised or even moved by the story.

"I learned a little of his background," he added. "His father died in prison a year after Sasha was born. He was some kind of common criminal—burglary, I think. Sasha and his sister were taken away from their alcoholic mother when he was two."

"He has a sister?"

"Two years older and in another orphanage outside Moscow. According to the people where Sasha lived, he was too young when they were separated to remember her and doesn't know she exists."

"Is he in good health?"

"He passed the adoption physical. Mentally, emotionally—" Jarrod shrugged "—that's another matter."

He took a sip of tea, suddenly losing interest in the food on his plate.

"He'd never been to school before I brought him here, never received any formal instruction at all. He can only count to five in Russian, doesn't know the names of colors, though he can distinguish one from another well enough, and needless to say, can't read or write."

"Was he abused?" she asked, having pushed her plate aside, as well.

"As best I can determine, he wasn't. I'm sure he was disciplined, but for the most part he seems to have been simply warehoused and ignored. His days were regimented. He got up to a bell, lined up at a long table with the other children to eat at the sound of another bell. Then they were marched to a row of chamber pots to relieve themselves."

She closed her eyes, as if trying to block out the ugly image—little children being herded like so many sheep. He remembered their narrow faces, their mournful eyes. Lost little souls. They'd grow up never knowing love. Many of them would become alcoholics and drug addicts, petty criminals and prison inmates—and they'd die young. And, he reminded himself, not for the first time, he couldn't save them all.

"I'd like to blame the people who run the institution," he continued, "but that wouldn't be fair. The staff I met seemed like decent people, but there were less than a dozen of them to care for over a hundred kids ranging from infants to six-year-olds. They barely had enough time or resources to attend to basic needs, much less nurture or hug the children."

Nina toyed with her iced tea glass. "You said there were children up to the age of six," she mused. "What was Sasha doing there if he was seven?"

Jarrod shifted in his seat. "He was almost six when the bureaucracy paired him up with me. Since he was scheduled to leave for good, they decided not to transfer him to the next institution, where he would start school. They didn't want to disrupt his life twice in so short a period. It was a reasonable, even a benevolent decision, I suppose. What they hadn't factored in was how long it would take—over a year—for me to get all the i's dotted and t's crossed for the adoption."

"So Sasha was left with much younger children and never given a chance to go to school."

Jarrod raised one shoulder and let it drop. "Is it any wonder he's behind? At a period when a child is starving for knowledge and direction, he was denied those opportunities."

Nina stared at the napkin she was twisting into a tight knot. "You've assumed a heavy burden."

"Adopting him is the best thing I've ever done."

Her blue eyes warmed, and for an instant he felt he had connected with her.

"Is he a discipline problem?" she asked a moment later.

"I almost wish he were."

She crooked a brow.

"Sasha does whatever I tell him, maybe

because he doesn't know how to argue yet. I should probably be careful what I ask for, huh? Teach him English and he might give me back talk."

Her return smile this time was wan, unconvincing. "If he's as intelligent as you think he is, he'll learn English with or without my help. I think you know that. All I might be able to do is accelerate the process."

He nodded. "He's already picking up words. The books I've read recommend speaking in short declarative sentences and asking simple, positive questions. He seems to understand more and more every day, but he rarely says anything in return."

"It'll come," she assured him. "You told me on the phone that you put him in public school. Is that the best place for him?"

"Probably not, but I don't have any choice. I applied to several private institutions where they have smaller numbers and give more individual attention, where I reckoned they'd be better equipped to deal with issues of foreign language, but his IQ is a major stumbling block. Because Sasha scored so low, they won't accept him."

"There are private institutions that deal with slow learners."

"Unfortunately, they have waiting lists longer than my arm. The few that have openings are way beyond my means, and the state doesn't subsidize them, or at least not enough. We're talking about a minimum of fifty thousand dollars a year."

"But Sasha does have a learning disability, right?"

Jarrod flexed his jaw. "We don't know. We only know that at present he's unable to communicate ideas, not that he doesn't have them or can't learn them."

She frowned. "Maybe so. I'm not qualified to assess the situation. I'm sorry, but I really don't think I'm the person you need."

Impulsively he reached across the table and took her hand. "Nina, you're my only hope." Several people at other tables glanced over at his raised voice.

"Look," he said more quietly, withdrawing his hand, "I don't expect you to perform miracles. All I'm asking is that you help him learn English. That's the major hurdle right now. We can't even talk to each other."

When she didn't say anything, he went on. "Just give it a shot for a couple of weeks. Let's see what kind of progress he makes. If nothing else, you can act as our translator."

"Two weeks isn't very long," she said. "If he is a slow learner, we may not see any progress in such a short time."

"A month, then."

"I don't know…"

"You can stay at my place. The guest-house is a separate building that I think you'll find quite comfortable. A living area, bedroom, full bath and a small kitchen. Ideal for one."

She hesitated and that encouraged him. "Nina, I really need your help. You said you do a lot of freelance translating. The job I'm offering isn't full-time, just a few hours in the afternoon and evening. I can't afford to match what you were probably earning in Atlanta, but I can furnish you a place to live for free and give you all day to work for your other clients. That should make up for some of the difference, and if you're willing, I'd like you to take your evening meals with us. That'll save you time and money, as well. If it doesn't work out, you won't have lost anything."

She gazed up at the ceiling, her expression thoughtful, then she met his eyes. "I'll have to meet Sasha first."

He blinked slowly, then expelled the breath

he'd unconsciously been holding. "Thank you," he said softly. "You'll love Sasha, I promise."

Her smile offered no commitment.

## *CHAPTER TWO*

JARROD CHECKED HIS WATCH. "SASHA WILL be home from school in less than an hour. If you don't mind, I need to stop at the grocery store on the way."

"Sure," she said. "I'll follow you."

A mile down the road he turned into a convenience store parking lot. She pulled her silver BMW Z4 up beside his green-and-white Jeep Cherokee and rolled down her window when he walked over. He leaned down, his face mere inches from hers, and she caught the hint of woodsy aftershave.

"I'll only be a minute," he said, his arm resting on her door frame. A nicely muscled arm, she noted. "No need for you to come in. Chicken grilled outside this evening all right with you? I can fix something else if—"

"Chicken is fine."

She watched him walk away, and allowed herself the pleasure of enjoying the sight. He was tall—she'd noticed that when he'd appeared in the doorway of the restaurant—and he obviously took care of himself. She doubted there was an ounce of fat on him.

His hazel-brown eyes had flashed with righteous anger and deep compassion when he'd talked about his son and the other children at the orphanage. A man of contradictions. Friendly, yet aloof. Determined—he'd persevered through years of maddening bureaucracy to adopt an orphan—yet vulnerable in his love for the boy.

She liked his mouth—full, sensuous and intriguing with a hint of humor. It was hard not to stare when he spoke. Kissable?

She wasn't about to go down that road. After Lorenzo she'd resolved not to get involved with a business associate, much less an employer, ever again.

Jarrod was as good as his word, coming out of the store in less than two minutes. He grinned at her as he climbed back into his vehicle. She was still contemplating his smile when he turned off the highway onto a country road through woodlands. Towering maple, oak and pine trees hugged the narrow two-lane road that wove up and down hills. A few minutes later he pulled into the long driveway of a modest shingle-sided house. Nothing fancy, but it had a homey air Nina found appealing. Too isolated for a growing boy? Maybe. But it might also provide sanctuary for a kid overwhelmed by a strange new world.

She parked behind Jarrod's SUV and switched off the engine, just as he opened her car door for her. In his left hand he had the groceries he'd just bought.

"I hope you like vanilla ice cream. It's Sasha's favorite so far. With chocolate sauce."

She chuckled. "Sounds like a normal kid to me."

He led her to the back porch, as if she were a familiar friend rather than a first-time guest.

The inside of the house was no more extraordinary than the outside. The kitchen held the usual complement of white-enamel appliances, and was large enough for a table by the double window overlooking the backyard and the dense green forest beyond.

"Let me put the ice cream away before it melts," he said, "then I'll show you around."

The dining room held an oak table under a shiny brass chandelier, four chairs and a glass-fronted cabinet.

An earth-toned sofa and love seat as well as a leather recliner faced a green marble fireplace in the living room.

"Come take a look at Sasha's room." He waved her toward a hallway with paneled wooden doors on both sides. Motioning to the first door on the right, he said, "That's my room," and kept going. The next room contained a single bed against the wall with a red print coverlet on it—drums and horns, carousel horses and puppy dogs. New-looking stuffed animals were neatly clustered around a toy chest, along with a soccer ball and hockey stick. Little Golden books filled a shelf above a maple writing table. The carpet was a brilliant blue, the curtains a darker shade. The room was cheerful and boyish—and much too neat.

"Does he play with his things much?"

He shook his head. "Not really. Of course, he doesn't understand baseball or football yet, and there aren't any kids around here to play with."

"Get him an Erector set and Lincoln logs."

"You're right. I should have thought of that."

As they started back to the living room, Nina caught a glimpse of what had probably been the master bedroom across the hall. Seeing her interest, he invited her inside.

"This is my office."

The room was distinctly masculine and had apparently been expanded to incorporate what may have been a small porch. The extension had windows on three sides, forming a large bay that brought the outdoors inside.

Facing it was a long writing table with the usual accessories—a banker's green-shaded lamp, a tray containing pens, a jelly glass crammed with pencils, a telephone and a work basket with only a few papers in it. The desk chair was brown leather and high-backed.

On the right was a similar table, but this one held two computer flat screens, pull-out keyboards and a printer. The towers were neatly stowed underneath.

Beyond the extended workspace were handsome, matching polished wood file cabinets and a TV.

Turning, Nina found a solid wall of bookcases filled with mostly hardcover books. In front of them were two matching leather wingbacks separated by a table with a brass lamp.

More than an office, it was like a den. Inspiring confidence and security.

"You haven't told me what you do for a living."

"Nothing very glamorous. I'm a CPA. I

worked for a large accounting firm in Raleigh for several years until my mother got sick. I came back here to look after her and took a job with a local insurance company, where I expanded into investment counseling. I did some speculating on my own in the dot-com market, was lucky enough to pull out just before the bubble burst. Made quite a killing, too. I'm semiretired now, manage my own portfolio and those of a few select clients."

"If I hang around," she said, "I may have to switch my account to you."

"I'll be glad to advise you, but if you're comfortable with your current financial manager stick with him—or her. I got rich quick—well, sorta—but I was lucky. I don't recommend my clients speculate. Go to Vegas, if you want to gamble. The market has enough pitfalls without shooting craps with stocks."

She chuckled, pleased with his candor. "I'll keep that in mind."

She surveyed the room again. "You spend most of your time in here, don't you?" She could picture him ensconced in one of the wingbacks, legs crossed, a book in hand.

"I did until I brought Sasha home. We

watch TV in the living room now. He's sort of figured out without my telling him that I'm to be left alone when I'm in here. That doesn't happen very often, though. I do most of my work when he's in school or after he's gone to bed."

A man with priorities and a sense of order.

"Now let me show you the guesthouse," he said.

They went out the back door. Across the pine-studded lawn stood a double garage with a picturesque cottage attached to it. It didn't appear to be as old as the main house, but it was by no means new, either.

"I helped my father build this for my grandmother." His expression softened. "At least he said I was a help."

Her thoughts went back to the restaurant. She remembered the feel of his hand when he'd asked her to help him with Sasha. It wasn't callused, but it had a leathery texture that suggested a man who wasn't afraid of a day's work in the outdoors.

His smile faded. "Gram passed away before it was finished, so Dad used it as his office until he died a year later. After I went off to college, my mother rented it out. The extra income helped and she felt safe having someone close by. I continued to sublet it after she died, but the last tenant moved out just before I brought Sasha home, and I never got around to advertising it. Now I'm glad I didn't."

She glanced up at him as they approached the covered entrance. The sun dappled his dark hair, and she had a sudden image of what it must look like mussed from sleep in the morning.

He used the key he'd taken off a hook in the kitchen and unlocked the door. The inside was stuffy, so he left the door open and raised a window.

The decor was tastefully simple and essentially neutral. The pale gray walls and white woodwork were appropriate for the limited space. The sitting room furniture was economical, showed modest wear but appeared to be clean and in good condition. A narrow passage between a white-tiled bathroom and a compact kitchen led to a bedroom of the same dimensions as the living room. It held a double bed flanked by nightstands, a dresser with a mirror, and a rocking chair. Louvered closet doors lined one wall, casement windows the other. When Jarrod opened them, Nina could hear birds twittering and crickets chirping.

"There's a washer and dryer in the garage,"

he said. "You can get to them through the kitchenette."

"Cozy," Nina muttered. Not luxurious, but a single person could be comfortable here.

"Central air and heat," he added. "If you agree to stay, I'll have a crew come in tomorrow to clean the place."

"I like it," she said, and saw hope brighten his eyes. Still, she didn't want to offer false promises. "When does Sasha get home?"

He looked at his watch. "In about ten minutes."

She walked back through the passage, brushing close to him, suddenly aware of his size. Six-two at least.

Back in his kitchen, she accepted the offer of a soft drink.

"How long ago did your mother pass away?" she asked.

"It'll be three years in February. She was a heavy smoker and had been suffering from emphysema and congestive heart failure for years. Pneumonia was the last straw. She was sixty-two."

So that was why he was so adamant about not smoking. "And your dad died when you were a teenager?" So had hers.

"I was eleven." Jarrod's eyes looked somewhere faraway. "It was a Saturday. We were hurrying to finish the yard work so we could go fishing. We'd been looking forward to it all week. Then he just keeled over. They say he was dead before he hit the ground." Jarrod snapped back to the moment. "A massive coronary."

Nina pictured him as a young boy running to the man he obviously adored, wondering what was wrong. Did he blame himself, imagine there was something he could or should have done to save him?

"He was thirty-three."

Younger than she was now. "No brothers or sisters?"

Jarrod didn't actually slump as he leaned against the counter near the sink, but something about his posture gave that impression. "I had a brother two years older than me. Jimmy was killed in a car crash when he was sixteen, the night of his junior prom."

She cursed herself for opening so many old wounds. "I'm sorry. It must have been tough on you and your mother."

His shrug was philosophical, but not his eyes. "It was all a long time ago."

They heard the air brakes of a large vehicle stopping outside.

"That'll be the school bus." Jarrod put aside his soda can, opened the refrigerator and removed a pear from the crisper.

"He's always hungry after school. I have to be careful, though. He'll eat the seeds if I don't watch him."

Less than a minute passed before the door opened and a boy with straight, pale blond hair, keen blue eyes and a clear, milky complexion stepped inside. Jarrod had said he was about to turn eight, but from his height and scrawny build, Nina wouldn't have thought him more than six. At seeing her, he stopped abruptly in his tracks.

"Sasha, this lady is here to meet you," Jarrod said.

Nina forced a smile to put him at ease. *"Privyet, Sasha. Kak ty pashivayesh?"* Hi, Sasha. How are you?

His eyes went wide. His mouth dropped open, and his books tumbled to the floor. He backed away, bumped against the edge of the counter and nearly fell.

"Sasha?" Jarrod blurted with alarm.

"Are you here to take me back?" the boy asked Nina in Russian, his voice small, scared. Tears tumbled down his pink cheeks.

Nina's heart broke. She'd meant to make

him comfortable by speaking in Russian. Instead she'd terrified him. The image of her father flashed before her eyes. Her heart began to pound so hard that for a moment she thought she might be sick. If only she could convince this fragile kid she understood his fears, but that *his* were groundless.

*"Nyet,"* she said softly in Russian. "No one is going to take you away, Sasha. Your father is very pleased with you. He's very happy that you've come here to live with him. This is your home now."

"What did you say to him?" Jarrod demanded. He'd already moved up to the boy and crouched before him. "He never cries."

"He thinks I've come to take him away. I'm just reassuring him." She closed her eyes and felt a tear course down her cheek. What had they done to this child to make him cower at the sight of a strange woman, at the sound of his own language?

"There's nothing to be afraid of, Sasha," Jarrod murmured, but the trembling boy looked past him, staring in glassy-eyed terror at Nina.

Jarrod wrapped his arms around him and hugged him tightly, but the child's stiff posture didn't soften.

"There really is nothing to be afraid of, Sasha." She repeated Jarrod's words in Russian. "You are safe here. You like living with Mr. Morrison, don't you?"

He nodded shyly. *"Da,"* he said in a leery voice.

"Has Mr. Morrison been good to you?"

*"Da."* He was still tentative.

"Do you want to stay here with him?"

*"Da, da."* More enthusiasm, but she could see his mind working. *Is this a trick?* How many times before had he been lied to?

"Do you like school?"

He only nodded this time, obviously giving the answer he thought she wanted to hear.

"What are you learning there?"

He didn't respond, but his eyes never left hers. She could feel him assessing her.

"Mr. Morrison is your father now, Sasha. He loves you very much."

The boy's rigid stance relaxed only slightly. "Are you going to be my mother?" he whispered.

The question jolted her, then settled like a knife in her heart. She wanted to be a mother, to love and be loved unconditionally. A few more years and the possibility would fade like so many other dreams.

Now this confused child was asking for her love. His world had been cold, heartless, uncaring, yet he seemed to know what was missing in his life.

How should she answer him? It would be cruel to hold out a promise, then snatch it away when it was time for her to leave.

"I'm just visiting," she said, trying to sound upbeat. She waited for a response, a reaction. He merely stared at her. "Your father asked me to come here and help you learn English. Would you like that?"

Longing filled his sad blue eyes. He nodded sheepishly. *"Da. Pazhaluista." Yes. Please.*

She hunkered down beside Jarrod, gently squeezed Sasha's shoulder and said in English, "I'll take the job."

JARROD GOT HIS FIRST TASTE of Nina's language skills a minute later when he told Sasha to go change out of his school clothes. The words had hardly left his mouth in English when they were coming out of hers in Russian. Sasha gaped at him, then they both stared at her.

"Never heard simultaneous translation before?" she deadpanned innocently.

"Not up close and personal," Jarrod replied. "That's amazing."

Sasha said something.

"He wants to know how I do that," she reported.

Jarrod grinned. "Tell him it's magic?" He reached up with his right hand and plucked a coin from behind Nina's left ear. "Like this."

It was her turn to gape.

Sasha's face beamed.

Jarrod winked at the boy, extended his left hand and pulled another quarter from his son's right ear. The youngster's grin widened. Jarrod handed him the coins.

"Has he ever done that before?" Nina asked in Russian.

"Sometimes," Sasha answered.

"Pick up your books and go change, Son," Jarrod instructed him. "Then we'll play some basketball, if you want."

Nina repeated it, and the boy dashed off to his room, his step considerably lighter than when he'd come in.

"You didn't tell me you were a magician," she said to Jarrod.

"Just amateur stuff."

"Well, you're good. Where did you learn it?"

"My dad tinkered with sleight of hand.

Claimed his secret desire was to run away with the circus. He taught me a couple of tricks." He wagged his eyebrows. "I have a few more up my sleeve. Want to see them?"

She laughed and thought about the tingling sensation she'd felt when he'd touched the delicate skin under her ear. Just ticklish, she told herself. Nothing more. "Maybe later."

"Can we go to see Ruff?" Sasha asked Nina in Russian a minute later. He'd changed into blue shorts and a yellow T-shirt.

Nina translated, then asked Jarrod, "Who's Ruff?"

He laughed. "My neighbor's dog. It's five minutes on the path through the woods, if you don't mind the walk. I'll introduce you. Sasha can play with Earl's sheltie, then we'll come back and I'll fix dinner." His face brightened. "Better yet, we'll take everything over there and eat with him."

"He won't mind you just barging in with a dinner guest he's never met?"

"He'll welcome the company."

After sixteen years in this country Nina found there were times when the informality of Americans still baffled her. Where she'd grown up this kind of presumptuousness would never have been tolerated.

She helped Jarrod place the chicken into a cooler and fill a canvas tote with corn on the cob, a bag of brown rice and the makings for a tossed salad. At the last minute he snagged a couple of flashlights from a kitchen drawer.

"You're sure your friend won't mind? Maybe he already has plans for dinner."

Jarrod shook his head. "Trust me. He'll be thrilled when we show up, especially with vittles in hand."

The woods were cool and sun-dappled. The sounds of birds flitting and squirrels scampering, and the clean smell of pine and earth were tonics. She'd been a city girl all her life, liked the human energy in tall buildings and horn-honking traffic.

"Do you visit this man very often?" she asked Sasha as they started off.

"I throw sticks. The dog carries them to me in his mouth."

Then the child was gone, bounding ahead of them, turning to his right and left as different things caught his attention. A stick, a stone, a colorful leaf, a pink flower. Nina wondered if he had ever gone on excursions outside the orphanage, or if his entire world had been confined to the institution. She also noticed that Jarrod watched him carefully but didn't try in any way to inhibit him. She liked that, the father's willingness to let his son explore on his own.

Suddenly Sasha stood still, transfixed by something on his arm. As they drew closer, she saw it was a caterpillar. He peered at it and placed his index finger in its path. He smiled up at Nina when it inched onto his finger. He studied it intently.

"What do you have there?" she asked.

"I don't know," he said.

"It's called a caterpillar," she said, still in Russian. Then she gave him the English word. "Can you say it?" She repeated it slowly.

His attempt wasn't bad for a first try.

*"Ochen khorosho,"* she told him. "Very good."

He looked up at her and smiled again before redirecting his attention to the creature in his hand. Then he rested his finger on the branch of a bush and let the caterpillar creep away. A moment later, Sasha ran ahead, the encounter all but forgotten.

"You've won a friend," Jarrod said in his soft drawl. Nina had been aware of him hovering behind her. "He doesn't often smile, but he did at you. Twice. Thank you."

She shrugged. "I didn't do anything."

"A little kindness goes a long way." They resumed their walk. "With few exceptions, his world has been a hostile one."

"Yet he's so gentle."

"Strange, isn't it? You'd expect him to be angrier."

"Maybe you've had a calming effect on him."

"Not me. Maybe this place. Some people think growing up in the sticks is boring. I never have. The countryside's full of life, yet so peaceful. After I came back I wondered why I'd ever left."

She listened to the forest sounds. "It is serene, isn't it?"

"A great place to bring up kids."

Nina would have liked to pursue the conversation, ask him why he'd never married, since he seemed to relish his role as Sasha's father, but they'd come to a clearing.

The neighbor's house was similar to Jarrod's and might have been built by the same developer fifty or sixty years before. Like Jarrod's, it appeared to be in good condition, the one difference being the ramp up to the back porch.

The door opened and a tricolored sheltie came bounding toward the visitors, barking.

Sasha ran full-tilt toward the dog and threw his arms around the animal's neck. Nina was sure she saw the dog smile.

"He has a pal," she said to Jarrod.

He nodded. "They get along very well. I thought he might be afraid of dogs, but he isn't. Of course, Ruff is pretty old and gentle."

Nina glanced over at a young man in a wheelchair in the doorway.

"Hi," he called out. "You must be the tutor." He rolled down the ramp, stopped and extended his hand. "I'm Earl Slater, in case he hasn't told you."

"Nina Lockhart." His grip was strong and confident. "I apologize for showing up here uninvited."

"Jarrod brought you, so you're welcome. Thanks for coming." He looked at his friend, who had the cooler in one hand and the tote in the other. "What do you have there?"

"Supper," Jarrod announced. "Chicken, corn on the cob, salad. Darn, I forgot the dressings. I'll get the fire started and go back for them."

"I have plenty," Earl said. He looked up at Nina. "I assume your being here means you've taken the job."

"On a trial basis. For a month. After that, we'll see."

"Good." He watched Sasha with the dog. "He's a great kid, but he's having a tough time figuring things out all by himself."

Earl took the canvas bag from Jarrod, placed it on his lap and swiveled back toward the house. His long brown hair was gathered at the nape of his neck with a rawhide thong.

While Jarrod kindled a fire in the grill and Sasha played fetch with Ruff, Nina joined Earl in the kitchen, modified to be wheelchair friendly. He put the rice on to cook; she shucked the corn.

There was plenty of time before the chicken was ready, so the three adults sat in the backyard, sipped cold beers and watched the boy and the dog.

Sasha lofted the stick into the air with no great strength or accuracy. The sheltie bounded delightedly after it and returned at a trot. Sasha patted him on the head gently, removed the stick from his mouth and threw it again. The two seemed perfectly content to repeat the process endlessly. Judging from the wag of the dog's tail and the glow on the boy's face, the best part of the exercise for both of them was when Sasha petted the animal.

"I had to take Spanish in high school," Earl

said. "I could learn the words, read and write them, but when anyone talked to me in Spanish, they might as well have been speaking Greek or Swahili. All the sounds seemed to run together, and I couldn't tell where one word left off and another began."

Nina smiled. "Some people have an ear for languages, others don't."

"Where did you go to school?"

"Columbia. Received my bachelor's and master's degrees in linguistics."

"How many other languages besides English and Russian do you speak?" Jarrod asked.

"French and German fluently, and I can get along fairly well in Spanish, Italian and Dutch."

"With those talents and qualifications," Earl said, "what are you doing in North Carolina? You should be working at the U.N."

She laughed. "I had an offer when I was still in college. The head of the political science department had a couple of visiting academics addressing his class, one Russian, the other East German. They read their lectures in English, but their command of the language wasn't up to handling the Q and A session afterward, so I was asked to interpret for them. When the session was over a professor pointed out that I'd been simultaneously translating throughout the exchange. I hadn't even been aware of doing it. He referred me to the head of the U.N. interpreters, who offered me a position on his staff after I graduated. I turned it down."

"Why?" Jarrod asked. "It sounds like a dream job."

"It can be, but it can also be limiting. And consider the consequences if I were to make a mistake. I could start a world war."

Earl laughed. "Somehow I doubt that, but I see your point. Pretty high pressure. Still, there must be other, better paying jobs than tutoring a little boy in Misty Hollow."

She smiled ruefully. "Better paying, yes. But more important?"

Jarrod flashed her an appreciative smile.

At last their dinner was ready, and they took their places at the picnic table under a spreading oak tree. The day's heat had waned, but not enough to make the air chilly.

Nina watched Sasha. With an elbow securely propped on either side of his plate, he hovered protectively over his food as though someone might yank it away. Using both hands, he began cramming salad into his mouth.

"Sasha, wait," Jarrod said, not harshly but firmly.

His son halted in midmotion and looked up, on alert, his mouth full and open. Jarrod handed him a fork, which Sasha clutched like a shovel—or a weapon.

Nina leaned over and adjusted it. "This way."

Sasha tolerated the correction, but she could see impatience.

*"Myedlenno,"* she said when he returned to wolfing down his rice. "Slowly."

"If he didn't eat quickly in the orphanage," Jarrod explained, "other kids would steal from his plate."

"Sasha," she said in Russian, "nobody is going to take your food away from you. *Ponimayesh?" Do you understand?* "You don't have to eat so fast. If you want more, you can have it."

He gazed at her, his mouth again open with food in it, then he closed it and chewed less rapidly, but she could see it was hard for him to control the impulse to hurry. Gobbling was the only way he knew to eat. She also appreciated Jarrod's patience in not pushing the issue of table manners. First Sasha would have to gain confidence that he wasn't going to be hungry before he could learn the finer points of etiquette.

When she wasn't observing the boy, Nina found herself studying the two men. She guessed Earl to be in his late twenties. The nature of his affliction wasn't clear. She'd seen him move his legs when he'd put the groceries in his lap, so he wasn't paraplegic. In fact, he looked quite healthy. His thick hair was shiny, his lively eyes a soft brown. He was obviously intelligent and quite good-looking in a youthful sort of way.

After helping Earl clean up, the three guests set off for Jarrod's house, this time with flashlights at the ready.

Jarrod carried the now-empty chest, Nina the folded tote bag. For a nerve-racking moment as they trekked through the woods, she had the urge to intertwine her fingers with his, like two old friends, like…

She shifted the tote to her inside hand.

The man intrigued her, but he was her employer. She'd have to remember that. He was also more than ten years her senior and from a very different world than hers. They had so little in common.

Maybe that was the fascination.

She'd caught him studying her during the

course of the evening, not the way an employer observes an employee, but the way a man looks at a woman. She should have been offended, but she wasn't.

All perfectly natural, she told herself. Two unattached adults of the opposite sex. It didn't mean anymore on his part than it did on hers. Nothing to worry about.

## CHAPTER THREE

JARROD WATCHED AS SASHA darted ahead with his flashlight, stopping every few feet to focus the beam and examine some dark recess.

"You're probably wondering about Earl. He has muscular dystrophy," Jarrod told Nina. "He was diagnosed about five years ago."

"I've heard of the disease, but I really don't know anything about it."

"It's actually a group of muscle-deteriorating disorders. The type Earl has is called Limb-Girdle MD."

"Is there a cure?"

He shook his head. "There are treatments that can slow the progress of the symptoms, but there's no cure."

"Explain this…limb-girdle."

"It affects the long muscles of the chest and shoulders, as well as the hips and thighs, rather than the shorter muscles of other parts of the body. And it's confined to voluntary muscles, not automatic ones like the heart and those that work the lungs, though with time they can be affected, too."

"He looks so strong and healthy."

"For the most part he is. He was always athletic, stayed in shape and took good care of himself."

"So what caused it?"

"It's usually genetic, except in his case they haven't been able to find a family history of the disease. His mother remembers an uncle who walked funny, so they think he may have had early symptoms, but he died in an accident when he was fairly young, so nobody really knows."

"Is that how Earl learned he had it? Trouble walking?"

"His stride became more like a waddle, and he began losing strength in his legs." Jarrod called to Sasha to stay on the path. The boy looked back and either understood the words or was able to figure out what they meant, because he complied.

"What's the prognosis?"

"It can only get worse, though how long that'll take no one can predict. He was an adult when he started showing symptoms, so deterioration is likely to be slow, but again, there's no guarantee. Exercises help keep existing muscles in shape but can't correct damage already done."

As they walked, the shadows lengthened. Soon they'd have to turn on their flashlights. Jarrod was tempted to take Nina's hand to guide her along the path he knew so well, but he wasn't sure how she would react, and he didn't want to do anything that might make her uncomfortable. He needed her too much—for Sasha—to chance scaring her off.

"In Earl's case," he continued, "so far the disease is confined to his legs. He can walk with canes or crutches but he's very unsteady. Rather than take a chance of injuring himself, he uses the wheelchair. Unless someone comes up with a miracle cure, he'll be in it for the rest of his life."

She made a soft sympathetic sound.

"He goes to therapy three times a week," Jarrod stated, "and does exercises at home to maintain his upper body strength. But even that's a delicate balancing act. If he works out too hard he risks straining muscles, which could cause damage he won't be able to recover from. On the other hand, not exercising risks weak muscles atrophying."

After a moment she said, "He seems to be

handling his condition well. What does he do for a living?"

"Computer engineer. Got his degree from the University of Chicago. Works at home now, but right after he graduated, he was recruited by one of those big software firms in California, married a sexy sales rep—"

"He's married?" He hadn't been wearing a wedding band.

"Was. About a year later he found out her after-hours meetings with clients involved playing games with hardware and software not included in the company's catalog."

"Ouch."

"Yeah. Ouch. That was about the same time he was diagnosed with MD."

"You're very protective of him, aren't you?" An endearing quality, she was tempted to add. "Your friendship obviously means a lot to him, too."

"We're fifteen years apart in age, so I didn't know him when we were growing up, but he's like the kid brother I never had."

"He's from here?" It didn't surprise her. His drawl matched Jarrod's perfectly.

"He grew up in that house. After he was diagnosed, he decided to come back here—that was about three years ago—and bought the place from his parents, who are retired now. They live in Florida most of the year. He has a housekeeper who comes in three times a week. Mrs. Burgess does the cleaning and laundry, stocks the pantry and keeps his refrigerator well supplied with her home cooking."

Nina studied Jarrod's profile in the rapidly fading light. His features were strong, masculine, determined, but she'd detected vulnerability, too. He was a man who cared very deeply for the people in his life: his father, his more recently deceased mother, his friend, the boy he had adopted. Yet he'd never married, and again she wondered why.

They reached the clearing where his house stood bathed in silver-gray twilight. Sasha was swinging from a rubber tire hanging from the branch of an oak tree.

"Does he ever run out of energy?" she asked, watching the skinny kid kick as high as he could.

"He's always on the move, always examining things. Once his immediate curiosity is satisfied, though, he moves on to something else. He only stops when I put him to bed. Within two minutes he's sound asleep."

"Has he been tested for Attention Deficit Hyperactivity Disorder?"

"No, but the principal and the school counselor have mentioned the possibility of ADHD. In the classroom he's always getting up and looking at things. I'm sure part of it is sheer boredom, because he doesn't understand what's going on."

"He must know he's supposed to stay in his seat, though."

"Of course he does, Nina," Jarrod exclaimed, "but given a choice between listening to someone lecture in a language you don't understand, and checking out how a pencil sharpener works, which would you choose?"

"I see your point. You have to admit though that he is disruptive in class."

"I know, but even if he has ADHD the solution isn't to put him on drugs, as I've been advised. That won't help him, it'll just warehouse him again. He's had enough of that." Jarrod paused, his eyes glued on the child. "Sasha needs to be allowed to explore. That's why it's essential for him to learn English as soon as possible, so the school and I can channel his energy, not suppress it."

"I'll do my best, Jarrod, but he's starting off at a terrible disadvantage. I'm not sure that learning English will compensate for years of neglect. They say the first seven years of a person's life are the formative ones. The truth is Sasha may never recover."

Jarrod took a deep breath. "You're not telling me anything I don't already know." His anger softened to worry. "But that won't stop me from doing everything within my power to give him a chance to reach his potential and be happy."

Nina touched his hand. "And I'll do what I can to help."

ON THE TRIP BACK TO Atlanta the following morning, Nina installed a book-on-tape in her cassette player, a romantic suspense by one of her favorite authors. The stories usually made trips race by, and made her feel she'd done more than simply cover distance. This time, however, she realized after a few minutes she had no idea what the narrator had been saying. Her mind was too occupied with the place and the people she'd just left. She rewound the tape, returned it to its case and found a soft rock station, which she turned down low. What she really needed to do was think.

About Jarrod. About Sasha. Even about Earl. She could sympathize with the young man confined to a wheelchair. She understood what it was like to be restricted, to feel powerless.

Her father had chosen a career, a profession that had made her a permanent outcast, but he'd also done what he felt he had to do to protect his family, to make their lives better. For many years he'd succeeded.

Then times had changed and a crumbling social order had caught him in its juggernaut. He'd been idealistic, tried to be progressive and do what he'd thought was right, but he couldn't change entrenched interests.

Nina would always remember the look in his eyes the morning they'd come to take him away. He'd known he would never return, and so did she. He'd kissed her mother in a way Nina couldn't remember him ever doing before. Their affection had always been reserved in front of her. That morning he'd offered a glimpse of how he'd really felt about his wife of twenty years.

Then he'd come to Nina, his Ninochka. He'd taken her hands in his and peered at her. His smile should have been sad, but it wasn't. The glow in his gray eyes had been filled with love and pride and hope, not for himself—there was no hope where he was going—but for her.

"Don't think too badly of your old man," he'd said. "Remember the walks in the park, laughing as we tasted snow on our tongues, the first warmth of the spring sun on our backs." Then he'd leaned forward and kissed her on the lips. "I love you," he'd said, his voice only then quavering.

A minute later he was gone. Nina and her mother had stood like pillars, tears running down their cheeks. They never saw him again.

Tears clouded Nina's eyes now, and she would have pulled over to the side of the road had it not been deserted. She did take her foot off the accelerator, though, as she wiped her cheeks.

Her papa hadn't been a saint. She'd long suspected he'd done things he could not and would not talk about, and that she didn't really want to know. People had died because of him. In a sense they'd suffered so that she wouldn't. It was wrong, but theirs had been a closed system. For a few to prosper, others had to go without. For some to live, others had to die. She hadn't made the rules, and neither had her father.

A year later, after Nina was safely in the United States, she'd received a letter from her mother announcing her papa had died in the gulag several months earlier. The end had been swift, painless, her mother had assured her. He hadn't suffered. They could at least be grateful for that.

Grateful?

Why now, after all these years, was Nina thinking about her father? He and Jarrod Morrison had nothing in common. She wasn't even sure her papa would have liked this bourgeois capitalist, and she was pretty sure Jarrod wouldn't care for the party hack, the state apparatchik.

So why was Nina's visit with a rural American reviving memories of her urban parents and the life she'd left behind?

The answer was obvious. Sasha. He looked like so many of the children she had seen from her father's limousine on her way to school, to dance class, to singing lessons, on the family trips to their country dacha. Small kids trudging along the streets of Moscow or the edges of the roads outside the capital city. Children with whom she had nothing in common—except humanity and a hunger for something they couldn't define.

She had to laugh, not for the first time. The classless workers' paradise had been neither classless nor a paradise. Her father had tried to bring about change and had perished. Her mother had gloried in its privileges and survived.

And Nina? Had she perished or survived?

OVER THE NEXT TWO DAYS Sasha underwent a kind of metamorphosis. Until now he'd been almost completely silent, but spending an afternoon talking with Nina seemed to have opened a floodgate. The following morning and afternoon after school he rattled on almost interminably in Russian, even though he knew Jarrod and Earl didn't have the slightest idea what he was talking about.

"Well, we know his vocal cords work all right," Earl said, as the boy chattered to Ruff, who seemed delighted with his young companion's long monologues.

"I'd give anything to know what he's saying," Jarrod responded. "Probably things he wouldn't say if he thought I could understand him."

"Maybe it's best you don't know then," his friend replied. "He may be running off about what terrible breath you have."

"What?" Jarrod cupped his hand in front of his mouth.

Earl laughed as he wheeled into the kitchen. He was still snickering when he returned with soft drinks for all of them.

"You're so easy," he said, handing him a cold, sweaty can.

Jarrod shook his head, pretending to be annoyed, but after a few seconds he chuckled, too.

"You like her, don't you?" Earl asked.

"Of course I like her. Anyone who can help Sasha gets my vote."

"I think you know that's not what I meant. She's a beautiful woman, Jarrod, and unless I'm misreading the signals completely, she likes you, too."

"I hope you're wrong," Jarrod said. "I have a son to raise. I'm not interested in romance."

Earl's grin revealed pity under the humor. "Maybe you don't think so, but that's not what your eyes say every time you look at her."

"As you said, she's a beautiful woman," he admitted. "Of course I look at her. I look at a lot of pretty women."

"Uh-huh."

"But, I'm too old for her. She's thirty-four. I'm forty-five."

"Yeah. What was I thinking of?" Earl bounced the heel of his hand against his forehead. "You're old enough to be her... brother."

Jarrod wagged his head again. This was all foolishness. He barely knew Nina. Of course, over the next month, if she stayed that long, he'd get to know her better. But she was his little boy's English teacher, he reminded himself. That was all. No point in complicating matters.

Of course, she would be living in his guest-house, right outside the back door. Sharing her evening meals with him and Sasha. The prospect of sitting across from her evening after evening was both appealing and disturbing. It had been a long time since he had been with a woman, even longer since he'd lived with one. Desire battled with common sense. His son needed a tutor. Perhaps even more, Sasha needed *this* tutor, this woman who seemed to mysteriously bond with him. Jarrod had said he would do anything for his son. He was about to be tested.

NINA ARRIVED BACK at Misty Hollow the following Saturday afternoon. Jarrod was amazed that she was able to cram all her possessions in the sporty little convertible: three suitcases on the passenger side, two hanging bags and a few boxes in the miniscule trunk. She commented that with a sports car one learned to travel light.

"I should have warned you there's no cable service out here, and I don't have a satellite dish, so if you're a TV junkie—"

"The vast wasteland?" She grinned and he was reminded of how much he liked to see her smile. "I'm not. A good book, music, and I'm quite content."

"What kind of music?"

"Almost anything, as long as it isn't ear shattering. My favorites are classical, folk and country. A strange combination, I know, but it works for me."

He smiled. "Not so strange. If you like bluegrass you've come to the right place. This is Appalachia, after all. We have some of the finest fiddlers and banjo pluckers in the world within a fifty-mile radius, and every spring there's a downhome jamboree in Asheville. We'll have to take Sasha to hear it."

Nina tilted her head to one side. "Has he shown any interest in music?"

"He seems to like it when I put on the car radio, but I haven't noticed any particular fascination with it."

"I wonder how much he got to hear back home," she commented.

A picture of the orphanage popped into Jarrod's mind. No way could the cold, sterile surroundings Sasha had come from be considered home. It was merely the place where the child had lived.

That evening at the dinner table, Jarrod learned more about his son than he had in nearly two months. For instance the boy had had only three changes of clothes and two pairs of shoes. Jarrod had known that Sasha, like the other older children, had been assigned regular chores around the place. What he hadn't known was that his son's job had been cleaning out chamber pots every morning and evening.

"That must have been very unpleasant," Nina said to Sasha.

He shrugged. "Not as bad as polishing the windows. The matrons were really strict about the windows. Made the kids do them over and over. They didn't bother with the pots. Just wanted to make sure they were emptied. I got finished quick so I could go outside."

Nina translated his response for Jarrod.

He shook his head in disgust. "The irony, of course, is that clean chamber pots are a lot more important than sparkling windows."

Nina was skillful in drawing the boy out. Though Jarrod couldn't follow their conversations, he figured she was telling him as much about herself as she was asking about him. Jarrod wished he could understand what she was saying. Even chattering in a foreign language, she fascinated him—the exotic sounds tumbling from her mouth, the twinkle in her eyes when she recounted something that made the boy laugh… For the first time, Jarrod envied his son, envied Sasha the private world he was sharing with this woman.

LIFE SETTLED INTO a routine over the next two weeks. Nina found herself enjoying the charm of the guesthouse, especially the bedroom, where a wall of windows seemed to bring the woodland in. Only reluctantly did she finally draw the drapes last thing before climbing into bed every night.

She received a contract for translating a series of romances into Italian and French. The schedule was tight, so the work kept her busy. She also found the novels fun to read. Because she spent so many hours at a desk or writing table, she'd long made it a habit to break up the day with physical exercise. In the city that had meant jogging or a trip to her health club. Here she found another diversion that was much more pleasant.

Jarrod, she quickly learned, ran the three-mile round trip to the lake every day at lunch-time and ended his fitness routine by shooting hoops. On Tuesday he caught her watching and asked if she'd like to join him, forcing her to admit she'd never played the game.

"Come on," he said. "I'll teach you."

He was wearing a tank top that exposed his broad shoulders and muscular arms. Her fear of looking like a complete spastic was quickly counterbalanced by the distraction of sharing the improvised court with him.

Predictably, she was uncoordinated and clumsy in her approach to the basket.

"Let go of the ball at the top of your jump," he said, and demonstrated what she was doing wrong and how she could correct it.

Her second attempt was an improvement, her third even better.

"You sure you're not setting me up? You've done this before."

"Never," she insisted. "But I did play volleyball in college."

He laughed. "Okay, how about some one-on-one."

It was, of course, too soon, so the score

was completely lopsided. Still he did allow her a few points. More interesting was the body contact they made. She had to admit she enjoyed the mild collisions.

Finally, she'd had enough, and he went to get a couple of bottles of water from his refrigerator. They stretched out on the cool grass in the shade of a towering maple.

"Did you play professionally?" she asked.

"No. I had a basketball scholarship in college and was competent but hardly star material," he admitted, "maybe because I never saw it as more than a game. The tuition assistance was the real driving influence."

She liked his frankness and his modesty.

"Have you ever gone white-water rafting?" he asked.

She pictured a huge rubber boat tumbling precariously through boulder-strewn rapids. "I went tubing once, but I've never been rafting."

"Would you like to try it? October is only a couple of weeks away when the season shuts down till spring. I thought we might take Sasha up to the New River in West Virginia this weekend."

The invitation was tempting. "Does he know?" The boy hadn't said anything to her, and she would have expected him to be bubbling over with excitement about it.

"I want to make sure I can get reservations first. Come with us. It'll be fun. How about it?"

She really didn't have to consider the question very long. "I'd like that."

and she would have expected her to be both
using her skills to delineate about any other...

Appliances make such a ... can get delivered...

Baby. Come a ... it ... I thought I would it...

She's only doing ... have to ... to ... the store...

have you ... and ...

## CHAPTER FOUR

"SASHA, IT'S TIME to get up." Jarrod jostled his son's shoulder. "S-a-s-h-a."

The boy gave a grunt of annoyance.

"Sasha…"

No response.

"Time to go white-water rafting."

His eyes opened.

"Come on, Son. You can sleep in the car, but we don't want to be late. Hurry up and get dressed."

Jarrod returned to the kitchen and was filling a thermos with hot coffee when Nina came in the back door.

"Brrr. It's chilly out there."

He smiled. "It'll warm up."

He'd never seen her this early, slightly rumpled from a short night's sleep. Not an unpleasant sight at all, he decided.

Sasha slept in the back seat on the two-hour drive to West Virginia. The sun had been up only an hour when they arrived at the mountain resort that offered hiking trails, fishing, spelunking and various forms of boating on the broad, brown New River. Jarrod checked in at the headquarters, got directions to the rafting departure point and continued through the densely forested mountains to a settlement.

By now Sasha was wide awake, all-eyes, and jabbering away to Nina in Russian, pointing to things, people, and asking one question after another.

They were each issued gear—a life preserver, safety helmet and oar. Everything fascinated the boy. Jarrod kept waiting for some sign of hesitation, some hint of fear. He detected none.

They were assigned to a ten-person raft, along with a family of six—grandparents, parents and two daughters. Their guide was a young woman from Wisconsin, named Hannah.

Preparations seemed interminable. Jarrod got out the sunscreen and helped Sasha apply it. Nina then repeated all the rules and safety precautions to the boy, who nodded impatiently and tapped his feet. Jarrod had to smother a laugh. He'd never seen his son so excited.

At last they received the go-ahead, lifted the massive pontoon and stepped into the cool water. Shoving off, they helped one another into the raft and paddled away from shore. Hannah gave them several maneuvers to practice as they gently floated downstream toward a section of churning water.

"You okay?" Jarrod asked Sasha, who was sitting immediately ahead of him on the gunwale.

"*Da, da,*" Sasha said, nodding enthusiastically, his face beaming. "*Khorosho, khorosho,*" which Jarrod had learned meant good.

They hit the turbulence. The bow went up, then nose-dived. Water splashed in, spraying those in the front. First there was an audible collective gasp, then laughter. Sasha's was louder than anyone's.

The current accelerated, sweeping them through a neck and down a mini waterfall. This time the entire craft was awash, with everyone wet. Jarrod looked at Nina, who was sitting across from them. She, too, was laughing.

During the next two and a half hours, they navigated a variety of rapids, some of which looked more intimidating from a distance than they turned out to be. The excitement level never ebbed, however. By the time they paddled over to a clearing in the dense pine forest for lunch, they were ready for a break, though no one was willing to be the first to admit it.

Three other rafts joined them on the riverbank. One was carried ashore and overturned to use as a table. A large cooler was produced from the second craft, and a pair of big beverage urns from the third. Within minutes lunch was being served buffet style.

Nina had taken off her life vest and hung it on a tree branch to dry. Jarrod had to control an urge to stare. Her powder-blue T-shirt was wet enough to cling.

"Should we fix Sasha's plate for him?" she asked.

Jarrod gave the question a moment's consideration. "I think I'll let him do it himself, so he can see I trust him. We'll have to watch him, though, and guide his manners. He's not used to being able to take whatever he wants, and with so many other people around, he may feel threatened."

She nodded. "Let's go over the rules with him first."

Jarrod called Sasha to the side. Carefully, they explained how everyone would go through the line and select the food they wanted.

"Take only as much as you'll eat," Jarrod told him, as Nina translated. "You can have all you want, but it'll be better to take less the first time and come back for more when you finish that. Do you understand?"

He indicated he did.

"Nina, you go first. Sasha will be behind you. I'll bring up the rear."

As they inched along, she explained what the different foods were, and took small portions for herself. Following her example, Sasha took exactly the same things in the same proportions. Jarrod complimented him as they moved along. They got glasses of lemonade from one of the big urns, and the three of them moved to a fallen log and sat down across from the family from their raft.

"Eat slowly," Jarrod advised his son through Nina.

To his relief, Sasha did exactly as he was told.

"Is that Russian you've been speaking?" the grandfather asked Nina.

She confirmed that it was.

"I thought so. I grew up speaking Czech at home. Haven't used it in years, but I can sort of understand what you're saying. Is he adopted?"

Nina conversed with him in a language Jarrod could only surmise was not Russian. The man's face lit up, and they both laughed.

"You didn't mention Czech in your list of languages," Jarrod said when the man excused himself to get more lemonade.

She laughed. "I'm not fluent, not even proficient. I can get by, that's all."

He suspected she was being modest.

Sasha finished his plate.

"Would you like more?" Jarrod asked.

He nodded. The kid had a good appetite, though he was still skinny.

"Go ahead and get whatever you want."

"Are you coming with me?"

"You can go by yourself, unless you need my help."

"I'll go with you," said the older of the two girls. She was about twelve. "I want another cookie."

"He's a cute kid," the girl's mother said. "Shy, though."

"He's only been in this country a couple of months," Jarrod explained. "Everything is still very new to him."

Sasha returned a few minutes later with a

large helping of macaroni salad and two oat-meal-raisin cookies.

"Is it all right if we go for a walk?" Jarrod asked Hannah after Sasha had finished and they'd disposed of their paper plates and cups. They'd be hauling their trash away with them.

"Sure," she said. "Stay on the road, though. There are a lot of nasty brambles and poison ivy in the woods. You don't want to get tangled in either of them. Please be back in about twenty minutes."

Jarrod, Nina and Sasha strolled the dirt road that jackknifed the steep hill, eventually coming to a railroad track on a ridgeline a quarter of the way up the mountain. They'd seen several long coal trains on it earlier in the day. In the distance now they could hear the warning whistle of one approaching.

"Let's stay here," Jarrod said. "We don't want to be stuck on the other side when it's time to head back."

They watched the train approach. Sasha had never seen one up close before. The two heavy diesel locomotives rumbled loudly and made the ground shake as they passed.

"It's big," he said.

Jarrod searched his son's face for signs of fear, but saw only fascination.

Loaded cars were still clacking by when they finally turned to rejoin the group.

With the exception of one large chute that had everyone yelling and laughing, the second stage of their adventure was less hair-raising, and they drifted easily down the broad stretch of river.

"I'm going for a swim," Hannah announced. "Anyone want to join me?"

"Me," the younger of the two girls shouted.

Nina explained to Sasha.

"Have you ever been swimming?" Jarrod asked him.

He shook his head.

"Do you want to try it? You have on your life vest, so you'll be fine."

Jarrod saw him waver. This was a new challenge, and much as Sasha wanted to take it, he was scared. The older of the two girls jumped off the bow of the raft and spun around frantically.

"I'll go with you," Jarrod told Sasha.

The boy's eyes lit up. "Okay."

"Is the water cold?" the grandmother asked.

"Freezing," the girl answered with chattering teeth.

"Still want to go in?" Nina asked Jarrod.

"I'm game, if Sasha is."

The grandfather plunged off the side and paddled around for a minute. "It's not bad after the first shock."

Jarrod decided to take the plunge. The icy mountain river took his breath away. "It's pretty cold," he told his son. "You don't have to come in if you don't want to."

The little girl jumped in and screamed. Sasha watched her and her sister splash each other. "I'll come in."

He stuck a foot in the rippling brown stream. His eyes went wide with doubt.

"Just jump in," Jarrod suggested. "Don't try to do it gradually. That just makes it worse."

The boy was obviously skeptical.

Jarrod held out his arms. "Go for it."

Taking a big breath, Sasha jumped feet-first, went under for a second, then bobbed to the surface, choking and sputtering.

"You okay?" Jarrod moved beside him.

The kid looked terrified.

"Just relax, Son."

Sasha had his elbows pinned to his sides. His teeth were chattering.

"Move your arms and kick your feet."

Nina translated from the raft.

Dubious but determined, Sasha complied.

"You're doing great," Jarrod assured him.

The two girls were laughing and splashing each other now, but they kept their distance from Jarrod and Sasha.

With the bulky life jackets on, it was impossible to do much more than dog-paddle. After another minute, Jarrod lifted Sasha to the side of the raft. Nina pulled him in, and Jarrod climbed aboard after him.

He smiled at his son and patted him on the shoulder. "What did you think of it?"

"It's cold," Sasha said.

"It isn't always. Next time we go swimming it'll be warmer, I promise."

Their clothes went from dripping wet to soggy by the time they reached the end of their adventure. A bus was waiting to take them back to the resort center. After returning their equipment and saying goodbye to the other family, Jarrod tipped their guide and they climbed into the Cherokee.

Their cabin contained two bedrooms, two baths, a common room with kitchenette and laundry facilities. Jarrod let Sasha and Nina shower first. Standing on the back deck overlooking a pond, he watched small carp weave in and around a cluster of water lilies, while he listened to the sound of Nina's shower. He forced his mind to concentrate on his surroundings—the beauty of the mountains, the blue sky, the chatter of birds—and ignore images of hot soapy water streaming down her naked body.

The shower ended. Minutes passed. Finally he heard the screen door slam behind him. Sasha came out, dressed and smiling.

*"Otyets?"* Father? "Can we…go…*yescho raz?"*

Nina appeared behind him. "Again."

Sasha nodded. "Can we go again?"

Jarrod looked at her scrubbed faced and wet hair. *Beautiful…* He focused on his son.

"You want to go white-water rafting again?"

His face lit up and he bobbed his head.

"Another time. Definitely."

*"Zaftra?* Tomorrow?"

Jarrod shook his head. "Not tomorrow, but next summer when the water is warm."

Nina translated.

Sasha's enthusiasm turned into a scowl. "I want to go tomorrow. Why can't we?" he asked Nina.

She relayed the questions.

"Because we have to go home tomorrow. You have school Monday, and Nina and I have to work."

"I want to go again," he said more forcefully.

This was Sasha's first real request, and Jarrod felt bad about not being able to grant it. "We'll come in the summer. Now, how about we drive around these beautiful mountains and find a place to eat?"

They stopped for dinner at a family restaurant in the mountains overlooking a tiny lake, and ordered fried catfish and hush puppies. Sasha would have burned his mouth on the piping hot food if Nina hadn't cautioned him. Jarrod was pleased how the boy paid attention to her. As a reward for good table manners Sasha got a small dish of vanilla ice cream with chocolate sauce for dessert.

Later that night Jarrod read him a bedtime story and watched him slip off into peaceful slumber.

Nina put aside the book she'd been reading when Jarrod joined her in the common room.

"An exciting day," he remarked, as he settled into the armchair across from her.

She nodded. "I thought you'd like to know what I've learned about him so far."

He studied her and the warm but wary expression in her eyes.

"From your tone I suspect it isn't encouraging."

"I wouldn't go that far," she said, "but he's starting off with definite limitations. His command of Russian is at best rudimentary."

"He's not even eight years old, Nina, and he's never received any formal training."

"I understand that, and I'm taking it into consideration, but even so his language skills are substandard. He speaks more like a child of three or four than one of seven or eight. His grammar is primitive, his vocabulary extremely limited."

"Are you saying you think the low IQ is accurate, after all?"

"I honestly don't know about his IQ. It's probable that he was never given the opportunity to improve, that no one ever pointed out the mistakes he was making or tried to teach him new words. But the fact that he didn't pick up more on his own is a bit troubling."

"Can you give me some examples?"

She paused for a moment to frame her response. "He always uses the present tense instead of past or future and doesn't put the proper endings on words." She propped her fingers together and touched them to her lips. "Let me see if I can give you an equivalent in English. Instead of saying he went to school yesterday, Sasha would say 'he go to school yesterday.' Instead of 'he will go to school tomorrow,' he says 'he go to school tomorrow.'"

Jarrod frowned. "A lot of people use bad grammar. I would understand what he means."

She nodded. "And that may be the point. He is understandable, so no one ever bothered to correct him. I started out speaking to him in very simple sentences and gradually made them more complex. He didn't seem to have trouble following me, so that's a positive sign. When he does have difficulty, it seemed to be because he doesn't recognize the words I was using. He knows what a tree is, but he apparently never heard of an oak or a pine. He knows what fish are, but not the names of different kinds. Naturally, I wouldn't expect him to know what hush puppies are, but he didn't realize that French fries are potatoes or that coleslaw is cabbage."

Jarrod wriggled his nose. "So what are you telling me—that he's ignorant or stupid?"

"I'm not saying he's either." She softened her tone. "He can learn, Jarrod. I just don't know much or how quickly. I started him using several new words in Russian today. I'll find out tomorrow if he remembers them. My guess is that he will."

She kicked off her shoes and curled more

comfortably into the corner of the couch, tucking her legs under her. "I don't want you to feel left out of the conversation. Tomorrow I'll begin teaching him words in English, so the three of us can talk. You've done a good job so far, Jarrod. I want you to know that. He's picked up quite a bit. Your instincts have been right to talk to him in short, simple sentences."

DURING THE TWO WEEKS following the rafting expedition, Sasha seemed to break out of his shell and lose a good deal of his shyness, at least around Jarrod, Nina and Earl. Soon "sandwich" became "I want sandwich," then "I want a sandwich," and finally became "I would like a sandwich." Nina was especially pleased when he mastered the *th* sound and stopped rolling his *r*s. He still had an accent, but it was mild, and she assured Jarrod that it would likely disappear with time.

Everything was going very well when, on the third Tuesday, Jarrod received a telephone call.

"Mr. Morrison, this is Fern Keller. We have another problem with your son."

Minutes later, Jarrod tapped on the guesthouse door. "Nina?"

"What's wrong?" she asked the moment

she opened it. "Has something happened to Sasha?"

"I just received a call from the school. He's in trouble again."

"What kind of trouble?"

"I'm not sure. The principal refused to discuss it over the phone, but she wants me there right away. Will you come with me?"

"Of course. Let me get my purse and sweater."

Leaving him standing in the doorway, she ducked into the bedroom and came out wearing a cream-colored cardigan. With purse in hand she followed him out, snapping the door lock as she went.

"You weren't able to get any information about what's going on?" she asked.

He backed the Cherokee out of the driveway. "Other than to confirm he isn't hurt or curled up under his desk again, Mrs. Keller would say only that he's being detained in her office."

Nina looked over. "Curled up under his desk? Care to elaborate?"

Jarrod told her about the episode that had happened just before she'd interviewed for the job.

"Surely he's not still hoarding food," Nina

said. "I think we've convinced him he won't go hungry anymore. His table manners have certainly improved."

"When he's with us, but I imagine the school still seems a bit like the orphanage to him."

Jarrod pulled into the school parking lot. The receptionist in the office, a harassed-looking woman with salt-and-pepper hair pulled back in a bun, started to greet him, then saw Nina and hesitated.

"Sasha's English tutor," he said quickly.

"Oh. I guess that's okay." She nodded to the door behind her. "Mrs. Keller said for you to go right in."

Jarrod tapped twice on the opaque glass-paneled door and entered the principal's office without waiting for an acknowledgment.

Sasha was sitting on one of the shiny wooden armchairs against the far wall. His head shot up when he saw Jarrod. Last time the boy had been bewildered by what was going on; this time Jarrod thought he saw anger lurking behind the worry.

Mrs. Keller was sitting at her desk, hands folded in front of her.

"Thank you for coming, Mr. Morrison." She saw Nina and rose from her seat.

"Mrs. Keller, this is Nina Lockhart, Sasha's English tutor."

Nina stepped forward and reached across the desk. They shook hands quickly.

"What seems to be the trouble?" Jarrod asked.

The principal scowled, "Mr. Morrison, I cannot and will not tolerate theft in my school. This time your son has stolen food from the other children."

Jarrod's pulse speeded up. "Nina, why don't you talk to Sasha in here and get his side of the story, while Mrs. Keller and I step outside and I hear hers?"

The principal's mouth fell open. "Mr. Morrison—"

"Shall we discuss this in the next room? I'm sure Sasha will be more comfortable talking to Ms. Lockhart alone, and we won't be distracted by their conversation."

After a long moment's pause, she glared at Sasha and moved from behind her desk. "Very well."

The receptionist looked up and just as quickly refocused on her papers.

"Mr. Morrison, I don't appreciate you coming here and taking over my—"

"Why don't you just tell me what happened, Mrs. Keller? Let's see what we can do to resolve the problem."

She seemed uncertain how to react. He'd purposely shed the confrontational tone for a more conciliatory one. She could either accept his invitation to work together or risk coming across as petty and uncooperative.

"Sybil," she finally said, "would you please have the volunteer in the library relieve Ms. Peters in her classroom so she can join us?"

"Yes, ma'am." The receptionist picked up the telephone.

Mrs. Keller motioned Jarrod to an adjoining room that contained a row of filing cabinets and a long conference table with a dozen chairs around it.

Alicia must have been waiting for the summons, because she appeared within two minutes. The principal asked her to explain the situation.

"During our morning break, Bobby Smith complained to me that Sasha had taken the apple from his lunch bag. A minute later Sally Haynes came up and told me the banana she'd brought to school was missing. I found both pieces of fruit, as well as several packages of cookies and cupcakes other children had brought from home, in Sasha's desk."

"Since they didn't give him the food items," the principal interjected, "the only explanation is that he stole them. Mr. Morrison, we've had problems with him stealing food before."

"*Steal* is a very strong word. Last time he took rolls from the cafeteria, bread he would have been allowed to eat there. I'd hardly call that stealing. Has he done anything like this since then?" He directed his question toward Ms. Peters.

She shook her head. "No. Not that I'm aware of."

He turned to the older woman. "You suspect he has, though, don't you?"

"All I'm saying," she replied, "is that today's incident is consistent with his past behavior."

"Ms. Peters, how has he been behaving in class otherwise?"

"Actually, he's been doing much better lately. Still not on a par with the other children, of course, but considerably better than when he first arrived. That's one reason I find today's episode so distressing. He's starting to play with the others, too, something he didn't do before, and while his English isn't fluent, it's certainly better than it was. I thought he was making a real effort to fit in until this."

"Let's hear his side of the story," Jarrod said, "before we pass any judgments."

NINA SAT ON THE HARD wooden chair beside Sasha and settled a reassuring smile on her lips.

"Are you all right?" she asked in Russian.

He nodded.

"Tell me what happened today. Why were you brought to the principal's office?"

He shrugged. "They say I take food from others."

"Did you?"

"*Nyet,*" he snapped defiantly.

"Then why did they say that you did?"

He made no reply.

"Sasha, I'm not saying you did anything bad. I just want to know what happened."

"The teacher go to my—" he blurted, then halted, as if searching for a word.

"Desk?" she asked in English.

He nodded.

She told him the Russian word and asked him to continue.

"She say I steal things to eat, but I not."

"Then why were they in your desk?"

He looked her straight in the eye this time,

and she could feel him assessing whether she would believe him. "They give to me."

She'd expected him to say he didn't know, that he hadn't put them there. "I believe you, Sasha. Now please tell me why they gave them to you?"

"They say…I think they say they have no place in desk and want me to put in mine until they eat them."

Again Nina had anticipated a different response, that they'd just given them to him. It would have been natural for him to think they were his to keep, but he'd apparently understood they were only asking him to store them temporarily. Which meant his comprehension of English was better than she'd realized. Unless he was lying, of course.

"Did they say how long they wanted you to hold these things for them?"

"Until after lunch."

"And when did the teacher go into your locker?"

"During break."

"Why did she go there at all?"

"Because Bobby Smith say something to her."

"Do you think Bobby Smith told her you stole them?"

Again he shrugged, as if the conclusion was obvious.

"Was he one of the children who asked you to hold things for them?"

The boy nodded. "He first. Others come, give me, too."

Sasha had been bamboozled, and Bobby Jones was the ringleader. The cruelty of children always amazed her. The need to find a victim and inflict pain seemed to be a powerful drive in some kids.

Nina spent a few more minutes reviewing everything Sasha told her to make sure she had it right. Ten minutes later—convinced he was telling the truth—she rose from her chair, went to the door and told the receptionist they were ready.

## CHAPTER FIVE

JARROD FOLLOWED THE PRINCIPAL and the teacher back into the office. Sasha was standing next to Nina, his mouth thin with tension, his eyes wary. Mrs. Keller invited everyone to sit down, and slipped behind her desk.

"Sasha has something he wants to tell you," Nina announced.

Mrs. Keller glanced at Jarrod, then at Alicia Peters, who raised her eyebrows.

"Go on, Sasha," Nina said gently in English. "Tell Mrs. Keller what happened."

The boy stood up, as Nina had no doubt instructed him. "Bob—by Smit-th—" the *th* came out as two separate sounds "—gave me to put in desk for him…and others."

The principal frowned as she considered his words. "They gave you their fruit and their treats? Why did they do that?" She looked at Nina for the answer.

Sasha gazed up at Nina as well and said something in Russian.

"Too much," Nina prompted him.

"Too much in desks."

Mrs. Keller took another moment to consider his response. "Is he saying the other children gave him the things Ms. Peters found in his desk?"

"Exactly," Nina replied.

"But why?" the young teacher asked, as confused as her superior.

"I think it's called being set up," Nina stated. "I'm sure you've run into it before, kids taking delight in tricking their friends—or enemies—in order to get them in trouble."

"Bobby Smith," Alicia muttered, and shook her head in exasperation. "I should have realized. He can be mean to other kids. Yes, it's possible."

Jarrod looked at his son and felt a surge of pride. The boy had explained himself, haltingly and clumsily, but he had gotten his idea across in English. He'd used his new language to defend himself. An important first step. Jarrod glanced at Nina and saw she felt the same way.

"Who else was involved?" Mrs. Keller asked.

Nina asked Sasha in Russian.

"Bobby Smith, Sally Haynes and Morley Watts," he reported, speaking directly to the principal.

The names didn't seem to come as a surprise to either woman.

"We'll settle this right now," Mrs. Keller said. "Ms. Peters, please pull Bobby and the others from class and keep them separated. I don't want them talking to each other. We'll let them cool their heels for a while, then I'll interview them one at a time in here."

Alicia Peters left the room and returned a few minutes later with a boy who was a head taller than Sasha. He had quick, intelligent brown eyes.

"Why did you tell Ms. Peters Sasha Morrison had stolen your food?" Mrs. Keller asked him.

The boy's jaw dropped. "I…I didn't lie. He did. Everybody knows he takes food."

"He takes food. He doesn't steal it. You gave him your lunch to put in his desk."

"He's lying."

"Who is?"

"Sasha."

"I didn't say he was the one who told me you gave him your lunch."

Jarrod could see the confusion and doubt written on the kid's face. Fern Keller understood the intimidating power of making the boy face her in the presence of two other adults and the classmate he'd victimized.

"Whoever told you that is lying," he insisted.

"Why would they lie?"

That stumped him for a moment. Jarrod could almost see the time-honored excuse forming on his lips: *because.* But Bobby was obviously smart enough to know that wouldn't fly, not with Mrs. Keller, who at that very moment was peering at him with the force of a ray gun.

"I don't know, but they are." The defiant tone came out sounding more like a whine this time.

"So the others gave their lunches to Sasha Morrison, but you didn't?"

Bobby squirmed.

"Where was your lunch?"

This was a question he could answer easily. "In his desk," he said with apparent relief.

"I mean where did he get it?" she amended.

He shrugged. "I don't know."

"Then how do you know he stole it? Maybe," she speculated, "it was just lying around and he put it away for safekeeping."

"It wasn't lying around. It was in my desk. He took it."

"You just told me you didn't know where he'd gotten it. Which is true?"

He stared at her. "Uh, er, I don't know."

"Bobby, you're not telling me the truth. Sasha didn't take anything from you or anyone else. You and the others gave him your lunches for safekeeping, then told Mrs. Peters that Sasha had stolen them. You lied to her."

"I didn't," he said in a defensive voice, his eyes glistening with frustration.

"What you did was wrong, Bobby. Not only does it make you a liar, a reputation you'll now have to overcome, but it hurt someone who didn't do anything to you. I don't think your parents will be very pleased when they find out."

He sniffled and a tear ran down his face.

"You owe Sasha an apology and you owe one to the class for being a bad example."

"Please don't tell my dad." The sniffle had turned into a sob.

Jarrod saw Mrs. Keller hesitate.

"I'm going to call your mother and ask her to handle this. But," she added sternly. "if anything like this happens again, I'll have no alternative but to notify your father, as well. Do you understand me?"

"Yes, ma'am." He seemed greatly relieved, making Jarrod wonder what kind of relationship existed between parents and child in the Smith household.

"You may return to your class now."

The boy nearly ran out the door.

"Is his father violent?" Jarrod asked.

"Not physically, as far as I know," Mrs. Keller said, looking at Sasha to see how much of this the boy understood. "But I've heard he can be excessively strict. He'd probably ground Bobby for a year instead of a week or a month."

"And his mother?"

The principal shook her head. "The opposite, I'm afraid. She won't take any disciplinary action. She might even excuse what he did as nothing more than a childish prank. I can only hope compelling him to apologize in front of the class will make the right impression on him."

Jarrod appreciated her dilemma and respected her decision. It wasn't ideal, but the compromise was probably the best she could manage under the circumstances.

"Sasha, you, too, may return to your classroom," the principal told him.

"Wait." Jarrod motioned him over. Placing his hands on the boy's thin, narrow shoulders, he said quietly, "I'm very proud of you, Son."

Nina translated in the same intimate tone.

Sasha didn't smile, but his eyes glowed with a new light. He nodded in thanks, then dashed from the room.

"Would it be possible for me to address Ms. Peters's class?" Nina asked the principal.

"About what?"

"I'd like to tell them about Sasha, about where he comes from, what his life has been like, and let them ask him any questions they might have."

Mrs. Keller turned to Alicia with a raised brow.

"I think that's a wonderful idea. I'd like to hear his story, too."

NINA GAZED OUT at the semicircle of eager, bright-eyed young faces, introduced herself and explained that she was helping Sasha learn English.

"Does anyone here know where Sasha comes from?" she asked.

Three hands went up. She pointed to the girl with black, curly hair in front row.

"Russia."

"That's right." Nine walked over to a map of the world on a side wall. "Who can tell me where the United States is?"

This time half a dozen hands shot up. She called on a tall, lanky boy in baggy jeans to point it out and complimented him on getting it right. Before he returned to his seat she asked him if he knew where Russia was. He didn't, nor did any of his classmates.

Nina swept her hand across the great expanse of her motherland and explained how big it was.

"Sasha comes from a place near this city." She tapped the capital with her finger. "It's called Moscow, and it's the biggest city in the country. Maybe one day some of you will get to visit there. It's a beautiful city with churches and museums, plenty of restaurants and places to see. They have buses and streetcars and the most beautiful subway in the world."

"Do they have a zoo? With wild animals?" A chubby boy with shoulder-length brown hair asked.

She smiled. "They sure do."

"Did Sasha ever go there?" a Hispanic girl asked.

"Why don't you ask him?"

The girl was nonplussed for a moment, then turned to him and asked, "Did you ever go to the zoo where you lived?" Nina repeated the question in Russian.

"*Nyet.*"

"Is that Russian?" a dark-skinned boy in back asked. "It sounds funny."

Nina grinned. "Would you believe English sounds funny to Russians, too?"

"It does?"

"I know you probably have plenty of questions for Sasha, so why don't you ask them and I'll translate for you."

Immediately hands went up. Nina pointed to a red-headed girl in the front row.

"Why does he always gobble his food like a dog?" she asked.

Someone giggled.

Nina turned to Sasha and said in Russian. "She wants to know why you always eat so fast."

He struggled. "So they can't steal it from me."

"Because he's afraid someone will take his food away if he doesn't eat it quickly."

"Nobody cares about his food," a boy in the back row scoffed, "especially after he's had his hands all over it."

She translated to Russian. "They say you don't have to worry. Nobody will take it."

She addressed the class. "There's plenty to go around here, but in the orphanage where he lived the servings were very small and there were no seconds." She switched again to Russian. "Sasha, why don't you tell them what you had to eat over there?"

He enumerated the limited variety of food items, a diet heavy in bread and soup.

A boy said, "That's all?"

Another sing-songed, "Bo-o-ring."

"What was your favorite dish?" a girl asked, then added, "I really like sushi."

Someone in the back said, "Gag," while Nina was translating.

"*Goluptsy*," Sasha said.

"Stuffed cabbage," Nina explained.

The expressions on their faces suggested most of them didn't know what it was.

"But didn't you ever go to McDonald's or Pizza Hut?" a girl in a bright pink shirt asked.

"I never heard of those places until I came here," Sasha explained in Russian.

"Do you go to them now? Do you like them?"

He nodded. "They're good sometimes."

The kids seemed baffled that he wasn't more enthusiastic about their favorite food.

"Why did he live in an orphanage?" a boy called out.

Nina asked Sasha the question.

"Because I didn't have any family, not until I came here. I still don't have a mother."

Nina translated the answer and glanced at Jarrod, whose sad expression matched how she felt.

"What happened to them?" a girl asked.

Sasha shrugged. "Dead, I guess."

The children fell silent. A girl in pigtails on the far side of the curved row gazed at Sasha with glassy eyes. Several other children lowered their heads.

Alicia came to the rescue. "What about sports?" She asked enthusiastically. "What kind of games did you play?"

AFTER LEAVING THE SCHOOL, Jarrod and Nina headed home.

"It's lunchtime," he noted, "and Tuesday, which means Mrs. Burgess won't be coming to Earl's house to fix him anything. She only comes on Monday, Wednesday and Friday. How about we pick up barbecue for three, stop off at his place and tell him all about this latest crisis?"

"I didn't realize I was hungry until you mentioned food," she said. "Barbecue with Earl sounds perfect."

Twenty minutes later they pulled into his driveway.

"Y'all brought food," Earl said, sniffing the air. He hurriedly backed his wheelchair away from the kitchen door to allow them to enter. "Smells like heaven. You're either taking pity on a poor computer geek, or you want something."

"Cynic." Jarrod deposited the white paper bag with the Rack Shack logo on the kitchen table. "We just want the pleasure of your company."

"I'm not about to argue with a gift horse."

"Actually, they're baby back ribs," Nina corrected.

Jarrod removed a tray from a lower cabinet and snagged paper plates and extra napkins from the pantry.

Earl led them through the house to the front porch, where a ceiling fan hovered over a glass-topped, white wicker table and matching chairs.

A minute later, his fingers were covered

with sauce. "So what kind of trouble did Sasha get into this time?"

"How did you know?" Nina asked.

He chuckled. "I figured it was due. It's been two weeks now."

Jarrod shook his head but couldn't keep from laughing. Interrupting each other and filling in details like an old married couple, he and Nina recounted the morning's activities.

"Good for Sasha," Earl said. "How did the follow-on session in the classroom go?"

"I told them who I was," Nina replied, "and that I was teaching Sasha English. Then I offered to act as translator if they wanted to ask him any questions."

The three of them annihilated the ribs, leaving nothing but a pile of dry bones. Nina went to the kitchen and returned with disposable bowls and plastic spoons for the still-warm peach cobbler.

Earl took a juicy mouthful, closed his eyes and wilted. "Not quite as good as Mom's, but it's here and hers isn't. What kinds of questions did the kids ask?"

"Fortunately, only a couple about his parents," Nina said.

Like her, Earl knew Sasha's family history. How the boy would handle the full truth, when and if he ever learned it, was a troubling question. How do you explain to a kid that his father was a criminal and his mother a drunk, that he had a sister he didn't even remember?

"I think the time spent was well worth it," Nina said. "They got to understand him a little better, and vice versa."

Earl placed his empty bowl on the table.

"Détente is good," he said. "Almost as good as this meal. Thank you both." He grinned first at Nina, then Jarrod. "You realize, of course, that he'll get into a fight today."

"What do you mean?" Nina asked.

"Simple. Some of his classmates set him up, humiliated him, tried to get him into trouble. He'll take them on. That's what I would do."

"You're not serious," she said, but in a tone of denial, rather than conviction.

Jarrod scratched his cheek. "You're right. I should have thought of that." He looked at his watch and scowled. "Damn, too late for me to pick him up at school now. The bus will be here any minute. He'll be lucky if Mrs. Keller only suspends him. She'll probably want him expelled."

"Who's that?" Nina pointed to a car pulling up the drive.

Jarrod stepped to the screen door. A Ford

Escort came to a stop a dozen yards away. Alicia Peters emerged from behind the steering wheel and opened the back door. Sasha unbuckled himself and climbed out. His white shirt was torn, his knees scuffed, and there was a cut on his cheek.

"Oh, my God," Nina exclaimed.

"What happened?" Jarrod asked, as the two approached.

Ruff bounded to Sasha's side and gazed up adoringly, waiting to be petted. Acting as if the animal were the only friend he had left in the world, Sasha rubbed him behind the ears. The dog cocked his head for maximum effect.

"Sasha and Bobby Smith had, shall we say, an altercation," Alicia announced.

"Who started it?" Jarrod asked.

"I'm not sure. I figured there'd be trouble, so I tried to keep an eye on them, but they were already scuffling in the school yard by the time I caught up with them. I asked several of the kids standing around, but their answers weren't very helpful."

Nina stepped down from the porch and stood beside Jarrod.

He beckoned to his son. Sasha didn't cringe. In fact, his back seemed to straighten, as if he were prepared to defend himself.

"Tell me what happened."

Nina instantly repeated his order in Russian, though she felt certain in this case it wasn't necessary.

Alicia moved to the side, her eyes resting briefly on the man in the wheelchair on the screened-in porch.

Sasha bowed his head but said nothing.

"I asked you a question, Son, and I want the truth. Tell me what happened."

Again Nina's translation was instantaneous.

"I yell at him because he lie," the boy said in Russian. Nina repeated his words simultaneously in English. "He tell teacher I take food he give me."

"Did you yell at him in English or in Russian?"

The boy looked up and blinked. He stopped petting the dog. Clearly he didn't know.

"Did you hit him first?" Jarrod asked.

"*Da.*" Nina didn't have to translate that.

Earl appeared in the doorway. "Why don't y'all come in out of the sun?"

Alicia automatically turned at the sound of his voice. Jarrod watched their eyes meet and tension flick across her face as her eyes grew sad.

"I'll be on my way," she announced nervously. "I didn't mean to impose, but Sa-sha—" she refocused on Jarrod "—saw your Jeep and said you were here."

"Come inside," Earl called out again. "You, too, Allie. I promise not to bite."

Color rose to her face. Her lips parted, but no words came out.

"Please," Jarrod said. "I need you to help me sort all this out."

"Just for a minute," she murmured, "then I have to go."

Jarrod walked over to his son, placed a hand on his shoulder and ushered him toward the house. At the bottom of the steps, however, he drew him aside so the two women could precede them.

Alicia's face was a mask of tension as she walked past Earl's wheelchair.

"It's good to see you again," he said softly.

"Uh…nice to see you, too."

"Sit down." Earl reached for the nearly empty pitcher. "I'll be right back with more tea." Securing the damp container between his knees, he spun around and entered the house.

"I can't stay long," Alicia repeated, as she sat on the front half of the cushion in one of the wicker chairs.

Nina resumed her former place, which was

across from the teacher, while Jarrod remained standing, frowning at his son.

The silence lingered only a few seconds before Earl reappeared with a large tray resting on the arms of his chair. On it were an ice bucket, a glass for Alicia, a pitcher of tea and a bottle of water for Sasha. Alicia rose but then seemed uncertain what to do next. Clearly the wheelchair—or perhaps its occupant—flustered her. Jarrod leaned over, relieved Earl of the tray and placed it on the table.

"How come you brought Sasha home yourself?" Earl rested his elbows on the arms of his chair and folded his hands as he gazed up at her. "Why wasn't he on the school bus?"

"Mrs. Keller might have seen him if I'd let him stand around with the other kids, and I didn't think that was a good idea. She would have suspended him for sure, and I don't want her to do that. He needs to be in school with other children. It's good for them to interact with him, too."

"She's bound to find out what happened," Jarrod observed. He put an ice-filled glass of tea in front of her.

"Probably…" She fingered the sweaty base. "But by the time she does it'll only be hearsay."

"You won't tell her?"

"No." Clearly she didn't agree with her boss's handling of the boy. "And I can assure you Bobby Smith won't report it, either. His father would find out for sure then, and he'd be in real trouble."

"Does he look as bad as Sasha?" Jarrod asked.

"Let's just say Sasha gave as good as he got." Alicia couldn't seem to suppress a small smile. "And tomorrow it'll be obvious from their bruises that they were fighting each other. As long as Mrs. Keller can't prove it took place on school grounds, though, there isn't much she can do about it."

"I hope you're right." Jarrod turned to his son, wondering how much of the conversation he'd understood. "Why did you hit Bobby?"

"He lie," Sasha repeated sullenly.

"Yes, he did. But hitting you with words is not the same as you hitting him with your fists." Jarrod turned to Nina. "Do you have the saying in Russia 'Sticks and stones may break my bones but words will never hurt me'?"

"Something pretty close." She spouted the Russian. The boy nodded.

"Tell him no ice cream for the—" Jarrod

stopped abruptly. "Wait. I don't want to use food as a punishment. No video games for the next three days."

Sasha nodded when informed.

"Now go outside with Ruff and play," Jarrod said, "while I talk with Ms. Peters."

Boy and dog crowded the doorway, trying to escape. The screen slammed behind them.

"Thanks for doing this," Jarrod murmured. "I know you didn't have to. I hope you won't get into trouble on his account."

"Don't worry about me," she exclaimed. "He's a good kid. Fighting is wrong, but in the world he came from, it was probably necessary. I hope he learns that here it isn't." She rose from her seat, her tea untouched. "I have to go." Self-consciously biting her lip, she gazed down at Earl. "It was nice seeing you again."

A tiny smile curled the corners of his mouth. "Nice seeing you again, too, Allie."

"You're the only one who's ever called me that." She paused, as if she wanted to say more. With a slight nod she moved to the door, and after the briefest hesitation said, "Goodbye."

A few seconds later the Escort crunched down the gravel driveway and disappeared from view.

Jarrod observed the man in the wheelchair. His friend was working his jaw as he stared through the screen at the empty road.

"You didn't tell me you knew Alicia Peters."

"We went to high school together." Earl continued to gaze at the sun-dappled lawn, or was it at the driveway? "She was a year behind me."

Jarrod raised his eyebrows to Nina, whose expression signaled her own curiosity.

Earl laughed in self-deprecation. "We went together for a while."

"What happened?" Jarrod asked.

"She found someone she liked better." He spun around, wheeled back to the table and topped up his iced tea glass. Jarrod had the distinct impression he would have preferred a beer.

"He got her pregnant, then left town before the baby was born," Earl said to no one in particular.

"She has a child?" Nina asked.

"A girl." Earl gulped a mouthful of tea. "She must be about twelve years old now."

Jarrod shook his head. "She doesn't look old enough to have a twelve—"

"She's twenty-nine," Earl declared. "A year younger than me."

The arithmetic wasn't hard. She'd been sixteen when she became pregnant.

"Is she at least getting child support from the father?" Nina asked.

Earl rolled back toward the screen door. Jarrod followed his friend's gaze and observed Sasha. The boy was throwing a stick and the dog was happily retrieving it. As usual, both seemed content to go on forever.

"Her parents made her give the baby up for adoption at birth," Earl said. "I heard she never even got to hold it."

Jarrod grimaced. He'd struggled to adopt a child. To have to give one up…

"Do you ever see her?" he asked his friend.

"Not since high school." Earl spun around and reentered the house, ending the conversation.

## CHAPTER SIX

OVER THE NEXT FEW WEEKS Jarrod became very aware that life around the Morrison household was taking on a routine and a new dimension—the feeling of a family. While he did the dishes and cleaned up the kitchen in the evenings, Nina gave Sasha a lesson in English, then hung around to watch TV, play cards or some other game with them.

Sasha was enthralled by his father's magic tricks, and asked him to repeat them over and over. At first Jarrod let him watch, knowing he would inevitably concentrate on the wrong place, which was the secret to sleight of hand. Gradually he introduced his son to some of the easier tricks. Since he had to speak through Nina, she, too, became privy to the secrets. Her openmouthed wonder was—in some ways—even more satisfying than Sasha's. Jarrod liked sharing secrets with her, though there were some he would never reveal.

Through all this the boy was making tremendous headway with English, and according to Nina, his Russian was improving as well.

Jarrod signed Sasha up for the midget soccer team. Unless Nina was working to a deadline, she accompanied them to the practice sessions and made it a point to never miss a game.

"Next year will be a problem," Jarrod told her one afternoon when they were watching the team work out. "He'll be too old for the Midgets but too small for the next level."

"Size isn't that much of a factor in soccer, is it?" she asked. "Not like American football."

"No, but skill is. He doesn't have the physical coordination required to move up yet."

"There's still the summer," she reminded him. "Kids shoot up in spurts. Maybe by the end of school break he'll have developed better control."

"I hope so. He enjoys the game, and it's a great way for him to work off some of his energy."

"He's a good team player," Nina pointed out.

A fact that amazed Jarrod. He would have expected a loner who'd had to scramble for himself to be self-absorbed. But Sasha appeared to harbor no jealousy when other players did well or scored, and he didn't hog the ball as a few of his teammates did. The kid was a maze of contradictions, Jarrod mused. He hoarded food, yet would give it away without a second thought.

Jarrod had been stopping in to see Sasha's teacher every Friday afternoon for a report on his progress.

On the Friday night before the long Thanksgiving weekend, after Sasha was in bed and sound asleep, Jarrod and Nina were relaxing in front of the fireplace. She was curled up in the corner of the couch, while he was ensconced in his recliner.

"I almost invited Alicia to Thanksgiving dinner."

Nina's eyes twinkled. "Playing matchmaker?"

He tilted his head and grinned. "I'm a bit big to be playing Cupid, huh?" He gazed into her eyes. "Do you think I should? Invite her, I mean?"

"I think you'd better talk to Earl about it first."

"Yeah, that's what I was fixing to do."

While he and Sasha were helping Earl with yard work the next day, Jarrod posed the question to his friend.

Earl continued to rake leaves. "It's your house. Invite whoever you want."

Jarrod tried to read his subtext. Was it displeasure? Anger? When Earl didn't suddenly announce a change in his own dinner plans, but simply rolled away without another word, Jarrod concluded his reaction might actually have been one of approval.

The response he received from Alicia Monday afternoon was equally inconclusive when he extended the invitation and mentioned in passing that Earl would also be there.

"That's very nice of you." She finished gathering the papers left on the small student desks, then walked over to the whiteboard and began erasing the large capital letters printed there. With her back to him, she asked, "How is he?"

"Doing fine."

She continued cleaning the board. "It'll be nice seeing him again."

"Then you'll come?"

Her smile was tentative when she turned around. "What can I bring?"

Nina had prepared him for the offer. "How about a pie?"

Her smile became more natural. "Two pies. A mince and a pumpkin. Might as well break Sasha into the season right."

Jarrod laughed. "You're on. Come around three. That'll give us time to relax and visit before we sit down at five."

NINA DELIGHTED IN WATCHING Jarrod bounce around the kitchen Thursday morning. She'd shared holiday meals with friends and business associates over the years, but always as a guest. Aside from occasionally helping to set a table or toss a salad, she'd never actually participated in the preparation. Although she'd helped Jarrod fix some of their evening meals, this festive holiday cooking captivated her. Seeing how much he enjoyed it, she gave in to the curiosity that had been bugging her from the beginning.

"Why did you never marry?" She cut off the tops of celery stalks and stripped away the coarser threads from the larger pieces.

He glanced over from the sink, where he was rinsing the giblets. "I almost did once, a long time ago."

"What happened?"

If he found the question strange or invasive, he gave no indication. "Her name was Maggie. We were in college together and had been dating for a couple of years. Right after I graduated I offered her a ring."

He dropped the giblets and the turkey neck into a large saucepan, grabbed the top of one of Nina's celery stalks, added it to the stockpot, along with a piece of onion, and lit the burner underneath.

"She refused it?"

"No, she accepted it. She still had a year to go, so we planned the wedding for right after her graduation. But at Thanksgiving she gave me back the ring."

"Why?" Nina asked. "Didn't she love you?"

He returned to washing the inside of the bird. "It wasn't so much a matter of not loving as it was of wisdom."

She looked at him. "Meaning?"

"Maggie said she cared for me and believed I cared for her, but neither of us cared for each other enough."

Nina continued chopping celery into small pieces on a wooden cutting board. "Was she right?"

"Since I wasn't totally devastated, I guess she was." He said it lightly, but Nina sensed there had been more hurt there than he was willing to admit.

He laughed. "She went on to marry a New England fisherman a few years later, settled down and raised a slew of kids. Last I heard, she was about to become a grandmother. She'd probably make a darn good one, too."

He set a large iron skillet on the stove, added generous pats of butter and stirred them with a wooden spoon.

"My turn to ask the questions now," he said. "You told me you're a widow, but you've never said anything about your husband. Mind if I ask what happened? You don't have to answer if you don't want to. It's none of my business."

She dumped the chopped celery and onion into the frying pan. "He was killed in a car accident. We were married less than a year."

"I'm sorry."

"He was a good man."

"How did you meet?"

She paused. "He was an American businessman over in Russia. It was a marriage of convenience."

"A marriage of convenience? In this day and age? Were you—" He stopped, unwilling to ask the question.

"Pregnant?" She cleared her throat. "No, it was nothing like that."

He waited for her to continue.

"He was sixty-two years old. I was eighteen. I respected him, was grateful to him, but I didn't love him. We never had sex."

Jarrod had lifted the turkey out of the sink and placed it on the drain board. He was reaching for paper towel to dry it, but halted midmotion and gave her a sidelong glance. "I hope you're not going to stop there."

She went over to the coffeemaker and poured them both fresh cups, then sat at the table to watch him.

"I'd just turned eighteen when my father was arrested."

"Arrested? For what?"

"Crimes against the state. I'm not sure what the specific charges were. It was a scary time. The Soviet Union was falling apart. There were demonstrations everywhere—unheard of in those days—and life was becoming more and more difficult. Everything was breaking down. Consumer goods were in even shorter supply than usual. People were bartering what meager possessions they had just to live."

Jarrod could remember a few periods of shortages in this country—gasoline, sugar, beef—but there was always the feeling they were temporary and sometimes more contrived than real. It wasn't as if people were starving because they didn't have sugar cubes for their coffee.

"It must have been horrible," he said.

Nina sipped from her cup. "My mother and I were alone. My father had been our sole support, and of course we didn't have Papa's income anymore, so we had to live on what you would call welfare. Twice government checks never showed up. Because of my father's previous position, my mother knew a few of the American and British businessmen who came to Moscow."

Nina held the cup to her lips, fighting to repress the shudder that coursed through her whenever she thought back to those times.

"Two weeks after my father's arrest my mother arranged for me to marry John Lockhart, the vice president of a U.S. manufacturing company. He and my father had worked closely together and become good friends. John's wife had died several years before. His children were grown. He agreed to go through a marriage ceremony with me and then bring me to the States. After I had legal status here, we would divorce, and I'd be free to go my own way. I didn't want to do it. I hardly knew the man. He seemed nice enough, but how could I be sure? I resisted as long as I could, but my mother isn't someone you say no to."

"So what happened?"

Nina held her elbows close to her body as she bracketed her cup in a vicelike grip. "I married him, and he did exactly as he'd promised. We came to New York. He arranged for me to get permanent resident status and apply for citizenship. He also enrolled me at Columbia University. We were about to file for divorce a few months later when he was killed in a car accident."

"So much happening in such a short time." He sat down across from her and picked up his mug. "It must have been frightening. Did his family help you?"

Her thin smile was grim. "They couldn't wait to get rid of me. John left a substantial estate, valued at over three million dollars. As his widow I was legally entitled to half of it, which naturally didn't sit well with his kids. So they offered me a deal. If I would give up my claim to his estate, they would give me enough to live on for two years—if I was frugal—and they promised not to report me to immigration for committing fraud in order to get into this country."

"Hardball."

She tilted her head. "Now really. I don't blame them. John had never intended for me to inherit his money, and we all knew it. They were protecting themselves and were actually pretty generous to me."

Jarrod nodded. "Point taken."

"By then the situation back home had deteriorated even more," Nina murmured. "Because my mother was now living by herself, she had to give up our luxury apartment. You have to remember that the government controlled all housing, and there was a perpetual shortage of it in big cities like Moscow."

"Where is she now?"

"Still over there."

That came as a shocker. Jarrod had thought—assumed—both of Nina's parents were dead.

"Are you in contact with her?"

"We write."

*Strange,* he thought. All the mail came to his house, including Nina's, but he'd never seen anything from Russia for her. Apparently they didn't correspond very often.

"Do you miss Russia?"

She barely raised her shoulders. "I did when I first got here. I longed for the familiar, the predictable." She finally looked at him. "Do you have any idea how frightening freedom is?" She shook her head. "No, you take it for granted. It's your birthright. Well, let me tell you, it can be very intimidating and downright scary, if you've never had to deal with it. So many decisions. Where to live. What type of work or education to pursue. What make of car to drive. So much responsibility. In the world I came from other people made those decisions for you. Choices were very limited. The first time John took me to a supermarket and a department store I stood there gawking like a little kid. I couldn't believe it was all real. A dozen different kinds of bread. As many brands of soap."

Jarrod glimpsed the same forlorn expression he'd seen on his son's face. For a long time the boy had been overwhelmed by what he'd seen, and he'd been hesitant, even afraid, to touch things, as if the mere attempt at physical contact might make them disappear.

Jarrod stood and walked to the fridge. He removed a package of carrots from the crisper and put them on the counter. "What was the biggest decision you had to make?" he asked, turning around to face her.

She finished the last drops of her coffee and took the cup to the sink. "Hmm, let me think. John had given me a car, and I'd already set up my college goals. I guess it was trying to decide where to live."

"Did you always want to be a translator?"

"Ever since I started taking French in what you would call high school. The different alphabets, the different ways of conveying thoughts fascinated me from the beginning. Did you know we don't have articles, or the present tense of the verb *to be* in Russian? We don't say 'I am a student.' We say 'I student.'"

"Sounds confusing."

She chuckled. "Not nearly as confusing as not having a singular form of 'you' in English."

"Sure we do. 'You' is singular and 'y'all' is plural."

This time she laughed. "Yeah, and in New York it's you and yous, as in 'Where yous goin'?' It would have been a lot easier if you'd kept thou."

His eyes glimmering, he turned her just enough to hang his wrists on her shoulders. "It does have a lyrical quality. Dost thou love me, Nina?" he asked melodramatically.

She looked demurely up at him and matched his playful tone. "I love thee, Jarrod."

They gazed at each other for several heartbeats.

"Shakespeare had it right," she murmured.

As he peered into her blue eyes he was overwhelmed by awareness of the frightened little girl he'd seen a few minutes ago, and of an urge to protect her. More than protect.

He shifted his hands, drew her against him and planted a kiss on her forehead. "I'm sorry for all you suffered," he said softly, "but I'm glad it's brought you here. To us, to me."

She wrapped her arms around him. "I'm glad, too," she whispered, then raised her eyes to his. The look of surprise he saw there matched his own. He hadn't planned this, and she could hardly be accused of seducing him. Only of being seductive.

He had to know. The freedom of choice she'd mentioned suddenly vanished, and primal instincts took over. He lowered his mouth to hers. When she didn't pull away, he deepened the kiss.

Still she didn't resist, but splayed her fingers on his chest.

"We…" She was breathless, which was how he felt. Breathless and hungry for more.

He cradled her head against his shoulder and decided he liked the sound of "we."

She gripped his waist. He rocked her in his arms. This was the first time he'd held her, and the feel of her body against him stirred impulses. He was about to take another sample when she pushed—not all that hard—against his chest.

"The turkey…" she muttered.

"Yeah," he echoed, "the turkey."

He threaded his fingers in her hair, changed the angle of her head and kissed her again—no gentle exploration this time, but a hot, passionate assault. He took her soft moan as acceptance and plunged deeper.

"Papa?" Sasha called from the next room.

Jarrod and Nina separated like wrestlers at the end of a round. They were facing different counters, their breathing ragged, when the boy charged through the kitchen door.

Still lightheaded, Jarrod turned toward his son. Sasha was staring openmouthed at the huge bird sitting in a roasting pan.

"Want to help?" Jarrod asked.

Sasha had pitched in with a few meal preparations—shredding lettuce for salad, washing vegetables, measuring out rice or noodles under careful supervision, but it was obvious he had never seen the volume of food they were preparing today.

"Can I?" He was still gaping in astonishment.

"Sure, but first wash your hands really well."

Patiently, Jarrod explained what he was doing and why. Sasha had been mystified the night before when they'd baked cornbread but hadn't eaten it. Now his father let him crumble it and the white bread he'd also left to dry out in the cold oven.

"This is called stuffing," he explained, too aware of Nina only a few feet away. Rather than dwell on the taste of her lips and the desire ricocheting through him, he kept up a stream of chatter.

"I always use white bread and cornbread. Break them up into small pieces—" he demonstrated the size "—then we'll add the cooked onions and celery and some spices."

They began to fill the bird's cavity. Following his father's instructions, Sasha sprinkled the outside of the turkey with salt and pepper and watched as Jarrod slid the big roasting pan into the oven.

After Sasha went back to his room to play a new computer game, Nina helped Jarrod clean up the kitchen.

"We'll have leftovers for a week," she said.

"Yeah," he answered with a wide grin.

"That doesn't bother you?"

"Actually, for me the best part of a Thanksgiving or Christmas turkey is the sandwiches that come later that night. On soft white bread with salt and pepper and plenty of mayonnaise. Then there's fried stuffing for lunch the next day. My mother never seemed to run out of ways to use a turkey. Hot and cold sandwiches, hash, croquettes, soup."

"Was she a good cook?"

"Yeah—" nostalgia softened his eyes, though his movements didn't slow "—she was. Nothing very fancy or imaginative. What you would call downhome cooking."

"I'm sorry I never met her."

"She would have liked you. Mom had an instinct about people. How about your mother? Is she a good cook?"

Nina couldn't remember Lydia ever fixing anything more complicated than tea. They'd had servants to take care of everything else, but Nina decided not to mention that.

"It wasn't something she enjoyed."

"It's hard to be good at a task you don't take pleasure in."

As the day wore on the smell of turkey roasting in the oven filled the kitchen and crept through the rest of the house. It had grown cold outside, so Jarrod lit a fire in the fireplace, adding to the homey atmosphere.

Earl's Trans Am pulled into the driveway

just before three o'clock. Jarrod watched from the kitchen window, ready to assist if he was needed, but allowing the man to preserve his independence. Earl struggled to his feet and worked his wheelchair out from behind the seat, all the time hanging on to the door or roof of the car for balance. Only after he was seated did Jarrod let Sasha open the back door and dash out.

"Hey, Tiger, happy Thanksgiving."

Grinning from ear to ear, Sasha returned the greeting. He still had a trace of an accent, but he had mastered the *th* sound and was learning to soften his long *e*s.

"There's a dish on the passenger seat. Would you get it for me?"

Sasha eagerly complied.

"The Waldorf salad I promised. Can you carry it to the house by yourself?"

Sasha tightened his grip on the covered casserole and proudly trailed alongside his friend.

Wanting his neighbor to feel comfortable about dropping by, Jarrod had recently installed a ramp beside the three steps to his back porch—with Sasha's help—stirring memories of his own childhood. His dad would have loved Sasha, too. He'd been dead more than thirty years, yet Jarrod could picture the three of them working together. The image came so easily it hurt.

Earl worked his way up the ramp.

"Man," he said, rolling into the warm kitchen, "if I wasn't hungry before, I am now. This place smells great." He motioned for Sasha to put the dish on the table. "Got room in the fridge?" he asked Jarrod. "If not, we can just leave it outside. It's certainly cold enough."

"I'll make room." Jarrod opened the refrigerator door and rearranged bowls and other containers for the new addition.

Earl struggled out of his down-filled jacket and gave it to Sasha, who was waiting to take it.

"My, don't you look spiffy," Nina said with a bright smile.

Earl was wearing a rust-and-brown plaid Pendleton shirt that emphasized the breadth of his shoulders and his large hands. Sharply creased khaki slacks and shiny brown boots completed the image of a rugged outdoorsman.

"Nice threads," Jarrod agreed, turning back from the refrigerator. He suspected the clothes were new.

The front door chime sounded. Before Jarrod could react, Earl propelled himself to the dining room and kept going, finally halting in the entryway. Nina followed and stood at his side while Jarrod maneuvered past them.

He swung the door wide. "Right on time," he said. "I'm glad you could make it."

Alicia Peters smiled self-consciously, looking more nervous here than she ever did at school. Her eyes shifted past Jarrod to the man in the wheelchair. Then she looked back at her host.

"Thank you for inviting me."

Jarrod relieved her of a tray holding two golden pies, then moved aside so he could enter. She stepped into the room, her hands clutching the lapels of her blue wool coat. Tension had the air virtually crackling. Nina went up to her with a greeting and an offer to take her coat.

Alicia slipped out of it, her eyes once more moving to Earl.

"Hello, Allie," he said. Nina hung the outer garment in the small closet near the front door while Jarrod took the pies to the kitchen.

"Hello, Earl. Jarrod told me you would be here."

"You look even prettier than when we were in high school."

She blushed. "I'm much older now. In

mind and body." She started to bite her lip, then stopped. "How have you been?"

"As well as can be expected, I guess."

Nina could see the words I'm sorry forming on Alicia's lips. Wisely, she didn't voice them.

"Come on, Sasha," Nina said, "let's go baste the turkey."

ALICIA HAD ONLY RETURNED to Misty Hollow four months ago, tired of the frenetic pace and the stressful jobs she'd held in Boston, New York and Washington.

Until three weeks ago, she hadn't seen Earl Slater in thirteen years, but in the last twenty-one days she'd thought of no one else. He was as handsome as ever, this man she had rejected. He'd been kind, considerate, gentle. Fun to be with. She'd felt safe in his company. Yet she'd thrown all that away for someone else. In the end she'd given herself to a male—instead of a man—and had paid the price for her foolishness.

"Do you enjoy teaching?" Earl asked, his hands stroking the rims of his wheels, moving the chair back and forth an inch or two. He was as nervous as she was.

"Very much. I'm just substituting now, but I hope to get on full-time next year."

"What happened to your plans to become a lawyer?"

Her father was an attorney. "I took pre-law for a while in college, but decided I didn't really like it."

Her father would have expected her to join his practice. Living with him had been bad enough. She couldn't imagine working with him in a job that thrived on conflict.

Earl waved toward the couch. "Why don't you sit down? It'll be easier for both of us with our eyes on a level."

"Our hosts seemed to have abandoned us," she commented lightly, following his direction.

"I told Jarrod about us," he blurted out. "About what happened."

Her shame. She stared at her fingers, folded neatly in her lap. "Oh."

"He's a good friend," Earl said, sounding defensive.

"He seems like a good father, too." Suddenly she felt uncomfortably warm.

"Sasha must be quite a challenge in the classroom."

"One I haven't handled very well, I'm afraid. He's doing much better now, though," she said, "but that's because of Nina and Jarrod, not me."

"You, too." His tone held encouragement. How much she'd missed that part of him— the positive, sympathetic side. She shouldn't long for some sign of approval, of acceptance from him, but she did. Forgiveness was another matter.

"I understand you're a successful software developer now. You always were fascinated with computers."

"I'm lucky," he said. "It doesn't require physical dexterity beyond the ability to write and poke a keyboard, and there are accommodations for that when the time comes."

She hesitated. Then she realized that trying to ignore the wheelchair was foolish and pretending it didn't matter was insulting. "Will it?"

"I won't ever get better, Allie. I'll never improve. The best I can hope for is that my deterioration remains slow."

Once more she wanted to say, "I'm sorry." Again, she didn't voice the words.

"You never married?" he asked.

She stiffened subtly at the question. "No. You?"

"Briefly. It didn't work out."

"Kids?"

"No."

They lapsed into silence.

"Do you ever see her?"

She understood who he was referring to. "No."

"Do you know where she is?"

Alicia nodded. "It took me several years, but I found her. She's with a good family, has brothers and sisters and is well provided for. She doesn't even know I exist."

Earl's heart ached at the sadness in her voice.

"I'm sorry," he said.

"Don't be," she replied. "It's for the best."

There was another pause. "Why didn't you ever come to me?" he asked. "I would have helped you."

She flinched. "How?"

"I would have married you, if you'd have had me. I loved—" He broke off and sucked in a deep breath. "Maybe you're right, though. Maybe it was all for the best."

She jumped up and crossed to him, then stopped, unsure what she should do now that she was within touching distance. Her hand closed around his tight knuckles. "Would you really have asked me to marry you? After what I did?"

"Would you have accepted me if I had?"

"My father…" She backed up abruptly and turned away from him.

"Hey, everybody," Nina said, coming through the dining room door, "how about some eggnog or apple cider?"

Sasha followed, pushing a tea cart, with Jarrod behind him, his hands resting on his son's shoulders. They were both smiling.

"Everything smells so good." Alicia pasted a smile on her face. "I wouldn't want to spoil my dinner."

"It won't be ready for another hour and a half at least," Jarrod said. "We'll have plenty of time to recover our appetites."

## CHAPTER SEVEN

THIS WAS A MISTAKE, Earl thought as he sat next to Alicia at the dinner table two hours later. Being close to her, inhaling her fragrance, brushing his hand against hers when they both reached for the gravy boat, feeling her glance at him, stealing glances at her—it was all a monumental mistake. Ten years ago, even five, they might have had a chance together, but not now.

The world had changed course since they were in high school. Why had he told her he would have married her if she'd come to him? A foolish thing to say. Not that it wasn't true. He'd been seventeen, she sixteen—both kids themselves. What would they have known about caring for a baby?

He'd been fortunate. He came from a loving family. His folks might have argued about his marrying Alicia and raising someone else's child, but they would have supported him…them.

Her family was another matter. He hadn't heard the term "trophy wife" back then, but it would have fit Alicia's mother. At least ten years younger than her husband, Eldora Peters had struck Earl even then as shallow and vain, more cunning than intelligent. The problem, though, had been Alicia's father.

Arrogant, slick and ambitious, Walter Peters wasn't the kind of man who would have allowed his daughter to marry a poor nobody like Earl Slater, at least not without dominating their lives and making them miserable. In the end the marriage would have failed, and the child they had married to protect would have become another victim of a broken home.

Maybe Allie had been right. Maybe giving up her baby for adoption had been the best alternative, even though the agony of doing so must have been all but unbearable. To carry new life within her, to go through the pain and anguish of childbirth, and then give up that precious gift… He couldn't imagine it.

Still, a secret part of him had always wondered if they might have made it. If together they could have found the strength and courage to defy her father, severing the tie, if necessary. Earl wondered, too, what it would have been like to be a dad.

He'd never find out now. He envied Jarrod. Earl himself would have considered adopting, except no institution would give a child to a man in a wheelchair whose condition was just going to deteriorate.

"Sasha has a question he would like to ask you," Jarrod said from the head of the table.

"Ask away," Earl replied, smiling at the boy sitting across from him.

"Can…can I call you Uncle Earl?"

"Uncle?" He already was an uncle, several times over. "Sasha, I would be honored to have you call me uncle."

The boy grinned from ear to ear.

Alicia placed her hand on Earl's and squeezed. "That's very sweet of you."

Earl's face grew hot. He wasn't sure if it was from her words or the sensation of her touch. No chance contact this time; she was molding her hand over his. His pulse raced.

"This calls for a toast." Nina held up her glass of cider. "To Uncle Earl."

They clinked glasses and drank. Then, raising his, Earl said, "To friends and family."

IT WAS AFTER NINE O'CLOCK by the time Jarrod's guests left with generously stocked doggie bags. He offered to accompany Earl back to his house and help him get his booty inside, but he wasn't surprised when his friend turned him down. He, Nina and Sasha waved goodbye as their guests pulled out of the driveway, both cars turning right at the road.

Jarrod instructed Sasha to get into his pajamas, brush his teeth and call him when he was ready for bed.

"They had a hard time keeping their eyes off each other," Nina commented as she and Jarrod returned to the kitchen to finish putting things away.

"Under different circumstances I'd say they'd both end up in Earl's bed tonight, or at least doing some heavy petting on the couch."

"But they won't, will they? Do you think he…"

"Can he have sex?" Jarrod asked a bit uneasily. "My understanding is that muscular dystrophy doesn't change that, Nina."

Sasha appeared in the doorway, making Jarrod do a double take. How long had the boy been standing there? The word *sex* was used too often on TV. Jarrod wasn't comfortable with his son hearing it discussed at home. Okay, he was a prude, but he remembered growing up in blissful ignorance of sex and drugs. He treasured that time of innocence.

"Say good night to Nina," he told the boy.

"Thank you for my first Thanksgiving," Sasha said.

"It was a fun day, wasn't it?" she responded. He nodded.

"You were a great help today."

In spite of the smile on his lips, there was a faraway look in his eyes. Jarrod wondered what he was thinking. Was he recalling the monotonous life he had spent in the orphanage? His friends there? Was he sad because he couldn't share this plentitude and security with them?

Nina walked over to him and planted a kiss on the top of his head. "Sleep well, Sasha."

Unexpectedly, he threw his arms around her waist and pressed his cheek to her belly. The affection, so spontaneously given, obviously caught her completely off guard. She hugged his shoulders and held him tightly for a few seconds. Watching them, Jarrod could feel the emotion between them.

After Sasha had crawled between the covers, Jarrod tucked him in, picked up the current book from the bedside table, sat in the rocker and began reading. Within five minutes his son was sound asleep.

Jarrod gazed down at the boy as he did every night, awed that this youngster was part of his life. He worried about him, about how he would meet the challenges ahead. At this instant, though, all Jarrod could think about was how blessed he was to have this child. There would be difficult times ahead. Every life was filled with them, and Jarrod prayed he would live long enough and have the strength and wisdom to guide his son through them.

With a sigh, he turned out the light, closed the door and returned to the kitchen.

"It's sad, really." Nina balled up a piece of aluminum foil and tossed it into the garbage can near the back door.

"What is?"

"Earl and Alicia," she said. "They want each other so badly."

Jarrod grabbed a steel wool pad and began scrubbing the roasting pan he'd earlier left soaking in detergent. "Have you ever wanted someone that much?"

She frowned. "You mean felt something deeper than just having the hots for someone?"

He responded immediately. "Have you had the hots for someone, Nina?"

"Let's see, Sean Connery, Mel Gibson…"

Jarrod laughed. "I mean someone real, someone within reach."

"Oh, gee, you mean Mel Gibson isn't real? You think he's all done with computers?"

He shot her a wicked grin. "Afraid to answer my question?"

"No, I'm not afraid to answer your question," she parried in a singsong voice. "Sure, I've had the hots for a few guys. But I thought we were talking about feeling something deeper."

He looked directly at her. "Well?"

She put the last pieces of silverware into the wire rack, added detergent and set the dishwasher dial. "No." She hit the start button.

"No?" His face went blank, genuinely surprised by her response. "Surely you've felt something…"

"Have you?"

He wondered why she was so reluctant to talk about herself. "I told you about my fiancée, Maggie."

"You also said it wasn't real love, that you weren't at all heartbroken when you split up. Sounds like you were more in love with love than with her."

Should he tell her he'd had the hots for Nina

I. Lockhart from the minute they'd met? He certainly hadn't been in love with love when he'd met *her*. His adventures in that field had all failed. Besides, he had to focus on his new son. What he'd felt for her must have been lust for a beautiful woman. Nothing wrong with that, as long as he didn't act on it.

But after this morning's kiss, not acting was growing more difficult. Worse yet, his feelings were no longer simply based on lust. He didn't know exactly when they had gone beyond desire and become need, only that they had.

She reached up to put a bowl in an overhead cabinet. Seeing the swell of her uplifted breasts seemed to suck the air right out of his lungs.

"Let me help you." He leaped to her assistance, his hand shooting up beside hers. Her arm touched his. Her breast brushed his rib cage. His already racing blood pooled lower, heated, thickened.

Together they placed the china piece on the shelf. As she lowered her arm, he wrapped his around her. She coiled into his embrace, as though they'd been practicing the maneuver.

"Now where were we when Sasha interrupted us this morning?"

Her blue eyes twinkled. "Right here," she murmured. "As I recall, you were about to—"

The words turned into a whimper as his mouth possessed hers.

SHE'D LIED WHEN SHE SAID she'd never had the hots for anyone. She'd been captivated by him the moment he'd looked down at her in the café and introduced himself. Her heart had tripped when he'd covered her hand with his, and her breathing had hitched when he'd begged her to help him with his son. He still took her breath away.

He tasted of the amaretto coffee they'd been drinking. The kiss was inviting, demanding, filled with exotic sensations. Her pelvis instinctively moved against his, until she felt his granite hard response.

*Not again. I won't let this happen again.*

She broke away, her chest rising and falling in a desperate quest for oxygen.

"Nina—"

She pulled out of his embrace. "No."

"What's wrong?"

She turned her back, waiting for him to place his hand on her shoulder, as she knew he would. When he did, she didn't know if she should flinch or beg him not to let go.

"I…Lorenzo…"

He coaxed her around with those warm, gentle hands of his. They would have been easier to resist had they been forceful, demanding. But his touch was kind, solicitous.

"Who's Lorenzo?"

"I worked for…with him in Atlanta. I swore I'd never get involved with a colleague, an employer again."

Jarrod stepped back. "Is that how you think of me—as a business associate? An employer?"

"Of course not. It's just that—" She broke off, went to the refrigerator and dug two bottles of water from the back of the bottom shelf, aware of him watching her. She straightened and handed him one. "Let's sit down."

He twisted the top off his bottle as they took their usual seats across from each other at the table by the window.

"Tell me about Lorenzo." His manner was casual, but she didn't miss the discomfort in his gaze.

She took a long drink.

"He was the head of an anthropology team," she said. "He'd hired me to translate some old manuscripts. He was planning to use the results to apply for large grants from the government and from several academic institutions. He'd swing it, too. Lorenzo had already made himself a reputation for delving into controversial areas and confounding his opponents. He was well-educated, erudite and had that special quality that some celebrities and politicians possess—the knack of never talking to a stranger. One handshake and exchange of greetings and you felt you were the only person in the room with him."

"Sounds perfect. So what went wrong."

She made a self-deprecating sound. "I made the mistake of falling in love. We became lovers. It was stupid. I should have known better, but I was foolish enough to think he felt the same way about me." She gazed off into space.

"It wasn't until the end of the project that I realized it had all been a game for him. He expected me to support a certain theory he had, one that wasn't substantiated in the documents I was dealing with but which could be interpreted that way by distorting a few phrases and terms. When I refused, he ended the relationship abruptly and did his best to discredit me. I actually had to take him to court to collect my fees."

Jarrod took a pull from his beer. "You think I'll renege on paying you?"

She clucked her tongue and gave him a crooked smile. "Of course not."

"Then what?"

His hazel eyes searched, waited. "I like you, Jarrod. I respect you and want us to be friends, but I'm not ready to get involved with you—or anyone."

"Friends," he repeated dully.

"Just don't rush me."

THE MONTH THAT FOLLOWED flew by. Jarrod made no attempt to kiss Nina again, though he was certainly tempted. The next move, he decided, would have to be hers. He thought she was going to make it several times, but on each occasion she retreated.

Sasha had never experienced the Christmas season. The child's wonder at the colorful lights strung across Main Street and the number and variety of games and toys on display in shop windows reminded Jarrod that the season really was about children.

Sasha's face lit up Christmas morning when he came into the living room and saw all the presents under the tree they had decorated the night before.

He stood openmouthed, staring at the gaily wrapped packages with their bright ribbons and fancy bows, then he sat on the edge of the easychair, his hands folded in his lap.

"Aren't you going to open your presents?" Jarrod asked, exchanging grins with Nina as they sat next to each other on the couch in front of the tree. He picked up one of the boxes. "Merry Christmas, son."

Sasha didn't seem to know where to start, so Jarrod slipped off the ribbon and tore a corner of the shiny paper and handed it back to the boy.

A baseball mitt.

Sasha fondled it until Nina handed him another gift.

A Game Boy.

Minutes later, surrounded by new clothes and toys, Sasha reached under the tree, removed a present and handed it to Jarrod.

"For you, Daddy." There was both shyness and pleasure in the way he said it.

Something inside Jarrod tripped. Over the months Sasha had addressed him as *Otyets*, Russian for father, and once or twice as Papa. But this was the first time he'd called him Daddy. Why that particular word should affect him more than the others he couldn't say, but it did.

Hoping he wouldn't get sappy, Jarrod

pulled at the bow, added the ribbon to the pile on the floor, and slipped his thumb under the silver paper. He opened the cube-shaped box and removed a layer of wadded red tissue. Beneath it he found a cylinder, a pencil cup made from a tin can. Pasted to the outside were autumn leaves—mahogany maples, yellow oaks, pale green birches and a dozen others interspersed with dark green and rust pine needles. Over them all was a thick coating of shiny varnish.

"Uncle Earl helped me," Sasha said. "For your pencils and pens."

"It's beautiful," Jarrod managed to say around the lump in his throat. "I'll keep it always."

He opened his arms, and Sasha slipped into them. Jarrod hugged him tightly. His son had made him a present, unaware that his being here was the greatest gift of all.

"I love you, Son."

"I love you, Dad."

Jarrod's eyes welled. Not far away, Nina's eyes glistened.

After another moment, Jarrod released Sasha and held him at arm's length. "There's one more present for you."

Sasha looked up. "Another one?"

"Come with me."

Jarrod led him to the kitchen. Near the back door Nina had placed the large box she'd brought from the guesthouse a little while earlier. A big gold bow sat on top. Sasha didn't seem to notice that there were holes in the shiny red-papered sides just below the detachable lid. Jarrod helped him remove it.

The boy's blue eyes grew to saucer size and his mouth fell open. He stared without moving.

"It's a puppy, Son. You're very own dog."

Still the boy didn't move, mesmerized by the blond-coated pup scampering around in the confined space. It looked up at Sasha and made a sound that was somewhere between a bark and a whimper.

Jarrod bent down and picked up the wiggling creature and placed it in Sasha's arms. The pup immediately licked his cheek. The glow of pure delight on the boy's face compared with nothing Jarrod had ever seen before.

"She's only six weeks old," Nina said, "so she'll need a lot of care."

Sasha was giggling at the sensation of the young golden retriever licking his face.

"And a name."

Jarrod and Nina exchanged warm glances and returned their attention to Sasha's ecstatic expression. Baseball mitts, Game Boys, blue jeans and running shoes were all forgotten now as the two young creatures got to know each other.

"Can I call her Laika?" the boy asked.

"A perfect name," Nina exclaimed. "It has a variety of interpretations," she told Jarrod. "Think of it in terms of Rover or Fido."

He laughed. "Laika it is."

They spent the next few minutes explaining to Sasha his responsibilities toward the pup—making sure she always had water available, that she got enough of the right things to eat and was let outside regularly. Sasha wanted to do all of them at once and that very minute. Jarrod laughed. He remembered the dog his parents had given him for his sixth birthday. Champ, a mongrel pup his dad had rescued from the pound, had waited patiently for him at the back door every day after school and had slept in his bedroom even after Jarrod had gone off to college. He hoped Sasha's experience would be as happy.

"I have a present for you, too," Jarrod told Nina after they'd poured their second cup of coffee.

He reached into his pocket and removed a small box. Her breath caught in her throat. This wasn't… It couldn't be…

"Open it."

Her fingers trembling, she undid the silver cord and tore the shiny paper to revel a velvet-covered jewelry box. Her heart began to pound and a cry welled up inside her. No! she wanted to yell, but the word wouldn't come out. She snapped open the lid and nearly collapsed.

A beautiful pair of diamond earrings.

"Oh, Jarrod. They're lovely. Thank you so much."

Relief…and disappointment swept through her. "I have your gift at the guesthouse." An engraved pen and pencil set. "I was going to bring it over when I went to change for dinner."

He pointed up to the mistletoe hung in the doorway. "Merry Christmas, Nina."

His mouth met hers. She wound her arms around his waist. For a moment, she lost herself in the warmth of his embrace.

"Can Laika have pancakes with us?"

They split apart like two guilty teenagers. Nina watched as Jarrod, obviously trying for nonchalance, reached for a mixing bowl.

"Dogs don't like pancakes," he said. "It makes their toenails itch."

Nina gaped at him and barely managed to hold back her laughter.

THAT NIGHT JARROD experienced the kind of physical pain he'd had just before he and Glenda had split up. It started in the center of his rib cage and fanned out, then receded again—not quite as intense as last time, certainly not enough to justify calling 911, as he'd done then. The humiliation of that episode still rankled and left him feeling ridiculous and inadequate.

Glenda had been a firebrand fund-raiser with a big nonprofit charitable organization in Raleigh, a crusader who thrived on campaigns and conflicts. He'd met her at a party of one of his big investors. They'd laughed a lot, kissed good-night—and ended up in bed. Their affair had lasted two years. She was the most adventurous partner he'd ever encountered.

Her causes, however, turned into stridency. He agreed with her on the substance of most issues, but their arguments when they didn't see eye-to-eye came close to physical combat, and Jarrod eventually realized life with her would be one long crusade, sometimes side by side, but just as often across the barricades from each other. He wasn't sure he could match her drive or wanted to. She was exciting to be with but also exhausting. Secretly, too, he had wondered what would happen if he ever ran out of that same level of energy in bed.

They'd just had their most heated argument over yet another one of her causes. She'd slammed out of the house, and he'd decided to end their affair the next day. That night he experienced chest pains so bad he was sure he was having a heart attack. The medical staff was still running tests when she showed up at the emergency room. Solicitous, of course, but he'd overheard her ask the doctor what would happen if it really was a heart attack.

"Surgery may be indicated."

"What about drugs?" she'd asked.

"That'll be our first option, but sometimes medication alone isn't enough."

"I mean after surgery. Will he still be on medication then? Permanently?"

"Probably."

"Those drugs interfere with a man's ability to have sex, don't they?"

There'd been a pause. "They might, but there are treatments to remedy that."

"Thank you," she said with a kind of finality.

She'd ended their affair that evening, not in so many words, but with the sudden announcement that she had to go on a long fundraising tour and wasn't sure when she would be back. Her departure from his life shouldn't have been more devastating than his failed engagement to Maggie years before, but he'd been younger then, hale and hearty. He began to wonder, too, what it was that made him unable to satisfy a woman. With Maggie, it had been emotional inadequacy. With Glenda, it had been the prospect of sexual dysfunction. In both cases, the women weren't willing to invest in him as a life partner.

"All your tests came back normal, Jarrod," his physician had announced the following morning. "You're sound as a dollar. Have you been under any stress lately?"

Jarrod admitted that he was without specifying its source.

"Anxiety manifests itself in various ways. Given your family history and the trauma of seeing your father die of a heart attack when you were a kid, it's reasonable that you would react to tension in the form of chest pains, rather than, say, headaches or stomach cramps."

"Are you saying this was just a panic attack?"

"The pain was real," the doctor assured him. "It just had no physical foundation."

Jarrod left the hospital feeling like a jerk.

A panic attack. Nothing more. No problem.

Except that Glenda had left him.

On reconsideration, though, that was probably for the best. She could have driven any man to a heart attack—in or out of bed.

No problem. Except for the gnawing feeling of time slipping by, and he was completely alone.

He'd actually entertained the notion of adopting a child a year or so before he'd met Glenda, but his inquiries made it clear no one was willing to give a child of either sex to a single man. He'd filled out the paperwork anyway, but nothing had ever come of it.

Then, on that long night in the hospital after Glenda had walked out, he'd seen a documentary on the plight of Russian children in the aftermath of the political and economic collapse of the Soviet Union. Russian authorities were actively seeking people, including single parents, to adopt orphans. He still didn't meet the guidelines, since he wasn't a single parent, but this time he didn't give up. The search for Sasha began.

Now, a year after achieving success, the

physical pain was back. Was this the real thing or another panic attack?

Over what? Naturally he was anxious to see Sasha do well, but the outlook for the boy at the moment was very optimistic. There was no denying the tension between him and Nina, but that was attraction, not fear.

No, this wasn't a matter of nerves. This had to be the thing he'd dreaded all his life, the curse of his family history.

Maybe it was just as well Nina had rejected his advances. If this was the big one, it was better that they weren't involved. He'd already made arrangements for Earl's sister in Spokane to take Sasha if anything happened to him. She and her husband assured him their family would welcome the young orphan.

The pain receded. What Jarrod had to do now was stay away from Nina.

Tomorrow he'd make an appointment to see his cardiologist.

"YOU'RE FINE," the doctor assured him a week later, after running a battery of tests. "Everything appears to be perfectly normal."

So it was just another panic attack. Jarrod felt like a double fool. He'd passed all the physicals when he'd applied to adopt and been assured he was in excellent health. Now he was being told the same thing— again. But the pain had been real—just like last time. Real enough to keep him awake at night.

"Adopting a child on your own has put you under a lot of pressure," the cardiologist reminded him. "Sometimes pain is the body's way of telling us to back off, to take a deep breath and relax. Worry never solved a single problem."

This guy probably thought his patient was a hypochondriac. At this point Jarrod was beginning to wonder if he was right.

AT LAST THE SNOW MELTED and spring arrived. The azaleas and rhododendrons were in full, glorious bloom and the air was rich with the perfume of lilacs and wildflowers.

Jarrod was working on investment accounts in his office. The market had been rising slowly and steadily for months. The blue chips and established technology stocks he favored were continuing to grow at an even pace, making them ideal for long-term capital gains and current income. He'd also been watching a collection of newer high-tech companies and was beginning to transfer a portion of his liquid assets into them.

Even focusing on price-earnings ratios and quarterly dividend projections couldn't keep him from being aware that not too far away, in her snug little house, Nina was engrossed in her own project, the translation of a recent bestselling Italian novel into German. He pictured her deep in concentration, her head cocked to one side, her golden hair in slight disarray as she tapped a pencil against pursed lips and sought the perfect word or phrase to convey the essence of a thought from one language to another.

That she could function in multiple languages still amazed him, but then there was a lot about Nina Ivanova Lockhart that flat-out dazzled him. Her smile. Her laughter. The grace of her movements as she worked around the kitchen helping to get dinner ready. Her scent when they brushed by each other was enough to intoxicate a man.

Today, he was sorely tempted to abandon his stocks and bonds, cross the sun-dappled back lawn and invade her space. Except he knew she was doing her last read-through of the finished manuscript before sending it out in the morning. A few more hours to suppertime. He'd see her then.

After school Sasha went over to Earl's place with Laika. Earl had announced the day before that he'd be trimming bushes of dead wood and had invited Sasha to help. The boy had jumped at the chance. He'd grown very fond of his uncle over the past eight months.

At Laika's excited bark, Jarrod sprang from behind his desk to the open window. Sasha was running full-speed ahead of the dog toward the house. Nina opened her back door.

"Dad, Nina, quick," Sasha yelled in English. "Uncle Earl falled."

## CHAPTER EIGHT

JARROD AND NINA MET HIM in the backyard seconds later. Laika's tail was wagging furiously.

"Uncle Earl falled," Sasha repeated, out of breath.

"Fell," Nina corrected without thinking.

Jarrod bolted into the woods. "How badly is he hurt?"

"He not can get up," Sasha huffed. The dog was bouncing at his side, clearly enjoying this new game.

"Is he bleeding?" Jarrod asked over his shoulder.

"I not see blood."

"Is he conscious…awake?" Nina asked, immediately behind him.

"He make funny noise."

His heart pounding, Jarrod sprinted faster through the trees.

At the clearing Sasha darted ahead to the front of the house.

They found Earl sprawled on the ground, Ruff lying next to him, the overturned wheelchair an arm's length away. A long-pole pruning saw lay nearby, half buried under the foliage of a severed tree limb. Jarrod made himself slow down, momentarily concerned the sheltie might attack him, but as he approached with soothing words, the old dog edged away, his feathery tail swinging once or twice.

Jarrod knelt at his friend's side. "You okay? Are you hurt?"

"I'm sorry," Earl said.

Jarrod could see tears of humiliation forming in his eyes.

"Let's get you up. Nina…"

She had already righted the wheelchair and was moving it closer.

Jarrod straddled the prostrate man's narrow hips. "Put your arms around my neck." He grabbed Earl's hands to guide them. His friend let out a scream.

"My left wrist," Earl said between clenched teeth. "I fell on it."

Nina crouched at his other side. "Can you move the fingers?"

Earl's face was a mask of pain. "I don't think so."

They hadn't heard the Escort drive up until the door slammed and Alicia cried out, "Earl!" She raced to his side and dropped to her knees. "What happened?"

"I was trimming a tree limb," Earl said, his eyes tight shut, his face a mask of pain.

"We need to call an ambulance," Nina said.

"I'm sorry," Earl repeated.

"Nothing to apologize for," Jarrod assured him. "You're going to be fine."

His mind was spinning. Firehouse volunteers would have to be called out, businesses disrupted. "I can get you to the clinic before an ambulance arrives." He turned to Nina. "There are some cedar shingles behind Earl's garage, left over from when they redid his roof last year. Grab one that's at least a foot long—longer, if possible. Then we need something soft to wrap his arm—"

"I'll get that." Alicia jumped up and ran toward the back of the house.

"Bring something for a sling, too," Jarrod called after her.

"Is Uncle Earl going to be all right?" Sasha asked in a small voice. He was wringing his hands and staring at his friend on the ground. "I pulled on the branch. He told me no." He sobbed. "I wanted to help."

Jarrod could imagine what had happened. Earl sawing. Sasha jumping, grabbing the branch. The blade suddenly binding. The rhythm abruptly interrupted, and Earl tumbling backward.

"Now he won't like me anymore." A tear dribbled down Sasha's dirty face.

"I'll always like you, Tiger. You're my pal, my buddy," Earl said through his pain.

Jarrod reached up and pulled the boy against him. "You didn't mean to hurt Uncle Earl. Accidents happen. That's what this was. An accident. Sometimes when we try to help, it doesn't work the way we want, but we can't stop trying." He brushed back his son's flaxen hair. "Uncle Earl will be just fine, but we have to get him to the hospital so a doctor can fix him up. There's something you can do to help," he said brightly.

Sasha looked up, eager to redeem himself. "What?"

"Go inside and ask Ms. Peters to get a bag of peas from Uncle Earl's freezer."

"To eat?" The boy looked at him in bewilderment.

"I'll show you when you get back. Just ask her to bring them. Okay? Hurry."

Baffled, Sasha nevertheless dashed off.

Nina arrived with several sizes of cedar shingle.

"Perfect. Thanks. Now I need you to bring the Cherokee around. The keys are on the bureau in my bedroom. My wallet with my driver's license is there, too."

She hightailed it through the woods. Barely seconds later, Alicia returned. Her face was pale, her hands shaking as she held out an Ace bandage. She knelt by Earl's side and kissed his sweaty brow.

Sasha, hurrying up behind her, offered the frozen food. "It's peas and carrots."

"That's fine. Hang on to them a minute."

Carefully Jarrod placed Earl's already swollen wrist on the thin cedar board and stabilized it with the bandage, making sure he didn't apply too much pressure. Then he extended his free hand. "Peas and carrots, please, Nurse."

Sasha giggled and handed them over.

Jarrod placed the bag over Earl's wrist and secured it with the rest of the bandage. "A quick and easy ice pack," he explained.

The Jeep rolled up the driveway. Tall spindly pines prevented Nina from pulling very close to the men.

"I'm going to carry you to the car," Jarrod told Earl. "I'll try not to jostle you, but it may hurt."

Tight-faced and clearly in pain, he nodded. "I'm sorry to put you to so much trouble."

Gently, Jarrod and Alicia raised him to a sitting position. She'd found what looked like a small tablecloth, which she improvised into a sling. So he wouldn't put pressure on the injured wrist, Jarrod moved around to Earl's right side, placed one arm under his knees and the other behind his shoulders. The burden was lighter than Jarrod had expected. He carried him to the passenger side of the vehicle and set him on the seat.

"You okay?"

"Fine."

Jarrod admired his friend's courage. Earl was anything but fire. He arched back against the headrest, his face pale and bathed in sweat, eyes closed, lips thin. Jarrod fastened the seat belt around him. Sasha had already climbed into the back seat. The women started to get in, too, but Jarrod suggested they follow in Alicia's car, so they'd have two vehicles available.

Circling the front of the SUV, Jarrod whispered to Nina that she should drive.

The Misty Hollow Medical Clinic was

across the road from the Misty View Retirement Center. The staff was small but professional and had a doctor on duty. Jarrod bade Sasha stay with his uncle Earl while he ran inside, emerging a minute later with a nurse and a gurney. Nina pulled into the circular driveway just as Earl was being wheeled inside.

Jarrod tried to restrain Alicia from rushing into the examining room, but she wouldn't be stopped. Seconds later, Earl's angry voice could be heard ordering her to leave.

Her red-rimmed eyes were big with shock as she slipped onto the hard wooden bench in the reception area.

Nina put an arm around her shoulders. "He'll be all right."

Alicia curled into Nina's embrace and broke down in tears. "Why won't he let me be with him?"

Jarrod understood. He sat beside her and stroked her back. "He's embarrassed, Alicia. He apologized to me three times on the way over."

"For what?"

"He feels helpless. That's not easy for a man to handle."

"He's been injured. It could happen to anyone."

"You're right," Jarrod agreed, "and inside he knows that, but it's no consolation. He believes he fell in a situation where another man wouldn't have, and then he couldn't get up."

"What are they doing to Uncle Earl?" Sasha asked, his eyebrows drawn together. "Is he going to die?"

"He's not going to die, Son. I promise. They'll put a cast—that's like a hard shell—on his arm so it can heal, and when they take it off it'll be just like before. You'll see. You did exactly the right thing, coming and getting us so fast."

"He told me to. I wanted to help him—"

"You did help him, and I know he's very glad you were there with him on the drive here."

"I'm scared. He can't walk...."

Jarrod wrapped his arms around the boy. "He's going to be fine, Son." He almost said, "Good as new." But Earl would never be good as new and this mishap reinforced that awareness.

Jarrod found a well-worn kid's book on an end table. They read it together while waiting for word from the medical staff. An hour and a half went by before the doctor emerged.

Everyone stood. He waved them back to their seats and pulled up a plastic chair for himself.

"How is he?" Alicia asked, still teary-eyed. "Will he be all right? How badly is he hurt?"

The doctor, a man of around sixty with rosy cheeks and soft hands, smiled at her reassuringly.

"He'll be fine. He sustained what we call a greenstick fracture of the wrist. It's more uncomfortable than serious. Think of it as a crack rather than a break. He'll have to keep it immobilized for a few weeks while it heals, but there shouldn't be any permanent damage."

"What about the muscular dystrophy?" Jarrod asked. "Doesn't that complicate matters?"

"If the break were serious enough to require surgery, it might, but in this case he should fully recover."

"What about exercise?" Nina asked. "Doesn't he have to keep his muscles active in order to maintain them? Won't this set him back, cause permanent loss?"

The doctor nodded. "That would be a problem if the condition persisted or total immobility had to be maintained for more than six or eight weeks. We all lose muscle tone under those conditions, but we're only talking about two or three weeks, and he'll still be able to use his fingers and flex his elbow. There shouldn't be a significant degeneration of muscle tissue."

"Can we see him?" Alicia asked. "When can he go home?"

"If there's someone who can stay with him, he can leave now."

Alicia was on her feet, ready to invade the examining area.

The doctor also rose. "I've given him medication to ease the pain, so he's a bit loopy at the moment and will probably sleep through the night. He says he can take Tylenol. If that isn't enough tomorrow, give me a call, and I'll prescribe a mild narcotic."

"He won't ask for it," Jarrod said.

The doctor shrugged. "I suspect you're right. Still, it's available if he needs it."

A few minutes later a male nurse wheeled Earl out of the treatment room. Earl's blue cast ran from just below his elbow to the palm of his hand. Everyone's greeting was upbeat, but Earl's only response was a grumbled apology for disrupting everyone's day.

The nurse, a strapping guy in his mid-thirties, pushed him outside and lifted him easily into the front seat of the Jeep, secured the belt and said goodbye as if they were old buddies. Sasha again climbed in behind him.

"You feel better now, Uncle Earl?" he asked.

"Mmm."

"I'm sorry I didn't do what you told me. I didn't mean—"

Earl snapped out of his lethargy and turned his head. "It wasn't your fault, Sasha. It was mine. You didn't do anything wrong. Thanks for being there."

In the rearview mirror, Jarrod could see his son struggling to believe him.

Alicia stood on the passenger side of the SUV, her features strained as she stared at the man who refused to look at her. Jarrod cranked the engine to life.

Only on the trip home did he remember that none of them had eaten supper. He asked Sasha if he was hungry.

"No."

At Earl's house, the two dogs came scampering to greet them. Nina moved the wheelchair into place. Jarrod lifted his friend out of the vehicle and placed him in it. Sasha ran ahead and opened the back door.

Jarrod pushed Earl directly to his bedroom, where a trapeze was suspended over a low hospital bed.

Turning down the covers, he transferred the injured man and began unlacing his running shoes.

"Leave me alone," Earl snarled.

"Go on home, Jarrod," Alicia said as she stepped into the room. "Thanks for all your help." Her voice was confident. "I can handle it from here." She took over removing the shoes.

Earl shifted his head and glared at her. "What are you doing? Go away."

"You can't sleep in those dirty clothes," she told him firmly. "We need to get you into clean pajamas."

"Get out," he bellowed, anger and frustration giving the words a pitiful note.

"Sorry. Doctor's orders. Unless you want to spend the night in the hospital."

Ignoring his further protests, she strode to the bureau opposite the bed, opened the second drawer and removed a pair of light blue cotton pajamas. Her familiarity with the room and its contents put a whole new light on things. Suddenly Jarrod felt like a voyeur.

"I don't need you," Earl all but cried.

"That may be true, but I need you. I can't change my stripes, Earl. I'm as selfish as ever.

I want what I want, and that means you, and I'll do whatever it takes to keep you."

Jarrod backed out of the room, confident his friend was in good hands—and a bit envious.

THREE DAYS PASSED. Nina had sent her translation off to her publisher on schedule and had received another project, this time translating a new Russian saga covering the Great Patriotic War. She had been enthralled by the book in her native language and felt it rivaled Boris Pasternak's *Dr. Zhivago*. She hoped she could do it justice in English, and looked forward to the challenge.

She was setting up the manuscript template on her computer when she heard a tap.

"Hi." Nina pushed the screen door open. "Come on in."

"I hope I'm not disturbing you," Alicia said.

"Not at all." It was close to three o'clock. "Sasha will be home from school in a few minutes, so I'm ready for a break. He and Laika always stop by after he changes."

Alicia smiled. "That kid is doing really well. I'm glad. I just came by to invite everyone over for supper."

"Ah, the bear is emerging from his dark cave?"

"Yes, but he's convinced this is the first step toward helplessness." She accepted the can of soda Nina removed from the refrigerator. They popped tops simultaneously. "You know how important exercise is for him. He's afraid he's going to lose manual dexterity because of the cast."

"Is he?"

"I dropped in and talked to the doctor when I was out shopping today. He says it's very unlikely. There might be some temporary stiffness when the cast comes off in a couple of weeks, but Earl should be able to regain full use and strength of the fingers, wrist and arm."

"Still, the possibility of that not happening must be terrifying," Nina said. "For both of you."

"I told him it doesn't matter. I'm not leaving him."

"You're a brave woman," Nina said.

"I love him. I always have. I don't know how much time we have together. Maybe decades, maybe only a few years. All I know is that I want to spend all of it with him."

Nina covered Alicia's hand with her own. "I'm happy for you. If there's ever anything I can do to help…"

"Thank you." Alicia pressed her other hand

on top of Nina's. "What about you and Jarrod?" she asked. "It seems like you two were really hitting it off there for a while, then…" She shrugged. "Is something wrong?"

So even Alicia had noticed that Jarrod had withdrawn from her lately.

"His world revolves around Sasha," Nina said. "His son is the most important person in the world to him. He's a good father—"

"And a good friend," Alicia agreed. "I know this is none of my business, but have you had a fight or something?"

"What would make you think that?"

Alicia gave her a pitying look. "You both seem to be holding back? Why? What are you afraid of?"

"I'm not afraid of anything," Nina said defensively.

"Are you sure?"

"SASHA'S ENGLISH HAS improved tremendously over the past few months," Alicia said that evening as she set the picnic table in Earl's backyard. She had marinated shrimp and cubes of steak, and threaded them onto skewers with cherry tomatoes, fresh squash, small onions and slices of green pepper. Earl was turning them on the grill with his right hand. Jarrod was playing catch with Sasha while Laika and Ruff ran between them. The pup was already as big as Earl's sheltie. Ruff had at first snipped at the invader on his turf, but ignoring the bouncy, eager-to-please scamp was impossible, and after two days of aloofishness, the older dog succumbed to the youngster's entreaties to play. Now they were the best of pals.

"He has done well," Nina agreed, referring to Sasha.

"He's still in the lower quadrant of the class as far as grades are concerned," Alicia said, "but he's by far the most improved. If he keeps up the momentum, by this time next year he'll be in the top half, maybe even the top quarter of his class."

Jarrod came over, panting, dropped his mitt on the bench and poured a glass of tea. "I'd forgotten how much energy growing boys and puppies have. Ruff finally wimped out." He pointed to where the sheltie lay on the grass. "So I figure I can honorably take a break, too."

"Alicia says Sasha is doing really well in school," Nina told him.

"I talked to the principal yesterday," Alicia said. "She thinks it might be time to reevaluate him."

"You mean give him another IQ test?" Jarrod asked.

Alicia nodded. "Mrs. Keller thinks learning a new language so quickly suggests a higher intelligence than the initial test indicated. She agrees the language barrier and the trauma he'd just gone through could have skewed the test results the first time."

Jarrod was more than pleased, not only with his son, but with the improved attitude of the school officials. Fern Keller hadn't called to complain in months, and now she was taking a positive step toward accepting the child. Or was this an effort to get rid of him?

"The shish kebabs are ready," Earl called out. "Somebody get the rice."

SASHA WAS TESTED the following Thursday morning, in the conference room adjoining the principal's office. The session lasted over an hour.

Jarrod hoped his son would top the ninety mark and possibly hit a hundred, which would be sufficient for him to apply to private schools.

He scored eighty-five, a twenty point improvement over the original results, which was phenomenal but still below the threshold for normal. Everybody agreed with Jarrod that the boy seemed smarter than that, and they shared his frustration, but the test had been carefully administered, was considered highly reliable and could not be retaken for another two years.

"It's not all that bad," Nina consoled him. "He's fitting in much better with his class-mates, so maybe a private school isn't really important now. At least his learning experi-ence won't be disrupted."

Jarrod wasn't convinced. "I was hoping…"

She placed a hand on his. "He is who he is, Jarrod. Don't be disappointed because he isn't someone else."

She was right. He hadn't adopted Sasha because he wanted a genius, but because he was a little boy who needed a home.

"I THOUGHT WE MIGHT ALL take a trip together after school gets out," Jarrod said a month later over the dinner table.

"Sounds like fun." Nina grinned encourag-ingly.

"Are we going to Texas to see the jacka-lopes?" Sasha asked. "You said we could, Dad."

"You have one in your room."

Sasha huffed out a breath and frowned at his father the way children do at the density of grown-ups. "That's a stuffed toy. You promised we could go and see real ones."

They had been playing this game for weeks, ever since they'd watched a spoof about jackalopes on television. According to the tongue-in-cheek narrator, no jackalopes had ever been captured, though there had been hundreds of sightings of them. The elusive creatures had an uncanny ability to vanish whenever anyone tried to look directly at them or photograph them.

Jarrod wasn't absolutely convinced the boy understood it was all a joke. Just about the time he concluded Sasha was savvy and putting him on, the kid would say something to suggest he was a true believer.

Like now.

"Maybe another time. I was thinking of a trip to Russia."

Sasha's fork clattered to his plate, his eyes went wide and his jaw sagged. "You want to take me back?" Tears streamed down his face.

## CHAPTER NINE

JARROD REACHED OVER and stroked his son's hair. "Just for a visit, Sasha. That's all. Two weeks and we'll be home again."

Sasha looked up with glassy eyes. "You won't leave me there?"

Jarrod shot a glance at Nina, saw she was holding her breath. How could he have been so dense? Or so cruel? "Of course not!"

Abandoning his chair, he knelt beside the raw-boned boy and put an arm around him. "Sasha, I'll never leave you anywhere. You're my son. I love you very much. I'll always want you with me. Always."

He pulled the child into his arms. To his immense relief, Sasha hugged him back. Tightly.

"We need to get going or we'll be late." Nina rose from her chair. "Come on, Sasha, finish up. You know how upset Coach gets when somebody isn't on time."

Jarrod looked up at her. It wasn't like her to

be insensitive to Sasha's feelings, but one glance at the closed expression on her face told him she was trying to hide her own feelings.

Sasha pushed back his plate. "I don't want any more."

"Are you feeling okay?" Jarrod asked. "Does your stomach hurt?"

"I don't want Coach to be mad," Sasha nearly snapped. "So may I be excused?"

Jarrod let the moment linger. "Yes," he finally said. "Go to the bathroom, then get your gear."

After Sasha left, he gazed at Nina, who was loading dirty plates in the dishwasher.

"I can understand Sasha's reaction," he said. "I should have handled this better. But I don't understand yours. Mind telling me what's going on?"

"Nothing," she said with an unconvincing shrug. She closed the dishwasher door and set the dial to Rinse.

Jarrod was about to ask for a further explanation when they heard the sound of the toilet flushing.

"We'll talk about this later." He turned to his son, who was just coming into the kitchen. "Got everything? Let's roll."

Between cheering the boy on and exchanging views with other parents, there was no opportunity for a private conversation with Nina during practice.

Back home two hours later, the three of them went through their evening routine: Sasha's bath; an English lesson, which now was as much a Russian lesson; a scoop of vanilla ice cream with chocolate sauce.

Nina started for the back door as Jarrod followed the boy to his bedroom.

"Hang around," he told her. "We need to talk. There's a bottle of the pinot grigio you like in the bottom of the refrigerator. Why don't you pour us both a glass and we can relax. Something's bothering you, and I'd like to know what it is. If it's something I've done—"

"It's not you. It's me." At his quizzical expression, she added, "I'll use the big glasses."

He read Sasha a bedtime story and wasn't surprised when the exhausted child fell asleep within minutes. He envied the youth his ability to drop off almost instantly. He spent most of his own nights now preoccupied by an awareness of Nina lying in the guesthouse, contemplating how easy it would be to step out the back door and slip in beside her.

He returned to the living room and joined her on the sofa.

They sipped white wine. A ritual. An evasion.

"About this trip to Russia…" he finally began, carefully placing the glass on the coffee table.

"I'm sorry, Jarrod, but I won't be going with you."

He swiveled to face her, crossed his arms and leaned back against the cushion. "Mind telling me why?"

"I don't want to."

He studied her profile, read an emotion he wasn't used to seeing there, one he could only describe as fear. "Not good enough, sweetheart."

She stared straight ahead, as if she hadn't heard him.

"I know I have no right to insist on an explanation," he said, "but I would like one. You seemed pleased about making a trip with us until I mentioned the destination. In fact, you appeared downright enthusiastic about it. Then, as soon as I said Russia, you pulled back. Why?"

She took a deep breath. "I just don't want to go there, that's all. I'd rather spend my time and money someplace else."

"This trip won't cost you a thing, Nina.

I'm footing the bill. As for the time, we're talking about two weeks, not two months. You said yourself you haven't had a real vacation in several years."

She offered him a watery smile. "You're very generous, but I couldn't allow you to pay for everything."

"Yes, you can, because I'm hiring you as my official translator."

She gazed over at him, her brow creased. "What—"

"I couldn't say anything in front of Sasha, but I have an ulterior motive for wanting to go to Russia, besides taking him back to the place where he was born."

Jarrod relaxed his posture, lifted his glass and took a sip of wine, then set the glass down again. "I told you Sasha has a sister."

"Two years older, but he doesn't know anything about her."

He nodded. "I want to see her, meet her, find out if she's all right."

"Are you thinking of adopting her?"

He shook his head. "I would if they'd let me, but they won't. First, under their rules, she's no longer eligible for adoption because of her age. Second, they'd never entrust a young girl to a single man."

Nina nodded. Bureaucratically, it was a wise decision. There were too many young girls throughout the world who were being forced into lives of pure hell. Sasha's sister wouldn't live well in an orphanage, but at least she would be protected from predators—presumably.

"So what's the point?" Nina asked.

"I want to make sure she's safe, see if there's anything I can do to help her." He shrugged helplessly. "I'm not sure what."

Nina remained silent.

"You know as well as I do that I won't be able to accomplish much over there by myself," he continued. "I don't speak Russian. Sasha might be able to help me find my way around the metro, but this situation isn't something I can entrust to him. I could hire a translator over there, but I'm not convinced how dependable they are." He rotated the wineglass, then looked up.

"I need you, Nina. I need someone I can trust to persuade them my intentions are honorable, that my goal is to help my son's sister. I may not be successful, but there's no point in even trying without you along."

She sighed. "I'm glad you're not putting me under any pressure." The attempt at light-heartedness only half succeeded.

"There's another reason," he added.

"What might that be?"

"You saw Sasha's reaction when I said we were going to Russia. The kid's terrified—"

"He's not convinced you won't leave him there."

"Why doesn't he believe me?"

"He thinks he did something really bad. He thinks he's responsible for Earl's broken wrist—"

"Earl and I have both told him—you did, too—that it wasn't his fault, that it was an accident."

"All he knows is that he was told not to do something, he did it anyway, and his best friend got hurt. He also thinks he let you down when he didn't do better on the IQ test."

"But I explained to him—"

"He's eight years old, Jarrod. He's gone from being totally ignored to having someone care about him. That's very precious to him, but it also puts him under a lot of pressure. He doesn't want to disappoint you."

"I told him the test results wasn't important."

"Right, and he's asking himself why you'd want him to take it at all if it didn't matter. All he knows is that the highest grade on a test is the best, and he didn't get the score you wanted, so he must be bad."

"I didn't handle that very well, either, did I?"

She smiled sympathetically. "You've been a great father to him, Jarrod. If you weren't he wouldn't be so worried about losing you. He's very insecure right now."

"Which is why this trip to Russia is so important. I need to satisfy myself that his sister is all right, and Sasha needs to learn he can trust me. But we can't do either if you don't come with us."

She scowled, lifted her glass, but didn't take a sip. She also didn't say no.

"So you'll come with us? If not for my sake, then for the boy's."

"You're persistent, I'll give you that." She let out a breath. "I'll think about it—that's all. I'll consider it. No promises."

*You may be able to turn me down,* he thought. *But I bet you can't say no to Sasha.*

"WHY WON'T YOU COME WITH US?" Sasha asked in Russian the following morning. "I don't want to go if you don't come."

Nina wasn't about to belittle his fear. He'd known only privation and loneliness in Russia. For him it was a place of internal exile, of indifference and friendlessness. For her it was a place of privilege and duplicity, loss and danger. Good reasons for neither of them to return.

The boy deserved a chance to overcome his demons. Maybe he wouldn't enjoy the trip, but that wasn't as important as discovering his father wouldn't abandon him.

She didn't want to rob Sasha of that confidence. Jarrod had made it clear he wouldn't take the child without her, that he needed her, not just as a translator but to help his son feel more secure.

And what about his sister? If Jarrod didn't go over there, she might be deprived of an opportunity, too. Did she remember having a brother? Did she wonder what had happened to him? Did she miss him?

It had been sixteen years since Nina had been home. She'd read every article, every interview, every human-interest story she could find about the political, economic and social upheavals that had taken place since she'd left.

She was being selfish, she concluded.

"Guess what?" she told him. "I'm going with you."

"Yay!" Sasha shouted.

Later, when he was outside playing with Laika, Nina informed Jarrod of her decision. He took her hands and smiled, making her wonder if he could see her nervousness. Then he kissed her, and for a moment she lost herself in the stimulating sensation of his lips on hers and the secure feeling of his arms around her.

"Thank you," he murmured, releasing her.

She was left to wonder that night if he was referring to the trip or the kiss.

THE SCHOOL YEAR ENDED five weeks later, and Sasha was promoted to the second grade. Jarrod made a big deal of it, taking him to Slink and Sloop's Amusement Center. He and Nina laughed at the boy's antics as he climbed the rope ladder and dived into a sea of rubber foam, rocked his car on the Ferris wheel and stuck the bright red cherry from his banana split on his nose with whipped cream.

As time for their trip grew closer, Nina became increasingly nervous, jittery, preoccupied. "If I didn't know you better I'd say you were afraid of going home, Nina," Jarrod commented. "What are you afraid of?"

She slouched against the back of the couch. "I haven't been completely honest with you."

"I've already figured that out."

The comment felt like a slap, one she knew she deserved. He'd been kind, generous and more with her, while all the time she'd been deceiving him. She hoped she could make him understand.

"I told you about how I left Russia. What I didn't tell you is that my father was Ivan Kamarov." She could see the name meant nothing to him. No surprise. Even in the old Soviet Union there weren't too many people outside the inner circle who recognized it.

"He was a member of the KGB."

This time Jarrod blinked slowly and gaped at her. "The secret police?"

"It…was really an internal intelligence service with police powers." She paused, amazed at the level of fear that rippled through her at the mention of those initials even after all these years. "And he didn't just die, he was executed."

"My God."

"My father wasn't a saint," she stated, "but he loved his country. He was also smart enough to see the system was falling apart, had been for a long time, and that it was about to topple."

Her hands were shaking, so she folded them

in her lap to hide the tremors. She had never told her story to anyone, not in sixteen years.

"For sometime, my father had been working with the forces of change outside official government channels. Because he was KGB, he was able to hide his activities—at least he thought he was. As it turned out, other agents had been monitoring his actions. One morning, while we were having breakfast, two of his associates came quietly to our apartment with orders to arrest him."

She bit her lips, trying to suppress the memory of that day. "I had just turned eighteen, old enough to understand by then who and what my father was, smart enough to realize he had hurt people, all in the name of a greater good. But he had always been a good papa to me, and I loved him."

She felt a tear escape, snatched a tissue from the box on the end table at her elbow and blotted it away.

"We lived in a large, luxury flat in one of the old apartment houses that had been built before the revolution. A prestigious address for the elite in what was touted as a classless society. After my father was taken away, my mother said we wouldn't be able to stay there much longer, that it was only a matter of time before we'd be evicted, and she might also be arrested. The question was whether I would be left to scavenge for myself or if I, too, would end up in Siberia."

Jarrod's brows drew together. "Why would they arrest you? You hadn't done anything."

"It didn't make any difference," she said. "In the old days whole families disappeared. It had started with the tsars, been perfected under Stalin and probably continues to this day."

Jarrod shook his head.

"My mother was certain it wouldn't be long before she ended up joining my father in the gulag. Common criminals had a chance of release from those frozen hells. They had fixed sentences. But political prisoners had little hope. Their sentences were indefinite and often ended only with death."

"What happened to your father?"

"He lasted six months, then he was shot trying to escape." She made a mocking sound. "As if there were any place to escape to."

She could see questions in Jarrod's eyes, but she needed to get this story out.

"Two weeks after my father was taken into custody, we were still living in our apartment, and we still had our servants. Mother had no doubt they were there to spy on us. I'd grown up knowing I had to be discreet, but my life suddenly became truly secretive. If the circumstances hadn't been so frightening, it might have been funny, hiding messages for my mother, retrieving hers from hidden places."

She wet her lips. "Mama was determined to get me to safety, and that meant out of the Soviet Union, beyond the Iron Curtain. Under the circumstances, there was only one way. She arranged for me to marry."

"John Lockhart."

She nodded. "What I told you earlier about him and his family was true. He was older than my father. Rich and powerful in his own way, and he held an American passport."

"What happened to your mother?"

"Three days after I left, she was thrown out from the flat with little more than the clothes on her back."

"How did she survive?"

"John had given her money when he married me." Nina laughed. "I guess you could call me a bartered bride. Anyway, he'd made sure she was provided for."

"You said she still lives in Moscow. Is that true?"

"Yes."

He wrestled with that for a minute. "Your mother lives in Moscow and you don't want to see her?"

"No, I don't," she responded.

He shook his head. "Why?"

"Let me tell you a little about my mommy dearest, Jarrod. She was the epitome of the ambitious political wife, always espousing the party line, always kissing up to the people above us—and their wives. She loved the spotlight and never failed to say the right things at social events. My father was trying to change the system, while she was praising it."

His features grew stern. "What are you implying?"

She pursed her lips and studied her fingernails. "I can't be sure, but…she might have been involved in my father's arrest."

"You don't mean that."

Nina laughed. "It's not unheard of. Remember, we weren't booted out of our plush quarters when Papa was arrested. We continued to live high, and Mother continued to dress like a member of the palace court. It wasn't until after I left that she was forced to move."

"But she got you out to protect you."

"Did she? Or was it because she was afraid of what I might say? I didn't know the details

of what my father had been doing, but I knew
he wasn't happy with the regime. My mother,
however, was heavily invested in seeing it
survive."

"You actually believe she was responsible
for your father's death?"

Nina looked away. "I don't know. I was
never as close to her as I was to him, and I
disagreed with her a lot. She always wanted
me to be the perfect little party girl." Nina
snorted. "Wrong term in English. Let me re-
phrase. Perfect model of young Soviet wom-
anhood. She didn't bake cookies or sew
dresses for me, but to be fair, until the last
year I would have said she was a decent, if
rather distant, parent. She only let me see
what she wanted me to. Once I started university my horizons expanded. I began to
suspect that none of it was about me or my
father. It was all about her."

"You could be wrong, Nina. Maybe she
had your welfare in mind all the time and just
didn't know how to express it. Not everyone
is comfortable saying I love you. Some of us
try to show it but can never quite get the
words out."

She thought about that, thought about him.
She'd been falling in love with him for

months. He'd made the first move, but after she'd held him off, he'd withdrawn, physically and emotionally. Yet the way he'd kissed her, the way he'd touched her in those fleeting moments of intimacy, the way he still looked at her, felt like more than just friendship. She tried to erase those images from her mind and concentrate on what they had been talking about. After all, she'd never said I love you, either—not even to Lorenzo. Because she didn't? Or because she was afraid of what would happen if she ever did.

Jarrod rose and sat at her side. His thigh rubbed against hers. She could feel warmth spreading through her when he took her hands in his.

"Conditions have changed, Nina. People change. Maybe it's time to reevaluate your assessment of your mother."

She shook her head. "Conditions change, Jarrod. People don't."

"Then we're all doomed," he declared. "If that's true, none of us can ever learn and grow. None of us can ever love."

His words stunned her. Shamed her.

He massaged the backs of her hands with his thumbs, while his eyes continued to search hers.

"All these years you've been running, Nina. Don't you think it's time you stopped and looked over your shoulder to see what's there? Maybe your fears are only phantoms, ghosts, and all you have to do is say 'Boo!'"

She gritted her teeth. "Don't patronize me, Jarrod. You weren't there. You don't know what it was like."

He continued to hold her hands as he slipped to his knees in front of her. "I would never do that, sweetheart. I care too much for you to ever intentionally hurt you."

Not love. *Care for.* Suddenly she wondered what ghost *he* was fleeing from. Who had hurt him so badly that he couldn't use the word, either, even though she was sure he meant it?

"I want you to come with us because I need you, Nina, because Sasha needs you. But most of all because it's time for you to conquer these fears and doubts that possess you."

He was probably right, but... The very thought of returning to Moscow made her break out in a sweat. God, she was a wreck.

Jarrod climbed to his feet and pulled her up. She leaned into his warm embrace.

"You asked me not to crowd you, to give you room. I've done that, though it hasn't been easy. Sharing our evenings together, sitting across the table from you, hearing your voice—it's been driving me crazy. Keeping me awake at night." He refused to let her look away. "Do you feel anything for me, Nina?"

"You know I do."

"I've wanted to make love to you from the moment I saw you sitting in that lunchroom." He smiled. "I couldn't admit it, of course, not even to myself."

She couldn't suppress a small grin. "I felt the same way."

"Lust," he said softly, his smile more intimate. "You were wise not to let us give in to it. But it's gone beyond that now."

She acknowledged the truth of what he said by breaking eye contact and lowering her head.

"What are you so afraid of, Nina?"

Her answer was soft, shy. "You. Me."

He tipped her chin up. "Do you trust me, Nina?"

It wasn't a question she was prepared for. "Yes." A simple statement, but one filled with doubt.

"Then come with me," he said, and led her to his bedroom.

## CHAPTER TEN

A BEDSIDE LAMP WAS the only source of light in Jarrod's room. He held her hand as he led her in. She was already familiar with the texture of his fingers, which were long, slightly roughened, strong. Heat spread through her when he stopped and spun her around to face him. She gazed up at his square jaw and parted lips. His scent, vaguely woodsy, wholly masculine, tripped something deep inside her.

She wasn't about to be passive, not after waiting this long. Placing a palm against his chest, she gently rubbed the hard-muscled flesh, felt his nipple peak, and began fiddling with the buttons on his shirt. The tempo quickly ratcheted up. He fumbled with her blouse. The sensation of his hands brushing against her breasts sent liquid fire to her belly.

"Wait." He broke away so fast her breath caught. He sprang to the open door, peeked outside, then closed it. "Sasha sleeps like the dead, but just in case…" Jarrod gazed at her, his eyes narrowing into a pirate's leer. "Now where was I?"

His lecherous grin made her skin tingle. "Unbuttoning my blouse."

"Oh, yeah, and you were doing something with my shirt."

She took a step closer. "Shall we resume?"

He tilted his head and, bowing, gave her lower lip a quick nip. "Excellent idea."

Before he got to her buttons, however, he caressed her breasts. His hands, warm and gentle, brought a soft whimper to her throat.

"A very good idea," he murmured.

Desperation raced through her. She helped him release the last button of her blouse, nearly tearing it off.

"Easy," he murmured, to slow her, then carefully slipped the fabric off her shoulders, planting a kiss atop each one as he did so.

Damn his patience. She wrestled with his shirt, tugged it from his pants, spread her fingers along the rippled skin of his rib cage. He sucked in a breath and held it as he squirmed out of his shirt and let the garment drop to the floor.

She fingered the fine dusting of his chest hair when he put his arms around her to undo her bra. Stepping back, he drew the flimsy piece of fabric away and gazed at her naked breasts. Her nipples instantly tightened. He brought his mouth down to one, sampled it with lips and tongue, then transferred his attention to the other. Wild sensations danced through her. Pleasure and desire. Want and need.

Now *she* was holding her breath. Her heart was pounding. She seemed incapable of movement when he undid the clasp at her waist and slipped her slacks down her hips. She'd already abandoned her sandals—no telling where they were. He took her hands and invited her to step away from the fallen clothes. Her world was spinning. She was dizzy and weak.

Somehow she found her voice. "You have me at a disadvantage, sir."

He chuckled at her lilting Southern drawl. His lips curled, his eyes twinkled. He shucked his loafers and toed them under a chair. Lifting each foot, he peeled off his socks and sent them flying in opposite directions.

He started unbuckling his belt. She sidled up to him and slowly unzipped his fly. A new surge of power possessed her when his chest expanded in his struggle for oxygen. His trousers dropped and he blindly kicked them aside.

"You're making me very uncomfortable," he muttered.

"Hmm. I can tell." Her tongue swept across her upper lip as her hand brushed the bulge of his briefs. "You seem to be under a great deal of pressure."

He moaned. "How very perceptive of you."

"Let's see if I can help." Laughing, she pulled down the soft cotton, stretching the elastic waistband over his stiff erection. "Umm, yes."

With his big toe he sent the underwear flying. "You're a vixen," he grumbled. Crouching before her, he yanked her panties down, then kissed her just below her navel.

Rising, he clasped her hand and dragged her to the side of the bed.

He didn't want this to end, not yet, not before he sampled more of her, and once they made full body contact he wouldn't last a minute, he knew. Coaxing her onto the bed, he knelt beside it, and with trembling hands began exploring her skin, the silken softness of her throat, the hollow of her collarbones, the warmth of her plump breasts. He explored the planes of her belly, the indentation of her navel, let his fingers travel lower…

She closed her eyes. Her breathing became

slow and deep. She bit her lips and writhed beneath his touch, but touching her wasn't enough. He rose, climbed on the bed, straddled her hips and began a long, slow, pleasurable adventure.

Starting with her ear, he curled his tongue in its convolutions. He kissed her and almost lost control when she responded hungrily, aggressively.

She audibly gulped for air when his tongue circled her nipples, and she bounced and rose to meet him when his mouth found its way between her legs.

He'd never before experienced the joy he felt when she convulsed under him. Pleasing her was rapture. It also had him throbbing with a need that was akin to pain. He wasn't sure he could last even long enough to enter her.

Suddenly remembering they needed a condom, he squeezed his eyes shut for a long breath and shifted off the bed.

Her eyes sprang open in protest. "What?"

He opened the drawer of the bedside table and scavenged for a Mylar packet. He'd bought several before the holidays. In anticipation. And now that longing was about to be fulfilled. His fingers fumbled. He cursed.

Nina clucked, took the packet from him and

used her teeth to tear the seal. "Do you need help?" She aimed a taunting smile at him.

"I don't think I could survive it."

Her eyes twinkled with mischief. "We'll have to risk it," she whispered, and sheathed him.

The respite had given him a chance of holding back—or would have, if she hadn't let out a near shriek when he entered her. She threw her arms around his neck, and together they went over the edge.

JARROD DOZED. In spite of the physical contentment of sexual release, he didn't sleep. He instead listened to Nina's measured breathing as she lay snuggled against him. His mind kept wandering to the story of her life in the Soviet Union.

How very different his formative years had been. He hadn't been brought up in privilege. His father had been a clerk in a local hardware store, who occasionally took odd jobs to earn extra money for Christmas presents or a week's vacation at the shore. His mother had been a homemaker when he was small, but she'd been forced to take a job as a receptionist in a doctor's office after Jarrod's father died. They hadn't been destitute, but they had been frugal. He couldn't have gone to college full-time if he hadn't received a basketball scholarship. His mother had insisted that even if he had to enroll in night school he would earn his degree. Education was the only way to make it in the modern world.

Which made him think of Sasha. Would he get to go to college? If the IQ test was accurate, it didn't seem likely. What kind of future would he have? A life of low-paying menial jobs? Of poverty? With careful planning and investing, Jarrod could mitigate that by setting up a trust fund. He'd have to start soon, though.

He was startled when the alarm went off at five o'clock. It was nearly a two-hour drive to the airport in Charlotte, and they had to get there at least an hour and a half before their flight to New York, then on to London, Berlin and finally Moscow. The entire trip would take more than eighteen hours. They'd arrive in the Russian capital in midafternoon.

Nina stirred. "What…" She fought to focus, then a smile spread across her face. "Hi."

"Good morning." He kissed her on the forehead. "Want to take a shower with me?"

The smile became a grin. "Yep, but I won't. Not this morning. What time is it?"

He told her.

She threw back the covers and levered herself out of bed. "I'll meet you in half an hour."

Jarrod's pulse spiked at the sight of her naked body. He hadn't planned on having to start the day with a cold shower.

She quickly put on last night's scattered clothing, blew him a kiss and disappeared through the doorway.

Sasha didn't wake easily. Jarrod had to call him twice. In the kitchen, he fixed him a bowl of cereal. They would have time for a more substantial meal at the airport.

Jarrod rambled as he poured his second cup of coffee. "I wonder if Moscow's changed much. Remember that street vendor where we bought the roasted chicken? Think he's still there? Those drumsticks sure were good. And the ice cream. Do you suppose it'll taste as good now that you've had American ice cream?"

Sasha kept his head down as he spooned up his Wheaties. "Will you bring me back?"

Jarrod encircled the child with his arms. "Of course I'll bring you back. You're my son. I'm your father." He turned the boy's face so he could look directly into his eyes. "I love you, Sasha. We belong together. Always."

Sasha shyly nodded. Jarrod could see he wanted to believe him.

Nina barged into the kitchen, breathless and rosy-cheeked.

"Come on, you guys. We have a big day ahead of us."

Twenty minutes later they pulled out of Earl's driveway, after dropping off Laika.

THE CHARLOTTE AIRPORT was bustling with business travelers and summer tourists. Enlisting the help of a porter, Jarrod got all their luggage checked in. It took several more minutes in line to confirm their reservations. No food would be served on the flight to New York, so the three of them strolled to a full-service restaurant for a hearty brunch.

Ever curious, Sasha seemed to thrive in the hubbub of the terminal. Now that he had a rudimentary command of English, a gregarious nature was beginning to blossom. There wasn't anyone he wasn't willing and eager to talk to, and Jarrod was amazed at how easily strangers warmed to the towheaded boy with the foreign accent.

Maybe things would work out after all.

They found only two seats together in the waiting area by their gate. Unconcerned,

Sasha wandered over to the plate-glass window to watch planes take off and land, taxi, dock, load and unload baggage.

Jarrod took Nina's hand. Her soft skin was warm in his grasp, and he wondered if his hands felt cold to her. They should be red-hot, the way his heart was thumping.

"I'm glad you're coming with us," he said. "I wish you were happier about it, though."

"I should have made the trip a long time ago. You're right. I have to stop running. Maybe I won't like what I find, but at least I'll know."

"I'm proud of you."

She couldn't remember the last time anyone had said that to her. Having this man say it was special.

After last night, Jarrod Morrison was extra special to her. He was making her want things she'd given up dreaming about. Someone to love. Someone to lean on. Family.

After her father's arrest she'd spent a lot of time looking over her shoulder. Even after she'd been brought to America, especially after John died, she'd waited for the knock on the door, for the announcement that she'd broken some law, any law. That she was going to be deported. Gradually the paranoia had subsided, but that had only left her feeling alone, not fully part of the society around her.

Maybe after this journey was over, things would be different from the way they'd been these past sixteen years. Maybe she could put the past behind her and live a normal life. No bogeyman following her.

The hours that followed would have been tedious for Nina and Jarrod if Sasha hadn't been with them. The little boy spoke with every passenger on the trans-Atlantic flight, some of them several times. Jarrod and Nina took turns reading to him and playing the games they'd brought along. Against the rules, he was even allowed in the cockpit, when the stewardess realized he was Russian.

They arrived at Sheremetyevo Airport, thirty-five kilometers outside Moscow, shortly after noon the following day.

Jarrod took Nina's hand as they entered the Jetway. Her fingers were ice-cold, and he squeezed them gently. She glanced at him and tried to relax, but all he saw was uncertainty and apprehension.

"Everything is going to be all right," he tried to assure her.

Her weak smile said *Thank you, but I don't believe it.*

They proceeded through Customs. The lines at passport control were long and slow-moving. The agents checking documentation and luggage wore green military-style uniforms. They were neither affable nor suspicious, and seemed completely immune to any sense of urgency or even of time passing. Fortunately, none of Jarrod's or Nina's luggage was selected for detailed inspection, so they were allowed to continue without further delay.

The main terminal was—as Jarrod recalled—cavernous, imposing, poorly lit and filled with acrid cigarette smoke. Because his father had been a heavy smoker, a factor in his early death, Jarrod had never taken up the habit. His single experiment with the weed had made him cough so badly he'd wondered why anyone would. He'd also forgotten how pervasive the use of tobacco in America had been before no-smoking ordinances had banned it from most public places. There were no such laws in Russia.

The PA system blared, almost unintelligibly, with information every few seconds in Russian and English.

Jarrod and Nina went immediately to the currency exchange, where they converted several hundred dollars into rubles. From there they walked to the information bureau and picked up handfuls of brochures about various sites of interest in Moscow, St. Petersburg and other parts of the country. Most of them were in English, but Nina found several in French and one in German that were not available in English.

"According to the woman behind the counter," she told Jarrod, "they have shuttle buses into the city. It's the cheapest way. Their schedule is sporadic, though. No telling how long we'll have to wait."

"We'll take a taxi."

Their cab was a Moskva, a large, black sedan. The engine pinged and gurgled but otherwise ran smoothly.

"I'm probably getting a very prejudiced view of this country," Jarrod said. "I've only been here in the summer, when it's green."

Nina chuckled. "You don't want to come in the winter. It's white and very, very cold."

She leaned forward and asked the driver something.

"*Vchera,*" he responded curtly.

She asked something else.

"*Zaftra.*" He answered just as abruptly.

"What was that about?" Jarrod queried.

"I asked when they last had rain. He said

yesterday, and that they expect more tomorrow."

"Friendly fellow," Jarrod commented.

She smiled. "He's paid to drive, not to carry on conversations."

On his first visit here Jarrod had found the people generally reserved rather than unfriendly. It took awhile for them to warm up, but once they did most of them were talkative and generous.

Sasha spent the time staring out the window, saying nothing. Traffic in the city was chaotic. Cars raced by in a mad scramble, weaving in and out of lanes, cutting each other off. The urgency and vitality were unmistakable and exciting, the feeling of a city on the move. They sped past businesses of every description: restaurants, clothing and shoe stores, some very smart and upscale, others clearly catering to less affluent customers. Casinos sported the same flashing lights and loud music found in Las Vegas and Atlantic City. Everywhere, people streamed by, coming and going.

The taxi pulled up in front of the hotel and a uniformed doorman stood by while they got out of the cab. Nina gave quick, curt orders and he instantly began to remove the luggage from the trunk.

The driver quietly informed Jarrod of the fare. When Jarrod showed confusion, the man repeated it in heavily accented English.

Nina instantly attacked him in fast, staccato Russian.

The man started to argue, but she shut him up with a wave of her hand. Taking a few ruble notes from the roll Jarrod had removed from his pocket, she handed them to the driver and turned her back on him.

Twisting his mouth, the cabbie made a comment Jarrod suspected wasn't complimentary, climbed back into his vehicle and roared away, leaving a trail of black exhaust behind him.

"What was that all about?" he asked Nina.

"He was trying to charge you three times the proper fare."

Jarrod chuckled to himself and didn't tell her it was pretty close to what he'd paid last year. He didn't have to understand the language to know she was in complete control of the situation.

Checking into his hotel last year had been a torturously slow affair. Jarrod had gotten the impression the staff were all new, that they'd never registered a guest before or even filled out a form. This time, with Nina giving orders, everything went much faster. Within minutes they were in the elevator on their way to the eighth floor. The bellboy opened the door and waved them into a spacious sitting room before rolling the luggage cart in behind them.

"This is a suite," Jarrod mumbled. "I asked for two adjoining rooms."

Sasha went over to the window and stared out at the distant golden domes of Kazan Cathedral.

"I had them make the change," Nina stated.

He raised his eyebrows. "This is nice, but I'm not really sure I can afford it."

"No extra charge," she said.

He blinked at her. "Do I want to know how you managed that?"

She awarded him an innocent grin. "I told them you were here evaluating accommodations for tourists as a personal favor to the Russian president, and that good treatment would be to their advantage."

"Nina, you know that's not true."

"That's all right. They know it isn't, too."

He was more confused than ever. "Then why—"

"Simple. I asked if a suite was available, then I bribed the clerk at the desk."

"I'm a babe in the woods." Jarrod snuggled up to her. "What do I owe you?"

She kissed him lightly on the cheek. "You can make it up to me it later."

THEY UNPACKED THEIR clothes. Jarrod and Sasha shared one bedroom, while Nina took the other.

"Do you want to rest and then go see your mother?" Jarrod asked her.

She shook her head. "Not today. Let's walk around for a while. I need to get reoriented. Besides, I'm bushed."

"How about you, Sasha?" Jarrod called out. The boy was again glaring out the window. "Want to stay here and take a nap or go for a walk?"

"Walk."

"Good." Jarrod smiled at Nina. She was putting on a brave front, but he could see worry in her eyes. "Let's go."

The bellhop greeted them effusively when they emerged from the elevator.

"You must have scared the hell out of the staff," Jarrod whispered to Nina after they'd exited the front door. Her personality was quite different here—forceful, almost haughty, not at all what he had expected.

"I just let them know who's in charge."

"Something your father taught you?"

The remark took her momentarily aback. "Actually, it's something my mother taught me."

"Well, it obviously works. Carry on as if you own the place and the people accept your role—and theirs."

They turned left on a side street. The pavement was chipped and cracked and coated with a layer of dirt, giving it a look of neglect, though there wasn't any of the trash and debris he'd seen in other big cities.

"Have things changed much?" he asked as a trolley bus hummed by.

"It's more congested than I remember," Nina commented. "Faster paced…and upbeat."

"Sounds like progress."

They approached a vendor who was selling ice cream.

"I bet Sasha would like some," he said. "How about you?"

"Yes. But let me buy it."

"Yes, ma'am. Just add it to my tab."

She chuckled. "I always loved buying ice cream in the summertime," she said after sampling it. "It seemed so…decadent, sinful somehow."

"Ours is better," Sasha commented after the first lick. He walked a few paces ahead of them, observing everything, and Jarrod suspected finding it all wanting.

"In the wintertime they sell roasted chestnuts on the street," said Nina.

They strolled on for several more blocks. Jarrod sniffed the air. "Do I smell peanuts?"

Around the corner they found a pushcart where an old man was roasting peanuts over a charcoal fire. The rich scent was tantalizing. With Nina's help, Jarrod bought a newspaper cone of the warm nuts for them to share.

Moments later they reached Red Square.

"Did you know it was called Red Square even before the revolution?" Nina asked.

"Really? Why?"

"It's called Krasnaya Ploshchad. Back in the days of Ivan the Terrible, *krasnaya* meant red and beautiful. Nowadays it only means red. Another form of the word, *krasivaya*, means beautiful in the modern language. So Krasnaya Ploshchad originally meant beautiful square."

"All this time I thought the Bolsheviks had named it. I never thought to ask what it had been called before then."

They wandered the streets and boulevards,

passing kiosks selling baked goods, drinks, theater tickets. Pushcarts offered gorgeous bouquets of colorful flowers. A man strolled by with a bunch of posies in one hand, an open bottle of beer in the other. The city apparently had no ordinance against carrying open containers. Or the citizens and the authorities simply ignored it.

Jarrod hadn't had time for much casual sightseeing with Sasha last year. He'd been anxious to get out of the country, paranoid that at the last minute the bureaucrats would change their minds and make him give Sasha back. He and the boy had been united one morning and on a flight out of the country the next afternoon.

The three of them returned to the hotel weary, jet-lagged, but pleased with their excursion. Sasha had asked questions from time to time, but mostly he'd just looked and listened.

Something else struck Jarrod as interesting. Sasha should have been completely comfortable with people who spoke his first language, but he almost never talked to strangers directly. More often than not he would ask Nina quietly and let her repeat his questions. Even more surprising was that he often asked her the questions in English.

They ate a light dinner at the hotel. The food was good, though not remarkable. The service was slow and rather formal, unlike restaurants back home, where waiters and customers often exchanged personal greetings and chatted. Here there was a clear demarcation between server and served.

At last they rode up to their suite. Jarrod supervised Sasha's bath and put him to bed. The boy's eyes closed as soon as his head hit the pillow. No bedtime story tonight.

"He's off to dreamland." He sat on the settee beside her.

"It's been a long day for him—two days, actually. I'm about ready to collapse myself."

"Me, too," Jarrod admitted.

She cozied up to him, leaned against his chest and stretched out her long legs. Almost relaxed, he realized, but not quite.

"Is it strange being here?"

She nodded. "You can't imagine. Sometimes, as we turned corners, I felt as if I had never left, yet it's been sixteen years."

"Scared?"

"I know I shouldn't be. Who I am, who I was doesn't matter to anyone here anymore. Maybe it never did."

He realized she was talking about her

mother, rather than government officials. "I hope you find that isn't true."

Nina tilted her head and smiled up at him. "Thank you."

They luxuriated in their shared warmth for several minutes, each with private thoughts.

"When do you want to visit your mother?" he finally asked.

Nina hesitated before answering. "Tomorrow, after breakfast."

"You have her address?"

"She lives on the other side of town, in a development that didn't even exist when I left here."

"Sasha and I'll go with you. We can window shop, or maybe there's a park nearby we can hang around in."

"I think I'd like the two of you with me when I meet her."

Jarrod wasn't sure that was a good idea. This should be a very private moment. But he would respect Nina's wishes.

"However you want to handle it," he said. "We'll be there for you."

## CHAPTER ELEVEN

As TIRED AS NINA WAS—her body ached with fatigue—sleep escaped her. The prospect of seeing her mother after all these years both thrilled and terrified her.

A knock on the door startled her. She opened her eyes and only then realized the room was flooded with light.

Throwing on her robe, she padded to the door and opened it.

"Good morning, sleepyhead." Jarrod looked downright chipper, and the scent of his after-shave made her want to drag him into her bed.

"What time is it?"

"Almost noon."

The statement made her blink. "Did you say noon?"

He smiled. "Sasha and I had breakfast a couple of hours ago."

"Why didn't you wake me?"

He laughed. "I tapped on your door but

got no response. I figured you needed sleep more than food."

"My beauty sleep," she muttered.

He touched her cheek, a featherlight caress that sent an electric charge straight to her heart. "There's nothing wrong with your beauty, sweetheart."

She caught his hand and held it as she kissed his palm. Their eyes met.

He cleared his throat. "I'll order you up some food. I can't remember the last time I ate a soft-boiled egg. The ham was decent. So was the bread. I wasn't crazy about the coffee."

"Right now even bad coffee sounds good."

"Get dressed." He kissed her lightly on the lips. "Breakfast will be here by the time you're ready."

She closed the door and stared at the clock by her bed. Almost noon. She'd slept nearly twelve hours.

She showered, put on a little makeup and dressed in a sea-green suit and white linen blouse. The outfit was conservative in the States. Here it would look foreign, but what could she do? Yesterday on the street she'd noticed young women sported tight leather mini-skirts, while their mothers and grandmothers still wore the kinds of outfits that hadn't changed in fifty years. The word *dowdy* came to mind. Nina had no dowdy clothes in her wardrobe—and hoped she never would.

By the time she entered into the sitting room, the coffee had arrived along with a fruit cup, ham, a boiled egg, toast, butter, jam and preserves.

She gulped down the coffee, which was heavily laced with cream and sugar, let Sasha have the fruit, and managed to nibble on a piece of dry toast.

"You really should eat more," Jarrod prompted.

"Maybe later."

"Do you want to call your mother first to let her know you're coming?"

"I don't have her number."

"Look it up in the telephone book."

She chuckled. "There is no phone book."

"Are you serious?"

She shook her head. "Besides, I wouldn't know what to say."

"How about, 'Hi, Mom, this is Nina.'"

Her strained smile faded quickly.

"Okay, finish your coffee, then the three

of us will take a taxi to her apartment." He tipped up Nina's chin. "We'll play it by ear from there."

OUTSIDE THE HOTEL, Jarrod walked down the street to a vendor who was selling flowers. He bought a lush bouquet of nine salmon-pink roses—they only came in odd numbers—and brought it back to Nina.

"I bet your mom would like these."

Nina accepted them. "I should have thought of that."

"You have other things on your mind right now."

She inhaled their sweet fragrance. "Thank you."

He touched his lips to her temple. "You're welcome."

The ride across town took longer than Jarrod had expected, not because the cabbie didn't drive like a New York hackie, but because of the apartment complex's distance from the center of the city.

They zipped through the established, formal core of the capital, through residential areas that were old and staid and had a worn, tired feel about them to more modern areas that somehow felt shabby rather than new. At last they came to a group of widely spaced high-rise apartment buildings that resembled the type of cold, utilitarian government projects Jarrod had seen in New York and Chicago. In those cities he would have been reluctant to enter them. Here he didn't know what to expect.

"I've changed my mind," Nina said as they screeched to a halt in front of one of them. "I can do this on my own. You don't need to wait. I'll get a cab back."

Jarrod climbed out and offered her his hand. "We'll wait."

Her stomach had been roiling all the way out here. She gathered up the bouquet and grasped his hand tightly. "That's sweet, but—"

"I see a play area." Jarrod waved toward a set of swings, a seesaw and a jungle gym. "Sasha and I will be over there."

Nina nodded. "She may not be home."

"You won't know until you check."

She tapped her foot, delaying.

"Go on, Nina. It's time." He bent and kissed her on the cheek. "We'll be right here."

Not nearly as bolstered by this assurance of support as she should be, Nina turned and entered the building.

JARROD TOOK SASHA'S HAND as they saun-
tered over to the play area.

Of the four swings, only two were intact.
Jarrod checked one out carefully before letting Sasha on it. He was pushing him when
a woman approached with a toddler in a
stroller. In her mid- to late-thirties, plump
rather than fat, she had a pretty face, dark
eyes, creamy skin and pink cheeks.

*"Zdravstuite,"* she said pleasantly, her eyes
not quite meeting his.

Jarrod recognized the formal greeting, but
knew he didn't have a hope of pronouncing
the word. He nodded to her and smiled.

She said something else to him, but he had
no idea what the words meant.

"What did she say?" he asked Sasha.

"She asked if we're moving in here."

"Tell her no, we're just visiting someone."

"You English?" The woman regarded him
more closely. "American," she decided.

"Yes." Jarrod nodded.

*"Ty russki?"* She gazed at Sasha. *You are
Russian?*

"I am American," he said in English, stunning Jarrod with the sharpness of his reply.

"But you speak Russian," she said in heavily accented English.

"A little," he acknowledged.

The woman frowned, clearly confused. She lifted her child out of the stroller and placed him in the other swing.

"Whom you here to visit?" she asked.

Jarrod debated. Should he tell her? Nina was beginning to make him paranoid. Neighbors spying on neighbors. But what was the point? The cold war was over. Americans weren't regarded as the enemy anymore. More like rich tourists.

"A friend," he said, and decided to change the subject. "Is that your son?" He motioned to the little boy. "How old is he?"

"Petya three years, five months." She rolled the *r*'s but spoke slowly enough to make the words quite intelligible.

"He's very handsome."

"Like his papa." She smiled, revealing uneven teeth. "How long you in Russia?"

"Two weeks."

"You see Kremlin?" She pronounced it *Kreml*. "And Red Square?"

"It's a beautiful city." Which was true in parts, like every other big city he'd ever visited.

"I live here always."

He considered the statement. What exactly did she mean? That she had always lived here? Or that she intended to always live here? He thought about Nina. Now that she was back, would she feel the same way, a longing to be home? Was it one of the reasons, besides her mother's presence, why she'd hesitated to return?

NINA ENTERED THE vestibule of the ten-story building. The air was close, stuffy. She studied the names beside the apartment numbers. Kamarov was in the middle of the list. Seven D. The button beside it, like many of the others, was missing.

Nina pushed on the door to the hallway. It should have been locked, but she wasn't surprised when it opened. Midway down the gloomy corridor were two elevators. A handwritten sign on one said it was out of order. She hoped the other was operational. What did her mother do when both were on the fritz? "I can't imagine her walking up seven flights of stairs with groceries," she muttered to herself.

The elevator was slow and made creaking noises, but moved steadily enough. It stopped on the fifth floor. The door opened but no one was there. She proceeded to the seventh and emerged into a narrow hallway with doors on both sides. The only sources of light were bare, low-wattage bulbs in wall sconces, and a dirty window at the end of the passage.

The tile on the floor was chipped, a few squares missing. The walls were covered with wallpaper, some of it peeling, all of it stained and dirty.

Nina made her way along the hall and stopped in front of the fourth door on the right. The slot for a name plate was empty. A piece of tape above it had Kamarov inked on it.

Nina's heart pounded, and the urge to flee was overwhelming. She turned to leave, but a stronger instinct compelled her to stay.

She was about to see her mother, the woman who had borne her, raised her and saved her life by sending her away. The person who might also be responsible for her papa's death. Jarrod was right. She couldn't come this far and not visit her.

Feeling so weak she feared her knees would give out, she stuck her nose into the flowers, drew strength from their cool fragrance. Then, raising her fist, she took another deep breath and knocked on the green steel door.

No answer. Maybe her mother wasn't home. Maybe she hadn't heard.

Her stomach in knots, Nina knocked again, this time harder.

*"Momentochku." Just a moment.*

Was it her mother? The muffled voice was indistinct.

The door opened. *"Da, shto—" Yes, what—*

The two women stared at each other for an eternity of heartbeats.

"Nina?" The question was an incredulous whisper. "Ninochka?"

"Mama?"

The flowers tumbled as the two women flew into each other's arms. Sounds, indistinct, muffled, came from both of them.

Lydia Kamarova at last pulled away and held her daughter at arm's length. Her cheeks were wet, her eyebrows drawn together above her watering eyes. "It is really you?" she asked in Russian.

Nina nodded through her own tears.

"Come inside. Come inside. Oh, let me look at you."

Nina picked up the bouquet and held it out to her mother.

Lydia accepted the flowers almost shyly and inhaled their scent. "They're beautiful. You remembered how much I like roses." She kissed her daughter on the cheek again.

Nina smiled thinly, ashamed that she didn't remember that detail at all.

"I'll put them in water. Then we'll have tea."

Nina studied her mother. Lydia had put on weight. Her hair, once meticulously coiffed and honey-blond, was a gray veil that hung down to her shoulders. The Paris fashions she'd once worn with such elegance had also been replaced by the same black attire Nina had noticed on other women on the street.

Yet there was something in Lydia's steel-blue eyes, the restless energy that Nina remembered so well. Circumstances might have changed and this flat might be a far cry from the tasteful quarters they'd once inhabited in the heart of the city, but this woman wasn't beaten. Nina felt unexpectedly proud of her.

Lydia took the flowers into the kitchen and put them in a large glass vase, filled it with water and returned to the living room, where she set it on a sideboard in front of a gilt-framed mirror.

"They're lovely," she said.

Mother and daughter hugged again, then Lydia wiped her cheeks and hurried back to the kitchen area. "Do you still like your tea with extra sugar?" she asked over her shoulder. "I bought some sugar just the other day. There's plenty."

"You remember?"

"Of course I remember. You are my daughter, I remember everything about you. Now tell me about your life in America. Are you happy? Why didn't you tell me you were coming? I could have prepared."

"The man I work for adopted a Russian boy. They're waiting downstairs. He invited me to come with him to act as his interpreter. At first I said no. I was afraid."

Lydia came over and caressed Nina's cheek. "It's in the past now, Ninochka. The Kamarovs are nobodies, forgotten." Her eyes twinkled. "Except at the factory." She glanced over at the mantel clock on a side table. "My shift starts in half an hour. I'll call in, get the day off…the week off. Wait here."

She dashed out the door, leaving Nina standing in the middle of the room.

She took a slow look around. The furnishings were modest, a mixture of old and not so old. There was a feeling about European rooms that was different from American, and for the first time Nina tried to define it. In the use of space perhaps. Ornamentation? Proportions? Whatever it was, she couldn't label it.

She spied two ashtrays on side tables, both of them half-full.

Lydia came back almost out of breath. "Nadia down the hall has the only phone on this floor."

"Was your supervisor upset?"

Lydia beamed. "I'm the union representative. I know the rules better than he does. Can you believe it? I'm a true member of the proletariat now. I work in a cardboard factory." She walked through a doorway into a tiny kitchen and began filling a kettle at the stained porcelain sink hanging from the wall.

"I get to argue with management," she said, talking through the empty window frame between the two rooms. "I tell them what they are doing wrong. The KGB—it's called the FSB now, but it's the same people—doesn't come pounding on my door to arrest me and lock me up."

"They didn't pound on the door when they came to arrest Papa, either," Nina pointed out. "They knocked politely and greeted you like an old friend."

Her mother stiffened. The brass faucet screeched as she shut the water off. With a blank expression she stared over her hunched shoulder at her daughter.

"You think I had something to do with that, don't you? I remember the way you looked at me after he left, as if I had betrayed him." She abandoned the kettle and came to her daughter. "Ninochka—" she clutched Nina's hand and squeezed it "—do you really believe that I could do that? My Vanya. I loved him. Except for you, he was the most important person in the world to me."

"Yet you sent me away." Nina despised the note of self-pity that crept into her voice, but how else was she to feel? Within two weeks she'd lost both her parents, her friends, her country, her entire world.

Lydia dragged her to the couch and pulled her down on it, still holding her hand. "Sending you away was the hardest thing I have ever had to do in my life, harder even than seeing your father go out the door, knowing he would never be coming back." Her eyes brimmed. "You were all I had left. Everything your father and I did was for you—"

"What did you do?" Nina tried to pull her hand away, but her mother refused to give it up.

"Listen to me, Nina. Your father and I knew for a long time, for years, that the Soviet Union was collapsing. The system had been weak for decades as the government spent money it didn't have, diverted resources from the things people desperately needed in order to create weapons we would never use—weapons that, if we did use them, would mean the end of everything, anyway. Ivan…your father was trying to make members of the politburo see reason, to get them to alter the course of events. He knew he was taking a chance when he distributed those subversive materials. I knew it, too, and agreed that it had to be done."

Nina frowned. "You were always spouting politically correct party slogans, kissing up to people who were dining on caviar while ordinary people were scrambling for bread."

Her mother's expression was sad. She lowered her head, then slowly raised it. "My little girl. My dear, sweet little girl." She squeezed Nina's hands tighter. "You were so young, so filled with idealism. You thought you could change the world by speaking the truth. Oh, sweetheart, I wish it were that simple." She met Nina's eyes and held them. "While your father was working behind the scenes with the forces who wanted real reform, I was trying to give him cover by playing the perfect Communist Party wife."

"You were in on what Papa was doing?"

"How do you think I knew to go to John Lockhart? Where do you think your papa got the information he was distributing?"

Nina stared at her mother. It had never occurred to her that her "husband" had been part of a conspiracy. She'd thought he was just an American businessman her father had befriended in his role as a government official. But of course nothing was that simple under the old regime. For John to get the lucrative contracts, he would have had to offer something in return. In this case, forbidden documents and an exit strategy, a plan of escape, asylum for his benefactor's daughter.

To his credit, John had never even alluded to such a deal, never made her feel like a pawn, like the bartered wife she'd joked about earlier with Jarrod. Her husband had been one of the hated capitalists, but he'd been an honorable man.

Looking back now, Nina realized it all made sense. John had been almost paranoid about getting out of the country the moment they were married, so much so that he'd scared her. The ceremony had been rushed, agreed to and performed nearly overnight. None of her friends had been invited to the registry office to witness it. He had insisted they leave as soon as the paperwork was signed, and he never again returned to the Soviet Union, though he'd spent a good deal of the previous seven years there.

Nina had always assumed her mother had been evicted from the apartment because she'd let her daughter marry a foreigner and leave the country. Now she wondered if Lydia had forced her to marry and emigrate because she knew they were about to lose their home and everything else. Had that happened, Nina would have ended up on the street, too, and there were few choices for attractive young women in that situation.

Oh, God. Was it possible that all these years, Nina had had it backwards?

"What did you do after you were thrown out of the apartment?" She dreaded the answer. Lydia Petrovna Kamarova had been a beautiful woman then. Had she been forced to use her beauty to survive?

"I managed," was all her mother said.

"The money I sent you…" Nina had resented the request for money that arrived a few weeks after John passed away. Apparently he'd been sending Lydia regular monthly payments, which had stopped when he died. Lydia had simply written that if Nina could spare a little money from time to time it would be greatly appreciated. Nina had sent it, but grudgingly.

"It saved my life. You were very generous."

Now Nina wanted to cry, to scream, to beg forgiveness. She had not been generous. She had been bitter and angry and stingy. "Oh, Mama."

Lydia opened her arms. Nina fled into them.

"I'm so sorry."

The two women wept.

"You're here now," Lydia soothed through her tears. "That's all that matters."

After a few minutes they released each other. Lydia rose, went to another room and came out with two cotton hankies. She handed one to Nina. They sniffled together.

"Things have gotten better. Truly they have. The work is good. The pay—" she shrugged "—it's not bad, and it's usually on time…"

"You almost sound happy, Mama." Nina was astounded that the sophisticated woman who had once been a member of the elite could be so content with a paying job in a cardboard factory.

"I guess…in a way…I am. The only thing that has been missing is you, and now you are here."

Nina inhaled deeply. Did her mother think she'd come back for good? America was Nina's home now. Perhaps she would always be a foreigner there, but the United States was where she felt she belonged, where she felt safe.

As if reading her mind, Lydia asked, "Is it a good place, America?"

"A wonderful place, Mama."

Lydia resumed making tea, and they talked for more than two hours, during which Lydia smoked almost incessantly. She insisted on knowing all about what Nina did, how she earned her living, how she lived. Did she have a car of her own? What kind of place did she live in?

*"Bozhe Ty moi,"* Nina exclaimed at last. *My God!* "Jarrod and Sasha are waiting downstairs. They must have thought I got lost or kidnapped."

"Go to them, bring them up. I want to meet them. I have plenty of tea and sugar, and piroshki for the boy."

SURROUNDED BY WOMEN and children, Jarrod had just made a handkerchief disappear when he spied Nina coming out the door of the apartment house. She strode toward him with her head held high, a smile lighting her face.

Sasha saw her a second later and ran to her. To Jarrod's surprise he spoke to her in English, though he had been jabbering away in Russian with several of the kids, friends he had made on the spot.

"Daddy has been doing magic tricks," he told her. "I helped him."

"And having fun, I see." She squeezed his shoulder affectionately.

Looking up at her, he asked, "Do we have to go now?" The question held regret.

"I would like you and your dad to come upstairs and meet my mother."

Jarrod slipped the coin he had palmed for the next trick into his pocket and observed the other women as Nina approached. She was better dressed than they were, in a fashion that was stylish and foreign, and she carried herself in a manner that made her stand out. He sensed curiosity and perhaps jealousy on the part of the housewives. They made little pretense of not staring.

The first woman Jarrod had met said something to her in Russian. Nina replied. He understood only the last word, Kamarova. Her mother's last name.

"Kamarova?" The woman raised an eyebrow. *"Nasha soratnitsa."* Then she prattled on in rapid-fire Russian.

Nina laughed, and the other women joined in. She then turned to Jarrod. "Will you come up? My mother wants to meet both of you, to thank you for bringing me here."

"I'd like that, too." He put out his hand to Sasha, who came over and took it. "Goodbye, ladies. It was very nice meeting you."

The children complained that he was leaving. He placated them by plucking a coin from behind each one's ear and giving it to them to keep.

They all chatted at once, and though he didn't understand the words, it didn't matter. The message was one of goodwill.

"You've been a hit, I see," Nina said as they walked to the apartment house, her arm in his.

"I'm a curiosity. I don't imagine they meet too many American tourists around here."

"The kids think I have the coolest dad." Sasha gazed up at him, his face aglow. "I do, too."

Jarrod ruffled his hair affectionately. "I think you're pretty cool, too, kid."

While Sasha fingered his hair back into place, Jarrod turned to Nina. "They wanted to know who we were here to visit, but I wasn't sure I should tell them, so I didn't. Is your mother okay?"

They reached the vestibule to the building.

"She's fine, Jarrod. I'm fine." Nina turned to him and beamed. "You were right. Times have changed. Thank you for making me come here."

"The terror is over then?"

"The terror is over." She took a big breath and let it out slowly. "Do you have any idea what that feels like, to stop looking over my shoulder?"

He remembered the pleasure on her face when the woman had said something about Lydia. "What did that neighbor say about your mom?"

Nina laughed. "They call her their warrior. Whenever something goes wrong around here, they go to her and she launches herself at the powers that be and gets the matter straightened out."

They entered the hallway. Sasha looked around, surveying it with what seemed a critical and disapproving eye, but he said nothing. They stepped into the elevator.

"Is this thing safe?" Jarrod asked, half in jest.

Nina shrugged. "As long as it is the only

one running. When they get around to fixing the other one, this one will break down."

He drew back. "Why wouldn't they service this one at the same time?"

"That's not how the system works."

"Sounds more like it doesn't work."

"Aha," she said, her lips twitching, "now you're getting it."

With a shrug of incomprehension, Jarrod shook his head. This was indeed a different world.

The elevator stopped on the fifth floor, but no one was there. They continued up. The apartment door was open when they reached it, a woman standing just inside. Even with her backlit it was easy for him to see where Nina got her looks. Her mother was perhaps two inches shorter and considerably stockier than her daughter, but she possessed the same Slavic chin, high wide cheekbones and keen blue eyes.

Nina started to say something in Russian, then stopped and smiled. "Sorry." She reverted to English. "Mother, may I present Jarrod Morrison, my employer, and his son, Alexander. This is my mother, Lydia Petrovna Kamarova."

Jarrod was surprised when the older woman

greeted him in English, mildly accented with echoes of a British pronunciation. She extended her hand. "I am very pleased to meet you, Mr. Morrison."

Her greeting to Sasha was warm and adult. She offered him her hand, as well. "Alexander Jarrodovich—" Alexander, son of Jarrod "—I welcome you and your father to my home."

Sasha was flustered as he shook her hands.

Small and neat, the apartment was cluttered, lived-in and comfortable, but it reeked of cigarette smoke.

Inviting father and son to sit on the firmly upholstered couch, Lydia waved Nina to one of the overstuffed easy chairs. A plastic tray crowded the small coffee table. On it was a plate of pastries, a small bottle of what looked like lemonade, and a tea service. She held out the assortment of piroshki to the boy, explaining that they were fruit filled, then proceeded to pour tea from a large pot into clear glasses in metal holders with handles. Having learned the protocol of names, Jarrod was careful to always address the older woman formally as Lydia Petrovna. She, in turn, called him Mr. Morrison. Jarrod knew at some point the formalities would be dropped, but it would be the prerogative of the older person to initiate the change.

"Nina tells me the city feels different now from when she left it," he commented, as he sipped his third glass of tea. Sasha had devoured three of the pastries.

"We had troubled times after the collapse. Transitions are always difficult, but gradually things have been getting better. I have this apartment all to myself now. There is plenty of food in the stores. The variety and quality has improved. More people own automobiles. Yes, life is much better than it was."

Their conversation rambled on for another hour, mostly in English, but occasionally in Russian and at one point in French. Nina had told Jarrod that her mother had entertained a good deal when her father was a government official. It hadn't occurred to him that she would be multilingual like her daughter.

"Will you come to dinner with us?" Jarrod asked.

Lydia didn't hesitate. "That's very generous of you. It has been a long time since I ate in a restaurant."

"Then we must take you to a good one, one you will remember."

Lydia smiled at Nina. "I will always remember this day."

"Tonight we celebrate with caviar and champagne," Nina said.

"I will wear the burgundy dress I bought in the bazaar and the brooch I managed to hold on to, the one your father gave me for my thirtieth birthday."

It was already past five when Lydia and Nina went into the bedroom. Jarrod switched on the small television set in the corner and waited for it to warm up. A black-and-white, he realized after switching a few channels on the dial. There was no remote.

He found a talk show, but since he had no idea what they were discussing or whether it was suitable for his son, he flipped to another channel. News. They showed film of a flood somewhere, a shot of the American president at a news conference, a story about a train crash—he surmised it was in India—and a series of commercials, one of them for a motor scooter.

He turned the dial again. A movie about the Second World War was on, or as the Russians called it, the Great Patriotic War.

He rotated the knob once more and this time couldn't help but chuckle. *I Love Lucy* dubbed in Russian. He left it, sat beside Sasha on the couch and watched the fifty-year-old sitcom. He soon realized the language was immaterial. It was the classic episode of Lucy in the chocolate factory. He and his son relaxed and guffawed together.

They were still laughing when Nina and her mother emerged from the bedroom.

Instinctively Jarrod rose to his feet and stared. Sasha, too, seemed affected, for he stood up, as well.

"My son and I will have the privilege of dining this evening with the two most beautiful women in Moscow."

Jarrod went over to Lydia, took her right hand and raised it to his lips. "Absolutely stunning."

The older woman blushed, then said she'd go down the hall to call for a cab. Before she left, she looked at her daughter and said something in Russian. Jarrod decided to wait until later to find out what it was.

## CHAPTER TWELVE

"WHAT WAS IT YOUR MOTHER said to you?"

Nina felt her face flush. You better grab this one by the hips and not let him go. That such a statement came from her own mother was shocking enough, there was no way she could repeat it to Jarrod, though it might have been interesting to get his reaction. "That you're a very charming gentleman," she muttered.

She could tell by the way he looked at her that he didn't quite believe it, but to her everlasting relief he didn't challenge her.

Fifteen minutes later they were hurtling into the heart of the city against the stream of outgoing traffic, arriving at the hotel in less time than the earlier trip had taken. Nina marched to the reception desk and rattled off instructions. The concierge kept saying *"Da, da,"* and bobbing his head obediently.

"What did you tell him?" Jarrod asked.

"To get us reservations at the Trident for

eight o'clock, and to have a car and driver here for us in an hour."

"Your father would be impressed," Lydia said to her in Russian, as they stepped into the elevator. "You've learned how to take charge."

"You were a good teacher."

Lydia rested her hand on her daughter's arm. "In spite of everything, Ninochka, he was a good man."

Nina patted her mother's hand. "I have only fond memories of him."

"Do you ever miss him?"

Whenever she thought of the world she'd left behind and reminisced about pleasant experiences, it was always with her father, holding his hand, sharing laughter and exciting adventures with him.

"Sometimes," she admitted. "Sometimes I want to turn to him and tell him things. 'Papa, guess what I did today?'"

"He loved you very much."

"He loved you." For the first time Nina appreciated what her parents had felt for each other. She'd been too selfish then to see it. Jarrod had helped her understand love was about other people.

"Have you found anyone else, Mama?" Nina asked, realizing only after the words were out that it was something an American might ask, but not a Russian. Such things were very private.

Lydia looked straight ahead and after a short pause said, "No."

Nina decided not to press. Her mother's personal life was just that.

The door opened and they stepped onto the thick carpet runner that stretched the length of the wide marble-floored hallway, a marked contrast to the apartment house they'd left. Inside the suite, Lydia surveyed the room and its furnishings with a few appraising glances. "It is good."

While the women retired to Nina's room so she could change clothes, Jarrod and Sasha did the same in theirs. Jarrod put on the dark blue suit he'd brought, the closest he had to formal wear, and helped his son get into his new tan suit. Jarrod had already learned that the boy enjoyed dressing up.

"Babushka is nice, isn't she?" Jarrod regretted that his own mother hadn't lived long enough to be a grandmother. She would have relished the role.

"She has good piroshki," Sasha said.

Jarrod laughed. Definitely normal. The way to a boy's heart was through his stomach.

They returned to the sitting room and were gazing out the window toward the onion domes of St. Basil's Cathedral when the women rejoined them.

Jarrod let out a low wolf whistle. He'd never seen Nina this dressed up. Calling her a knockout would be an understatement. Her shiny black dress came to just above her knees. The fine fabric hugged her narrow waist and crossed her curves in neat folds. Her hair was piled high on her head, exposing the diamond earrings he'd given her for Christmas. Subtle eye shadow accented the deeper tones of her eyes. Her rosy-red lips were tantalizingly kissable.

"I wish I were a linguist so I could tell you in a multitude of languages how beautiful you are."

Nina's face lit up. It didn't seem possible that she could be even more alluring, but the smile did it.

"I like the way you look," Sasha agreed.

"*Bolshoye spasibo*—" *Thank you very much* "—Alexander Jarrodovich," she replied with a feminine bow. "I like the way you look, too."

Jarrod stepped between the two women and offered each an arm. "Shall we go to dinner?"

AFTER AN ELEGANT five-course meal—they did indeed start with caviar and champagne—the four of them returned to the hotel. While Jarrod put his son to bed, Nina acceded to her mother's request and ordered up a bottle of dessert wine. The three adults sat and talked—about America, about Russia, about art and literature. Jarrod was impressed by how well-read Lydia was in several languages.

At some point she asked Jarrod to address her by her first name. She did the same with him. She had already asked Sasha to call her Babushka—Grandma in English.

In spite of Nina's obvious concern, her mother used the house phone to order up a second bottle of sweet wine. This was indeed a banner day and a cause for celebrating.

Rather than allow Lydia to return to her apartment at such a late hour, Nina invited her to spend the night in the second bed in her room. It was well after 1:00 a.m. by the time they finally said good-night.

Despite the late hour and jet lag, it took Jarrod awhile to get to sleep. Perhaps it was the later-than-usual rich evening meal or the syrupy wine that caused the heartburn. Whatever the origin, it was enough for him to wish he'd brought antacid tablets. He'd have to see if he could pick up some tomorrow.

The following morning Lydia volunteered to act as tour guide, and Jarrod happily agreed. First, they returned to her apartment so she could change clothes. Within seconds of getting out of the taxi, she was surrounded by a group of women, all of them talking at the same time.

"What's going on?" Jarrod asked Nina as they exited the other side of the vehicle.

Nina listened a moment and chuckled. "Word has spread that I'm here from America, and everyone wants to meet me—and you and Sasha," she added. "Apparently you two made quite an impression yesterday."

The leader of the group was a matronly woman by the name of Olga Igorevna. She hugged Nina as if they were close relatives, shook Jarrod's hand vigorously and nearly crushed Sasha with affection. She and the other women didn't speak English, so Nina's skills as an interpreter were put to a severe test, since everyone insisted on talking at once.

Sasha wasn't used to so many people hugging and kissing him. He looked a bit frightened at first, especially by all the cheek pinching, but he quickly recovered, decided he liked the attention and even hammed it up.

Lydia slipped away and went upstairs.

"Your mother is a saint," Olga informed Nina. "When things go wrong in our building, we know we can count on her to get them fixed. No one intimidates that woman. She'll take on the president himself if it's necessary."

Nina glanced over at the apartment house and wondered where exactly her mother was expending her energy. The high-rise certainly wasn't in very good condition.

Olga followed her gaze and grinned. "We're buying it, you know."

"Buying it?"

The others nodded, almost in unison.

"It was your mother's idea. The state wasn't maintaining it. She figured we could do a better job ourselves, so she went down to the ministry of public housing and told the minister personally that the tenants want to buy the building. He laughed and started to throw her out of his office, but she stood her ground, spouting reasons and statistics why he should agree. We're negotiating the price now."

That explained why the place was so run-down. The government wasn't interested, since it was giving up ownership, and the residents had no incentive to do anything that might increase its value.

"She's like that at work, too," added another woman. "All the mangers hide under their desks when they see her coming, because they know they can't win when she's on the warpath."

"But the factory is operating better, too," a third chimed in. "The bosses won't admit it, but they're glad she's there. She keeps them on their toes."

Someone laughed. "*Da,* running for cover."

Lydia reappeared in less formal clothes, carrying a small overnight-size cardboard suitcase. "I called Mikhail Sergeyevich," she told the women, "and informed him I'm taking the next three days as vacation time. He said he would fire me."

Someone inhaled sharply.

"I told him he couldn't because I know about the special fund," she said seriously.

There was dead silence. Then someone asked, "What special fund?"

Lydia shrugged and a grin played across her mouth. "I don't know yet, but you can be sure I'll find out." The others laughed.

"What did he say?" a woman asked.

"That I can take as much time as I need."

Everybody laughed again, including Nina.

Over the next three days they visited museums, parks and parts of the capital most foreigners never saw. Lydia was a charming hostess, full of enthusiasm, facts and anecdotes. Every evening, as they returned from dinner, she stopped in one of the many liquor stores and bought wine or cognac to close the day after Sasha had gone to bed.

On the third evening, Lydia retired to the bedroom soon after Sasha, and Jarrod invited Nina to sit beside him on the settee facing the window with its view of the city lights. He wrapped an arm around her and took comfort in the way she nestled against him.

"Your mother likes her liquor," he commented.

"She used to rant about the drunken behavior of some of the guests at our parties. I remember her sipping champagne, but I never saw her drunk, not even tipsy."

"She's had a hard life since then."

"I've let her down," Nina said.

Jarrod lifted his head off the back of the couch and peered at her. "Why do you say that? She loves you, and it's clear she's very proud of what you've made of yourself."

"But I haven't loved her enough in return. All these years I blamed her for Papa's arrest, even for his death, never stopping to think what it might have been like for her to be left completely alone. There were only the three of us. She tried in her own way to protect my father, and failed, but she did protect me, and I rewarded her with ingratitude."

He tipped her chin up, so their eyes could meet. "I don't think she has any regrets, Nina. If she had it to do over again, even knowing what would happen, I suspect she'd do exactly the same thing."

Nina bit her lip. "That only makes it worse."

Frowning, he asked, "How do you reckon that?"

"She gave up everything for me."

"Everything was taken away from her, Nina. She would never have let you go if she hadn't had to." He spoke softly, intimately. "Your mother may not be perfect, but she's a strong woman who loves you unconditionally."

"I wish I knew how to help her. I can send her more money, of course. That's not a problem. I should have been sending more all along, but what if all she does with it is buy more vodka?"

Jarrod kissed the top of Nina's head. "You've already helped her by coming here."

"We both have you to thank for that. I could have come back long ago, but I didn't. You gave me the strength."

"Nah," he said with a grin, "just a nudge."

She cuddled closer, her hand resting on his chest. "Thank you."

He could have made love to her right there on the couch if they had been truly alone. In an attempt to distract himself from the urge, he returned to the subject of her mother.

"Maybe the last few nights have just been an aberration brought on by the surprise of you appearing out of nowhere."

"I hope so," Nina muttered, but she didn't sound convinced. Neither was he. Lydia handled liquor with intimate familiarity.

"Ready for tomorrow?" Nina asked a few minutes later. Her proximity and her warm breath against his chest was having a predictable effect.

"Ready as I'll ever be, I guess. Thanks to your mother."

The apparatchik's widow seemed to have contacts everywhere. She'd called ahead to the orphanage where Sasha's sister was living, and wrangled grudging approval for the next day's visit. She had also arranged for Jarrod to hire a car so Nina could to drive them. Lydia would have accompanied them, but she couldn't stay away from work indefinitely.

"You sure you don't want to tell Sasha where we're going and why?" Nina asked.

"I'll tell him where before we leave," he answered, "but I won't say why. I don't want to tell him about his sister, not until I see how things stand. I can't be sure we'll get to meet her or what she'll be like. Another disappointment would only make matters worse. In the end we might decide he doesn't need to know."

"You're probably right. You could go there by yourself. It might make things easier."

He shook his head. "I wouldn't get anything accomplished without you, and leaving Sasha alone with your mother, a virtual stranger, might only increase his paranoia. He'd think it was a trick to abandon him. I can't do that to him. He'd never forgive me."

She agreed.

THE RENTAL CAR TURNED OUT to be a recent model Mercedes sedan.

The town of Cosmovo, forty kilometers north of Moscow, had been called something else before *Sputnik* and spacewalkers, but it had been changed in honor of the great achievements of Soviet science.

"Mom tells me there's talk of changing the name back again," Nina said, as they sped along the well-paved highway, "like they did with St. Petersburg. But many people think it would be an insult to history. Lenin may be out of favor, but the things the Cosmonauts accomplished deserve to be remembered and honored."

Jarrod concurred. "Have you ever been to Cosmovo?"

She shook her head and passed a slow moving panel truck. "Not that I recall. We had a car when I was young and sometimes we went driving, so it's possible I've been through it, but the name means nothing to me, and as far as I know it has no other claim to fame."

The village was a couple of kilometers off the main highway down a poorly maintained secondary road. The small community held a few shops and businesses, but was indistinguishable from hundreds of other rural settlements. A dirt lane that obviously didn't see a great deal of traffic led to the orphanage, on the other side of a hill.

As they topped the crest, Jarrod studied the compound below. It could have passed for a monastery, a convent, a private school or a reformatory. Bleak taupe walls surrounded a group of three-story buildings with faded red-tile roofs. A single portal in the front seemed to be the only entrance. Nina drove through.

"Is this it?" Sasha asked from the back seat. Dressed in casual clothes and running shoes, he stood out as a foreigner in his native land.

That morning Jarrod had explained that they would be visiting an orphanage north of Moscow. Sasha had instantly stiffened.

"For girls," Jarrod had added. "I just want to visit it."

"Why?"

Jarrod had put his arms round his son's shoulders and felt the tension in them.

"I told Babushka about the one you came from and that I send them money sometimes." Which was true; a check for a few hundred dollars every quarter. "She said this one might be able to use some help, too."

Sasha had considered the words, then

nodded, but Jarrod wasn't sure the boy believed him.

"This is it," he said now.

The courtyard was large and open, its center a grass quadrangle, worn down by traffic rather than a mower. In the middle stood a tall pole with colored streamers dangling from its top.

Nina killed the engine in front of the largest building where steps led to an arched doorway. A minute later a woman emerged. Dressed in black, with gray-streaked dark hair pulled into a bun at the nape of her neck, she appeared to be in her late fifties or early sixties.

Jarrod pointed to a set of swings on the other side of the yard. "Sasha, why don't you play for a few minutes while I talk to this lady?"

The boy clearly didn't want to leave his side.

"I'm not going anywhere, Son, I promise. You'll be able to see me the whole time."

Sasha considered a minute, then trudged across the grassy field, turning several times to look over his shoulder as if to reassure himself his father was still there. Jarrod waved and smiled.

Turning to the woman, he said, "Thank you very much for seeing us, Mrs. Poldarska. Especially on such short notice."

Nina had slipped into translator mode. The interpreter he'd had last year had had a very strong accent and—based on her choice of words and rather mangled syntax in English—he'd never been completely sure her translations were accurate in either language. With Nina he had no doubt.

"I don't quite know what it is you want, Mr. Morrison," she replied without warmth.

He explained that last year he had adopted Alexander Sergeievich Chudikov and had been told at the time that the boy had a sister, Anna, two years older, who lived at this orphanage.

The headmistress's frown indicated concern. "Anna Sergeievna Chudikova is one of our best students. She is, however, unaware of having a sibling."

"I have no desire to cause her unhappiness," Jarrod assured her. "Sasha has no memory of his sister or of his mother, for that matter. But I'd like him to meet his sister."

The woman shook her head. "Absolutely not, Mr. Morrison. I cannot allow it. Such a thing would only upset the girl. Imagine learning she has a brother she doesn't remember, meeting him, finding out he has a family, then watching him leave to live in America, while she must remain here. No, it's out of the question." She shook her head again. "I'm sorry you came all this way for nothing." She started up the steps.

When Jarrod reached out to touch her, Nina put her hand on his arm to restrain him, then spoke to the other woman in Russian. Mrs. Poldarska turned and listened. For several minutes the two conversed.

"She has agreed to let them meet," Nina finally explained, "providing neither is told of their relationship to each other. If, after we leave, you want to tell Sasha who the girl is, that'll be up to you, but under no circumstances is Anna to learn he is her brother. Do you agree?"

Jarrod nodded. "Tell her I am very grateful for her kindness and understanding."

The woman seemed mollified, though not completely comfortable with her own decision. "The girls will be coming out for their morning break in a few minutes," Nina translated. Then she added, "We need an excuse for Anna to be singled out to be with Sasha. Mrs. Poldarska tells me Anna is one of the best singers in their chorus, so I've suggested we pose as foreigners interested in their music program, and ask her questions about the type of training she receives."

To Jarrod it seemed a little far-fetched. "I really don't know how convincing I'll be. I can play a few tunes on the piano, but that's about the extent of my musical expertise."

"I'll improvise as we go along," Nina said. "Don't forget, we don't have to convince Mrs. Poldarska, only the girl."

He assented wordlessly, and she resumed her discussion with the headmistress.

"Have Sasha play at the maypole," Nina again translated. "Anna will join him there."

Jarrod strolled over to his son. The boy was leery, clearly apprehensive. "We'll only be a few more minutes. The headmistress wants us to meet one of the girls, then we can go."

Sasha was clearly worried, even scared, and that realization made Jarrod miserable. Trying to be upbeat, he pointed to the tall pole in the middle of the courtyard. "Do you know what that pole is for?"

Sasha didn't.

"Why don't you go over and check it out? Maybe someone will come by and tell you. Relax, Son." He squeezed his tight shoulder muscles, trying to reassure him. "We won't be long."

A minute later a gaggle of preadolescent girls streamed out a side door. Mrs. Poldarska called out, and a slender girl with long platinum-blond hair broke away from the group and approached them. Jarrod was sure he would have instantly recognized her resemblance to Sasha, even if he hadn't known beforehand who she was. Nina mumbled a translation as the headmistress instructed the girl. She was shy but polite, and clearly mystified at being picked to meet these Americans, who were introduced as Mr. Jarrod Morrison and Nina Ivanova Lockhart.

"Anna, these people are here to learn about our different programs. I told them what a good singer you are, and they asked to meet you."

The praise seemed to surprise the girl. Apparently it wasn't something she received very often, or maybe it was because the headmistress was personally complimenting her.

Nina took over and asked a series of questions. What part did she sing? Alto. How often did she practice with the group? Once a week. Who was their instructor? The math teacher. What kinds of songs did they sing? Anna gave her a short list, none of which meant anything to Jarrod, but all of which seemed familiar to Nina.

Finally, when she appeared to run out of questions, Mrs. Poldarska politely intervened.

"Anna, while I finish talking with our guests, I'd like you to join their son standing by the maypole."

Sasha was alone. The other girls had stared at him as they passed by on their way to another building. To Jarrod, the boy again looked like the lonely orphan he'd brought home last year. Maybe this was all a monumental mistake. Perhaps now that he'd met Nina's mother, he should have had her visit here and report back to him. But it was too late.

"It's impolite for us to leave him standing there all by himself," the headmistress continued. "Please go and talk with him, answer any questions he might have."

"It was very nice meeting you, Anna," Jarrod said through Nina, and held out his hand to her.

"Very nice to meet you," she replied, uncomfortably shaking his hand.

He could see the reaction on her face. Weird foreigners. Americans. He couldn't blame her.

She would have been four years old when she was taken away from her mother and brother, old enough to have at least a vague recollection of them, but her life had been traumatic then and no doubt later. What memories she might have could be negative, the kind healthy minds try to suppress. In any event, she showed no indication she knew who the boy was.

She appeared to speak to him timidly; he responded with equal diffidence, then he grabbed one of the streamers and followed her around the pole.

"What can you tell me about her?" Jarrod asked through Nina.

"As you can see, she's a very bright girl, good at her studies. She truly does have a lovely voice. With training I think she could sing professionally."

"How long has she been here?"

"At this facility four years. She was at a lower-level home two years before that. Are you familiar with her background?"

Jarrod gazed at the two children happily playing together. "I understand their father died in prison," he said, "and that their mother was an alcoholic, so the state removed them from her care."

He glimpsed sadness in the woman's face as she nodded.

"Does she have any memory of her parents?"

"None of her father. A little about her mother, I believe, but she doesn't talk about her."

"And of her brother?"

"I've never heard her mention him, though one of the other teachers may have. My personal interaction with the girls is limited, since my administrative duties occupy a good deal of my time."

Jarrod detected regret in the statement. She seemed to be a caring woman, rather than a bureaucrat.

They watched the children dance around the pole. Within minutes the two of them were laughing and swinging in arcs by the long ropes. Their pleasure in each other's company appeared genuine and carefree.

"You say Anna is a good singer."

"Quite lovely. Unfortunately, we don't have the resources to develop such talents."

"Is there any way I can help?" Jarrod asked. "Perhaps pay for singing lessons for her—"

The woman shook her head. "Mr. Morrison, I'm sure you mean well, and I hope you'll understand that we cannot accept contributions for individual children. They have so little, and to single out one for special treatment would not only be unkind to the others but would cause considerable strife."

He understood the dilemma. Keeping everyone at the lowest common denominator seemed preferable to letting one excel.

"Suppose I were to establish an endowment for girls who are good at singing, without specifically naming Anna, but with the tacit understanding that she would be one of its beneficiaries."

The headmistress thought a moment, then nodded. "I would say that you are very generous."

"Can you give me some idea what such a program might cost? Say, for a voice teacher to come here weekly to give lessons?"

After half an hour of discussion, he agreed to sponsor a professional voice teacher for a year, at the end of which they would reevaluate its benefits, not only for Anna, but for other girls who participated, as well.

"In exchange," Jarrod said, "I would like you to send me regular reports of Anna's progress, not just about her singing but in general."

"You shall have it," the woman said, smiling broadly for the first time. "You are a kind and thoughtful man, Mr. Morrison. Sasha is a very fortunate little boy."

She gazed at the two children playing. "I'm sorry, but, this visit must come to an end. Anna is already late for her next class."

She shook Jarrod's hand as strongly as a man.

"Anna," she called out, and gave instructions. The girl looked over, clearly regretful that she was being summoned away, but again she complied without protest. Calling over her shoulder as she went, she headed toward a side door.

"What did she say?" Jarrod asked Nina.

"She told Sasha she enjoyed playing with him and hopes he will come again."

Then, suddenly, Anna stopped, reversed course and darted back to her brother. Impulsively, she planted a kiss on his cheek, spun around and dashed quickly inside.

The knot that had been building in Jarrod's throat hardened. Sasha looked stunned, forlorn, as he stood by the maypole and watched the retreating figure.

Nina grabbed Jarrod's hand and squeezed it. A moment passed before she called out to Sasha for him to join them.

"Did you have a good time?" she asked in English as he approached.

"She's nice. Not like the girls in school at home."

Jarrod forced himself to take consolation in the word *home*.

"Maybe that's because she's older than the girls in your class," he pointed out.

They returned to the rental car. Jarrod climbed in the back seat with his son. "How 'bout we go to the ice cream parlor Babushka took us to yesterday?"

Sasha's response was less enthusiastic than Jarrod expected. "Okay."

As they pulled out of the courtyard, the boy looked out the rear window, clearly ready to wave, but there was no one there.

"Did the girl tell you her name?" Jarrod asked.

"Anna."

"No last name?"

He shook his head.

"Sasha, her full name is Anna Sergeievna Chudikova."

"Like my name used to be." He paused, and stared at Jarrod for several moments. "Why does she have the same name?"

The meeting had gone so well, Jarrod felt encouraged, but hearing the distrustful tone of his son's question he suddenly had doubts.

"Because she's your sister, Sasha."

His mouth fell open. "My sister?"

Jarrod wasn't prepared for what happened next. He'd anticipated surprise, disbelief, maybe even anger. What he saw were tears filling Sasha's blue eyes and coursing down his cheeks. "She's my sister? And you didn't tell me?"

Suddenly he raised his fists and started pounding on Jarrod's arm and chest. "She's my sister and you're going to leave her there? In that place? We can't. You can't."

He beat harder. The punches didn't hurt physically, for Sasha was small and not very strong, but their emotional impact was devastating.

At last the boy collapsed on the seat beside him, buried his face in his hands and cried as Jarrod had never heard him cry before. He was no longer the dry-eyed orphan who passively accepted life's cruelties.

"Anna's going to be all right." Jarrod stoked his back, trying to console him. "I talked to the headmistress and she promised to send me letters about her, so we'll know how she is. And I'll be sending money so she can have singing lessons. The headmistress said she's a really good singer."

"Why did you take me to that place? Why did you bring me back to Russia? I don't want to be here. I'm afraid of this place."

Jarrod gathered the boy in his arms and

soothed him. "There's nothing to be afraid of, Sasha. You won't be staying here. Next week we go back home."

"I want to go home now, and I want Anna to come with us."

"Sasha, if I could take her with us, I would, but they won't allow it. I promise, though, that she'll be fine. They'll take good care of her here. The headmistress promised me."

"It's a lie. They don't tell the truth in those places." He pulled away, curled up in the corner and said nothing for several minutes. Jarrod and Nina exchanged eye contact through the rearview mirror. Jarrod felt helpless.

"I wish you'd never adopted me," the child suddenly shouted.

A knife through the heart couldn't have hurt more.

Jarrod extended his hand to touch his son, only to have him slapped it away. "I love you, Sasha, more than you'll ever know."

More than he ever thought he would. How could he explain to an eight-year-old that he had adopted him for selfish reasons, because he was lonely, because he had no one who mattered to him or who cared about him? Could he ever convince the child that he'd found pure joy in caring for someone else, someone who really needed him?

"I thought you'd be pleased to meet your sister and know she's all right, but I guess I shouldn't have told you. I'm sorry. I want you to know, Son, that I do love you and I want you to be happy."

Sasha turned away from him and stared out the car window. A minute elapsed before he asked, still facing the glass, "Does she know about me, that I'm her brother?"

Jarrod's heart sank. His good intentions were turning to dust.

"No. The schoolmistress doesn't want her to know."

"That doesn't mean you can't be friends," Nina said from the front seat, her voice positive, upbeat. "I tell you what. When we get home I'll help you write letters to Anna. The two of you can be pen pals."

"Hey, that's a wonderful idea," Jarrod said brightly, grateful for her intercession. "What do you say, Son? Would you like to do that? I'm sure she'd love to get letters from America."

Sasha turned and flew at him again, his small fists once more pounding Jarrod's chest and shoulder. "I hate you," he shouted. "I hate you. I hate you. I hate you."

## *CHAPTER THIRTEEN*

THE NEXT THREE DAYS were among the most depressing and frustrating Nina had ever experienced. Sasha became snippy, snarly and downright rude. Her heart broke when she saw Jarrod trying his best to deal with the boy in a sympathetic way, but at the same time understanding that discipline was necessary if his son was to develop into a mature, responsible adult. Until then Jarrod had walked a very careful line between indulgence and generosity in giving the boy nearly everything he wanted and explaining why he couldn't have things when it wasn't possible. But Sasha was now challenging him at every turn, a classic test of wills.

The day before they were scheduled to fly home, Sasha was particularly obnoxious. He'd been markedly slow getting dressed that morning, then putting on the wrong clothes, sloppily, at that—totally out of character for a kid who loved to dress up, especially in new duds. Jarrod had to make him change twice, thereby delaying their day's excursion even more.

Conversations with him were virtually nonexistent. His answers to direct questions, when he was forced to give them, were curt and sarcastic.

"Sasha, tomorrow is our last day," Jarrod said that afternoon. "We're supposed to visit the zoo. I know you want to see the animals. Babushka is looking forward to showing you around. She says it's one of the best zoos in the world. But if you don't start behaving yourself, we're not going. Is that clear?"

Sasha looked up at him defiantly. "Yes."

"Yes, what?"

"Yes, sir," he shouted.

Jarrod shook his head. "You're not helping yourself by acting this way, Son. You're mad at me, and maybe you have a right to be. I made a mistake, and I've told you I'm sorry. There's nothing more I can do. But being upset with me is no excuse for being impolite, especially to Nina and Babushka."

Sasha simply gazed into space, as if Jarrod wasn't there.

For a few hours after that, however, the

tension seemed to ease, though not completely. Exhausted after a full day of touring churches and cathedrals, gardens and historical monuments, they finally went to dinner at a small restaurant near Chinatown.

As usual, Lydia ordered wine with dinner. Jarrod and Nina barely touched theirs, but by the end of the meal the bottle was empty. They took a cab back to the hotel. Sasha was sitting between Nina and her mother.

Lydia leaned over and pointed to a tower of the Kremlin wall, and was beginning to tell a legend about it when Sasha pushed her away.

"You stink," he snarled. "Get away from me."

Jarrod whipped around in the front seat. "Sasha!"

"Well, she does."

"Apologize to Babushka this minute."

"Why? She smells like an old drunk."

For a moment, all that could be heard was the rumble of tires over cobblestones and the honking of horns.

"Lydia, I'm sorry," Jarrod finally said.

The older woman's jaw was firm. She straightened her back, then stared out her window. Nina reached over Sasha's head and squeezed her mother's shoulder. "He didn't really mean it."

"Yes, I do. She smells like—" The boy abruptly broke off.

Was he about to say *like my mother used to?* Had the smell of liquor and tobacco on Lydia's breath evoked a long buried memory of neglect and maybe abuse?

Mercifully, they arrived at the hotel and the cabbie jolted the vehicle to a hasty stop. The doorman came to open the door and everyone piled out. Everyone but Lydia.

"Come on, Mama." Nina extended a hand.

"I'm going home," Lydia said, her own hands bunched in her lap.

Nina could see she was at the point of tears. "Jarrod, you and Sasha go on upstairs. Mom and I will join you in a little while."

Jarrod had already paid and tipped the driver. He met Nina's eyes, his expression one of solicitude and embarrassment.

"Go on," she urged him softly.

He glanced back over his shoulder as he ushered Sasha through the hotel entrance.

Nina again extended her hand to her mother. "Come on, Mama," she begged. "Mama let's go for a walk. It's a pleasant evening." Lydia remained still. "Please."

Reluctantly, her mother climbed out of the taxi. To Nina she looked suddenly very old and very tired.

"He's just a little boy," Nina said, as they strolled along the street and turned a corner.

They found a small coffeehouse. A solitary waitress, who seemed more annoyed by their presence than pleased at having paying customers, brought their cappuccinos and walked away.

"Sasha's mad at Jarrod for not telling him beforehand about his sister," Nina said, "so he's taking it out on everyone."

"He's right." Lydia lit a cigarette and filled her lungs with smoke, then blew it into the air over her head. "I am an old drunk."

"Mama—"

Lydia sniffled and dug into her purse for a hankie. She wiped her nose. "I'm sorry you came all this way to see me like this. *Staraya pyanitsa.*" *An old lush.*

"Mama, no. Please—"

"It's been hard, Ninochka." She studied the smoldering tip of her cigarette. "When I found out my Vanya…your father…that they had killed him, I wanted to die, too. I had lost everything. Him. You. The life we once had. I was so alone. My friends—people I thought were my friends—wouldn't even look at me. When I went to them, they closed their doors in my face without a word. Of course, they were afraid. I kept wondering what would happen to me. Were they coming to arrest me, too? I was scared, Nina."

"If only I had realized."

"There was nothing you could have done. At least I knew you were safe. Then you wrote and told me John had died. The money he sent me was all I had by that time. With him gone… You don't know how hard it was for me to ask you for help."

Nina felt absolutely rotten. If only she'd sent more, done more… On the verge of tears now, she struggled to stay strong, to listen and not judge. She'd done enough of that already.

"I knew you didn't trust me—" Her mother's voice broke.

"That's not true. I—"

Lydia waved her hand dismissively. "You suspected me of betraying your father. You two were always close. I used to get so jealous watching you together. I wanted to be a good mother. Really, I did, but somehow I never was."

"Of course you were. I remember the wonderful clothes you used to buy me and the parties for my birthdays. So many presents and cakes and sweets, and all the kids you invited to share them with."

Lydia tried to smile. "They were fun parties, weren't they? Organizing them was such a pleasure for me. Giving you things was easy, too. Your face would light up at the toys, the dolls and girlie things I bought for you. But at the end of the day, when your father came home, you always ran to him, and it was as if I was no longer in the house."

Nina had loved her father, wanted to be with him all the time. She'd never been aware of shutting her mother out, but she realized now she'd broken Lydia's heart without even thinking, then blamed her because the two of them weren't close.

"I didn't always drink, you know," Lydia said as she wrapped her hands around the warm mug. "Not until several years after you were gone. By then everything around me had collapsed. There wasn't enough food. No meat or fresh vegetables. Not even bread sometimes. But one could always find vodka and cigarettes. I didn't used to smoke, either. Remember?"

"I remember."

She lit a fresh cigarette from the tip of the

old one. "By then I'd sold all the jewelry your father had given me—except for the brooch. All the things he'd told me to hide in the months before he was taken away. We both knew it was just a matter of time." Lydia stared at her drink. "If you hadn't sent me money…"

"I should have sent more. I could have—"

Lydia covered Nina's hand with her callused fingers. "You saved my life. If you had sent more—" she shrugged "—maybe I'd be dead by now from drinking more." She offered a wan smile to her daughter. "You have nothing to be ashamed of, Ninochka, nothing to regret."

Her mother was wrong. At eighteen, Nina should have been able to understand.

"But things are different now," her mother added. "I have friends, a good job, enough food to eat. Enough money to buy a nice dress now and then." She tightened her hold on Nina's hand. "And you are here."

Tears streamed down Nina's face. With a shaky swipe of her hand, she rubbed her cheek. She had been frightened when she'd left sixteen years ago. Her heart had been in mourning for her absent papa. This time she would leave with a heavy heart for the mother she'd grown to love and to whom she owed so much.

"I can't stay, Mama." She felt as if she were twisting a knife in her mother's heart.

It was Lydia's turn to offer comfort. She stroked Nina's cheek and gazed into her eyes. "I know. I wish you could, but I understand this isn't your home anymore. I have seen you, a beautiful, mature woman, someone your father would be very proud of. You have a good life, and that makes me happy. I've gotten to see you again. That's all that matters. I didn't think I ever would."

"Come to America with me, Mama. You'll like it there. I earn enough money to support us comfortably. You won't have to work if you don't want to."

Lydia tilted her head to one side as she considered the offer. "Being together would be nice, wouldn't it?" She fell silent and seemed to turn inward for a minute. "Let me think about it."

Nina glanced down at their cold, untouched coffees and pushed hers aside. "I guess we better get back before Jarrod starts worrying." She threw some ruble notes on the table, and they rose from their seats.

"He's a good man." Lydia crushed out her cigarette and rose heavily to her feet.

"I think so, too."

They linked arms as they strolled back to the hotel.

"He's also a good father," Lydia said, her tone bright. "Tell him he shouldn't worry about Sasha. He'll come around, and he'll make his papa proud of him one day."

JARROD KEPT HIS HAND on Sasha's shoulder and guided him to the elevator. As they rose, the boy said nothing and neither did he, but the atmosphere between them was charged.

Inside the suite, Sasha started for his room.

"Sit down," Jarrod ordered.

"I have to go to the—"

"I said sit down."

Sasha turned and looked up at him, fear in his eyes. Jarrod had never hit him and never would, but he hadn't raised his voice at him in anger before, either, not like this. The boy cringed and complied.

Jarrod stared down at him. "What you said to Babushka downstairs was disgraceful. It was mean and cruel."

"But—"

"Keep your mouth closed and listen to me. Babushka has been kind and generous to you, and you have thanked her by insulting her and calling her names. I'm ashamed of you, Sasha. For the first time, I'm ashamed of you."

The boy teared up and stared straight ahead, his chin trembling.

"This is the last night Babushka will be staying with us because we're leaving tomorrow evening. When she comes up here in a little while, I want you to apologize to her, to tell her you are sorry, that you didn't mean to hurt her, and that you hope she'll forgive you."

The boy remained stock-still.

"Do you understand me?"

"Yes, sir." His voice was small.

Jarrod's anger subsided at the sight of this unhappy child he loved so much. He'd always known disciplining was a part of parenting, but that didn't make the task easier. Feeling like an ogre, he sat in the chair across from his son and wished he had some magic words that would make the pain and disappointment go away—for both of them.

"You're right," he said. "Sometimes Babushka drinks too much. It's a sickness, Sasha. She's had a hard life and sometimes that makes people sick. When Uncle Earl got the flu last winter, we didn't yell at him, did we?"

Several heartbeats went by before the boy shook his head.

"We don't call him names because he can't walk. Hurting Babushka with words won't make her better, either. It only makes things worse."

Sasha kept his head down.

"Look at me, Son." He waited for Sasha to raise his tearstained face. "I know you didn't say those things to Babushka to hurt her. You wanted to upset me. Well, the next time you want to get back at me, make sure it's me and me alone you hurt. I apologized for not telling you Anna is your sister. I made a mistake, but I didn't do it to hurt you."

"Why can't she come home with us?" Sasha begged in a childlike tone, reminding Jarrod just how young he was.

"I wish she could, Son, but she can't, and you'll just have to accept that. Nina's willing to help you write to her, and we can send her presents sometimes. But you cannot tell her you are her brother—"

"Why not?" he cried, anger resurfacing.

Jarrod softened his voice. "Because it would make her feel bad. Do you want to do that?"

Sasha mumbled, "No."

"Someday you'll be able to tell her, but not yet. For now you have to just be her friend. Being a friend is the very best thing you can do for her, because being a friend will never hurt her. Do you understand?"

He nodded miserably.

Jarrod moved to the sofa and put his arm around his son's shoulders. "I love you, Sasha. I love you more than anyone or anything in the world." The boy pressed himself against his side. They were still hugging each other when the door opened and Nina came in.

"Where's your mother?" Jarrod asked.

"She decided to go home. I got her a cab and paid the driver."

"Is she all right?"

Nina shrugged. "I hope so."

Sasha separated himself from his father and stood with bowed head facing Nina, biting his lip. "I'm sorry what I said to her."

Nina's expression softened. "She knows you didn't mean it." To Jarrod she added, "She decided to go back to work tomorrow, but hopes we have a good time at the zoo."

"Without saying goodbye?" He took a deep breath in frustration. "What time is her shift?"

"Afternoon, I think. Why?"

"Because in the morning, we're going over to her house, so Sasha can apologize to her in person."

LYDIA SAT IN THE BACK of the taxi and wiped her nose. She wished she'd drunk that cappuccino Nina had ordered. She was thirsty. But of course it wasn't coffee she craved. It was vodka. Nina had already paid and tipped the driver, so Lydia didn't have to worry about taxi fare. She opened her purse and riffled through her notes. She had enough for a half liter of the decent stuff and an extra tip for the driver to make the unscheduled stop to buy it.

What difference did it make if she got thoroughly soused tonight? She didn't have to go to work until tomorrow afternoon. She'd be sober by then, maybe even past the headache.

It had been wonderful to see Nina, but she would probably never see her again.

She thought about going to America. It would be nice being with Nina, but what would she do there? Sit in a house that didn't feel like home, with nothing to do while her daughter worked. What about all her friends here, the people who depended on her? Besides, after a while Nina would get tired of her always being around, underfoot. They'd get on each other's nerves, then they would fight, and they would both be miserable. Better to stay here where she belonged, where she knew how things worked.

Her little girl had grown up and didn't need her anymore. She hadn't needed her since the day John Lockhart married her and took her off to America. Ivan had been right in making the arrangements with him. Her Vanya was always thinking ahead, always concerned for the people he loved. What would he think of his family now? Would he be pleased with the way things had turned out? Yes, because his Ninochka was safe and happy. As for herself…

Lydia Petrovna Kamarova leaned forward and gave the driver instructions.

JARROD PRESSED HIS HAND against the center of his chest as he dialed up the Internet. The pain was more intense tonight. Because of his confrontation with Sasha? Most likely. His stomach was upset, his heartburn more sharp than last time. He'd taken one of the antacid tablets Lydia had recommended, but it didn't seem to be doing any good, and the pressure in his chest was more acute.

He had been monitoring the stock market every day since his arrival in Russia.

Several days earlier, he'd read an article

online that Pruit Delford, the founding president and CEO of Supertec Corporation, had announced his retirement. The news had come as a shock to the business world. Delford was in his early fifties, a relatively young man, and Supertec was his baby, one of the sparkling jewels in the golden crown of high-tech software companies. There was no mention that the one-time whiz kid might be in poor health, only that he wanted to spend more time with his family, a strange statement since Delford had no children.

Jarrod was immediately suspicious and had ordered his broker to sell all of his and his clients' stock in the company. Unfortunately, a lot of other people had the same idea, because the stampede had already begun, especially after word spread that the revolutionary software Supertec had been touting had failed all its preliminary tests. The share price plummeted from fifty-eight dollars to twenty-four within hours. Since he and Earl had bought at thirty-five, it represented a loss of capital, but not a devastating one. Supertec made up only ten percent of their portfolios.

What Jarrod found when he dialed up tonight, however, was much more serious.

The Federal Trade Commission, the Justice Department and several other government agencies had announced investigations into a dozen technology companies for a variety of reasons, not the least of which were conspiracy and price fixing. Supertec's stock nosedived to six dollars a share, and trading had to be suspended. The ripple effect in such a vital industry, nationally and internationally, was immediate and catastrophic. The entire market went into freefall, losing eight percent of its total value, and the bottom seemed nowhere in sight.

Instead of capital gains, Jarrod and Earl had accumulated massive losses. Even worse, the dividends those stocks generated died with them, and the incomes they had been living on plunged. Neither he nor his friend were left destitute, but they were reduced to the poverty level.

Jarrod was up and dressed before the others the following morning. He hadn't slept well. This trip to Russia had been a mistake, a major disaster. Except maybe for Nina. She'd gotten to see her mother and had reconciled with her, though finding out she had a drinking problem, hadn't been pleasant.

He felt sorry for Lydia Petrovna. The last

sixteen years must have been terrible for her—watching the world she'd grown up in crumble around her, seeing her husband taken away, never to return, then having to give her daughter to a foreigner without being completely sure what Nina's fate might be. The loneliness that followed had to have been nearly unbearable, especially when coupled with the fear that she, too, might be arrested at any moment.

Liquor didn't solve problems, but it did mask them, at least for a while. It brought numbness, and when people were in pain, sometimes that was the best they could hope for.

He called room service and requested a continental breakfast for two, as well as juice, milk and cereal for Sasha. When it arrived he tapped on Nina's door and poked his head inside. She was already sitting up in bed.

"Coffee's here, whenever you're ready."

"Thanks. How's Sasha?"

"I haven't woken him yet."

In the other bedroom, Jarrod gently shook the boy by the shoulder. "Time to get up, Son."

Sasha twisted, glanced up at him and just as quickly looked away.

"Last day, and then we're heading home."

It was after nine by the time they finished eating. Their flight wasn't for another twelve hours, but they had to be out of their suite at noon. The hotel had agreed to hold their luggage until they were ready to leave for the airport.

"First stop, Babushka's," Jarrod said, as they rode down in the elevator. "I hope she'll want to come with us to the zoo."

"The zoo? But you said…" Sasha looked up at him.

"I don't want to come this far and not see a world-famous zoo because you misbehaved," Jarrod explained. "In exchange I want you to tell me what you'll give up when we get home."

"Like what?"

In trying to come up with an appropriate punishment, Jarrod had remembered his mother's trick of making him choose. He'd learned later that he inevitably selected a penalty more harsh than she would have imposed, but it also indicated his own evaluation of his misbehavior.

"Whatever you think would be right. Something you really like or want to do. You don't have to tell me now, but by the time we get home I expect an answer. If you don't come up with something on your own, I'll decide."

Nina looked over at him and nodded pensively.

While the doorman hailed a taxi, Jarrod returned to the vendor's pushcart down the street and bought another bouquet, not as large as the first one. Five yellow roses.

He put them in his son's hands. "These are for Babushka. Give them to her when you apologize."

Sasha nodded and took the flowers.

Nina leaned over and smelled them. "They're lovely. She'll really like them."

None of the women and children they'd met in the playground on their first visit were around when the taxi dropped them off. They rode up together in the arthritic elevator, which again stopped at the fifth floor, though there was nobody there. Nina knocked on her mother's door. No answer. She knocked again, this time harder.

*"Chort vozmi." The devil take you.* The door flew open. *"Shto—"*

Lydia was wearing an old robe, her graying hair spiked in complete disarray, as if she'd just crawled out of bed. The smell of body odor and stale cigarette smoke assailed them.

*"Shto—" What?* She stared with a half-open mouth at the two adults in front of her, then looked down at Sasha.

"I'm sorry I was mean to you yesterday, Babushka." He held out the bouquet stiffly.

She covered her mouth with her hand and gazed at him with bloodshot eyes.

"I didn't mean to say those things."

Lydia squeezed her watery eyes shut as tears spilled down her cheeks.

"Why don't you two go down to the playground while I help Mama get dressed," Nina urged Jarrod. She took the flowers on her mother's behalf. "We'll meet you there in a few minutes. Okay?"

"Sure," he replied, as if nothing were wrong. "Come on, Son." He extended his hand. "Let's see if that swing still works."

Outside, he led them to a couple of benches near the play area. They sat. Saying nothing, Sasha gazed into space.

"She's sick, Son. You know she's a good person, but she has a sickness. I hope you'll be nice to her today—if she comes with us."

"Will she get better?"

"I hope so."

"I don't want her to be sick. I don't like it when she's sick."

"It's important that we're nice to her, so she won't feel so bad."

Over an hour passed before Nina and her mother joined them. Jarrod wondered how much black coffee it had taken to make Lydia presentable. However much, it had apparently worked. Except for appearing tired, she seemed her old self.

"Are you feeling better now?" Sasha asked her.

"Much better." She kissed him on the cheek. "I'm sorry I didn't have any piroshki for you today. I promise next time you come to visit me, I'll have plenty of them."

"We're going to the zoo. Will you come with us?"

"Why, I'd love to, but we better hurry. It'll be crowded. It always is."

To Nina's relief the rest of the day went without incident. She watched her mother very carefully. The woman was obviously coping with a bad hangover, but she handled it well. She also didn't press herself on Sasha, no doubt sensing polite distance was preferable to fawning and touching.

For his part Sasha was also on good behavior, but it was clear, at least to Nina, that he was still unhappy. She didn't know what Jarrod had said to him last night or this morning, but whatever it was seemed to have defused the standoff between them. That didn't mean they were at peace with each other, however, and she wondered how long it would be before the truce ended.

Lydia had traded shifts at the factory, so she was able to join them for an early dinner. They ate in a nice restaurant. To her credit, Lydia didn't even suggest wine for their last meal together, contenting herself with mineral water.

They engaged in small talk during the taxi ride to her apartment house afterward. How long the trip would take. Another eighteen hours. Where their layover would be this time. London. What time they'd be getting home. Before noon.

Despite Lydia's attempt to be upbeat, Nina sensed a sadness in her mother, and felt her own eyes fill.

At the apartment building, Jarrod helped Lydia out of the taxi.

"Nina, will you come up with me, please?" She turned to Jarrod. "Thank you for returning my daughter to me, Mr. Morrison. You have made an old woman very happy."

They kissed on both cheeks in the European fashion. "You're not an old woman. It has been my privilege to bring her and my pleasure to meet you. And it's Jarrod, remember?"

"You're very kind." He could see she was struggling to maintain her composure. Turning to Sasha, she extended her hand. "Alexander Jarrodovich, I am delighted to have met you. I hope when you get home you will think kindly of a foolish old woman."

The boy pinched his lips together and seemed unsure what to say. He held her hand, then said, *"Bolshoye spasibo—"* many thanks "—for being so nice to me," he added in English. His cool slipped and his eyes became glassy. "I'm sorry I—"

"Shh." She opened her arms to him and pressed him to her breast. "I hope you will write me a letter sometimes and tell me about your school and your friends."

"I will," he promised.

She let him go with a kiss on his forehead, and gazed unsteadily at Nina. "Come," she said, and turned to the building.

"Thank you for a wonderful day," Lydia said on the way up in the elevator. "I will always treasure it." The door opened and they walked in tense silence to the apartment. Inside, Lydia said, "Wait here. I'll just be a minute."

Nina could hear a drawer being opened and closed in the adjoining bedroom. A moment later her mother reappeared carrying a large photograph.

"Do you remember this?" Lydia asked, holding it up.

The portrait had sat in a large silver frame on the buffet in the dining room of their old flat: Lydia, Ivan and Nina on her tenth birthday.

"This was one of the few things I was able to snatch before they evicted me. I had to sell the frame long ago, but I kept the picture. I want you to have it."

"Oh, Mama." She hugged her. She had no pictures of her family. She and John had left in such haste that taking mementos hadn't occurred to her. "Do you have a copy?"

Lydia shook her head. "I don't need one. It's imprinted in my heart. So much is. But you have nothing to remember him by."

"Or you, Mama. I'll make a copy and send it back," Nina promised.

"That would be nice."

"Come live with me in America," Nina repeated.

Lydia held her daughter's face between her

work-roughened hands and peered into her eyes. "I promise to think about it, but for now my place is here."

Nina again hugged her mother, very tightly this time. "I love you, Mama. I love you so much."

"Be happy, Nina," Lydia whispered in her ear. "For him. For me. Be happy, Ninochka."

## CHAPTER FOURTEEN

SOMEHOW THE HOURS BETWEEN MOSCOW and New York went faster on the return flight, maybe because Jarrod knew what to expect at the other end. Home. There was no sense of urgency. If anything, there was a feeling of letdown.

He reclined his seat and closed his eyes shortly after takeoff, intent on sleeping, but unable to get comfortable. He'd never been airsick before, but he felt light-headed and slightly nauseated. They'd gone to a good restaurant and dined well for their last meal with Lydia. No liquor, of course, but the food had been rich. He'd probably eaten too much, and the tension of these past few days didn't help.

As the plane leveled off, the pain in his chest intensified, his scalp began to tingle and he broke out in a sweat. Could this be the onset of a heart attack? Should he tell someone? On an airplane at thirty-five thousand feet, there wasn't much anyone could do about it.

He flexed his left hand, then his right. No weakness, no shooting pains. Not a heart attack, he decided.

Gradually the pressure subsided. He began to breathe easier. When he got home he'd make another appointment to see his cardiologist.

He glanced over at Sasha, who was intently playing with his Game Boy. If Jarrod had learned anything it was not to take his son's intelligence or emotional responses for granted.

Nina sat in the window seat beside Jarrod, restlessly paging through a magazine. She wasn't even pretending to pay attention to the pictures or the articles.

"Glad you made the trip?"

She took longer to answer than the question seemed to warrant. "Yeah."

"You don't sound very happy about it."

She dropped the magazine to her lap, crinkling the pages. "You saw my mother."

"I like her, but then I'm a sucker for strong women. I can see where you—"

"She's an alcoholic."

"So she drank a little too much on a couple of occasions. I wouldn't call her an alcoholic. She never did or said anything that was inappropriate or embarrassing."

Nina sighed, reopened the magazine and resumed flipping the pages. "You don't understand."

He gently removed the periodical from her hands and stuck it in the pocket of the seat in front of her. "Don't understand what? Please explain what I'm missing."

Annoyance flared and subsided. She sighed. "My mother has a drinking problem, and it's my fault."

"How do you figure that?"

"She drinks, she's all alone and she lives in poverty. Isn't that enough?"

Jarrod took her hand and held it, though she was tense and unreceptive to his touch. "First of all, she's not alone. She has friends, plenty of them, who respect and depend on her, and now she has you back in her life. She lives in modest circumstances compared with twenty years ago perhaps, but I would hardly say she's living in poverty. I don't expect she would, either. If you want the truth, I think she's damn proud of what she's done with her life, and rightfully so. She's gone through hard times—"

"Without any help from me."

He tilted her head toward him. "That's not true. You sent her money and you have always been in her heart."

"I could...I should have sent her more."

"You gave her what she needed. That's what's important."

"I begrudged even that because I was angry at her."

"Nina, you were very young. You'd just lost your father and been sent off to a foreign country with a man you hardly knew. You were confused. You had a right to be angry."

"If I'd been a better daughter, she wouldn't drink the way she does."

"You don't know that. You can't." He smoothed the back of her hand. "People drink for a lot of reasons—because they're happy, because they're sad, because they're bored, because they feel harassed. Whatever the reason, it's always their choice. She doesn't blame you for any of the things that happened to her. You shouldn't, either."

She was silent for several seconds. "I'm thinking of going back," she said finally.

"I'm sure your mother would love to have you visit."

"To live."

Panic battled with anger. He didn't want to

lose her. "What about Sasha, your work?" he asked. "What about us?"

"Sasha's English is coming along fine. From here on out he'll improve on his own. He doesn't need me, not really. Besides, from what you've told me about this stock market slump, you won't be able to keep me on as Sasha's tutor, anyway. As for my work—" she gave a casual shrug "—I can do it anywhere, probably even more productively and with greater impact in Moscow, where I can keep up with the language on the street."

He had to find reasons, excuses, anything for her not to go. "Do you really think you'd be happy there?" he asked.

"It's something I have to do. My mother needs me, and, well…I have a lot to make up for."

"Invite her to America," he said.

"I have. She said she'd think about it, but I know she won't come. Maybe after I'm over there awhile I can convince her, but right now she isn't interested. Besides, we're not talking about outer space. I'll still come back to the States periodically."

His desperation increased. "What about us, Nina? What about you and me? Doesn't what we have count for anything?"

"Of course it does." She covered his hand with hers. "What we've had has been wonderful, and I'll always treasure it."

"But not enough to stay with me?" he asked. "Do I mean nothing more to you than a pleasant memory?"

"This isn't easy for me," she insisted, and pulled her hands away. "But it's something I have to do."

"I don't agree. Your mother's gotten along fine for sixteen years without you. Her life is richer now for having you back in it, but that doesn't require moving halfway around the world."

"It's my decision, not yours," Nina retorted. Then she reclined in her seat and shut her eyes.

Earl knew he hadn't been very good company the past week. The stock market plummet pressed heavily on his mind. Until a few days ago he'd earned decent money writing programs for major software companies. Combined with his investments, they'd given him enough to live comfortably in his circumstances.

Now, as a result of the Supertec debacle, not only was his capital in the giant corporation wiped out, but companies that had been hiring him as a freelance developer were suddenly running scared. He'd been stunned to get a message this morning telling him his biggest contract was being terminated. Everything was happening so fast. He'd be paid a cancellation fee, but it would be only twenty-five percent of the original project amount.

"I'll have to let Mrs. Burgess go pretty soon," he said later that night, as Alicia lay beside him in his bed. Making love to her was more than an affirmation that he was still a man. She was the only woman he'd every cared for unconditionally. He'd meant it when he told her he would have married her and helped her raise her daughter with all the love a father could give. But it hadn't happened, and now it never would.

"Why do you have to get rid of Mrs. B.?" she asked.

"Because I can't afford to help her."

"Surely—"

"Let me be the judge of what I can afford," he insisted.

He caught a glimpse of Alicia's face and the hurt she always tried to hide whenever he snapped at her. He'd done a lot of that lately, and he hated himself for it.

"I'm sorry," he said, and kissed the top of her head.

Suppose he couldn't find more computer work? It wasn't as if he could apply for a job at McDonald's. Maybe he should sell off some of his land, except it wouldn't bring much, and he'd lose the privacy he treasured. In the end he'd have to apply for government aid or let his family take care of him.

Without a hint of the pain he knew he'd imposed, Alicia cuddled against him. "We'll find a way."

He liked the sound of *we,* but he couldn't accept charity, not even from her. "If you're suggesting…I can't take money from you, Allie. What kind of man do you think I am?" The words slipped out artlessly. He bit his lip and turned his head away.

She reached over and tugged at his chin so that he had to face her. "The man I love. The man I'm hoping will marry me."

"Marry?" For a while he'd actually entertained the notion, but it had been a foolish fantasy. Saddling her with his physical limitations was one thing, but with his financial hardship another. "No," he mumbled.

She released his chin. "Because you don't love me?" There was that hurt in her eyes again.

"Allie, please don't do this."

"Don't do what? Tell you that I love you? I do, you know."

"I can't marry you."

"Why?"

How he wished he could get up and walk out of the room. But of course, if he were capable of that, he wouldn't be in the fix he was in.

"The biggest mistake I ever made was rejecting you," she said. "I've never stopped regretting it."

He gazed at her, stunned by what she was saying. "The past is over."

"I still love you," she said softly.

He stroked her arm, luxuriating in the smooth texture of her skin, the heat of her flesh. He wanted her. He always would. "Don't you see? It wouldn't be fair."

"You'll have to explain that to me, darling, because I don't know what wouldn't be fair about two unattached adults who love each other getting married."

"You deserve more, better—"

"I love *you*. There can't be more or better than that."

Anger, borne of a world he couldn't have, resurfaced. "You insist on making me say it, don't you? Okay, I will. We can't get married because I'm a cripple in a wheelchair."

WITH EARL'S HARSH WORDS still ringing in her ears, Alicia approached the gate to her parents' estate and paused. She wasn't looking forward to the confrontation she knew lay ahead. She'd never seriously challenged her parents' authority, except in one instance. They'd wanted her to terminate her pregnancy. In that particular case, she'd won, but she'd also lost. The single consolation she could take from the experience was the knowledge that her daughter was living a happy life. At least the child didn't have to contend with her biological grandparents.

Taking a deep breath, Alicia proceeded up the blacktop driveway to the imposing Georgian mansion.

A maid answered the doorbell. "Your father is in his office, miss. Your mother's on the veranda."

Alicia thanked her and took the central hall to the back of the house. Eldora Peters stood in the sunlight, wearing designer jeans, a red silk blouse, a big floppy straw hat and floral decorated work gloves.

She turned at the snick of the French door

opening. "Alicia, how wonderful to see you, dear." She placed her pruning shears on the glass-topped table and came forward, planted a kiss on her daughter's cheek and stepped back. "You look lovely. We'll have tea in the conservatory, and you can tell me what you've been up to, how you're enjoying teaching."

Under normal circumstances, Alicia would have complimented her mother on the rose garden. Eldora definitely had a green thumb. The place was a showpiece that had been featured in several national homemaking and gardening magazines. But Alicia wasn't here to discuss flowers.

"Let's have it in the study with Dad."

Eldora eyed her with dismay. "Is something wrong, sweetheart? You're not in some sort of trouble, are you?"

Alicia almost laughed. Was her mother afraid she'd gotten pregnant again? She wasn't sixteen and pitifully naive anymore. "Everything's fine," she said. "I just have something I want to discuss with both of you."

Her mother was clearly discomfited by the request, but she acceded without further question.

Her father, ever the gentleman, rose from

his chair and came from behind his massive desk. Even as he gave her a polite kiss on the cheek, Alicia could see him searching for an explanation for this unexpected appearance. She wasn't in the habit of dropping by casually. Her visits were always orchestrated, responses to telephoned invitations for holiday dinners or her mother's gala birthday parties.

"Alicia has something she wants to discuss with us, dear." Eldora picked up the phone on a side table and instructed the maid to bring tea and pastries.

Alicia's palms began to sweat as she took the proffered seat across from her father.

"I want to let you know I'm getting married," she announced. *As soon as I can convince Earl.* "I'd like your blessing and support."

"Oh, Alicia, that's wonderful," her mother gushed, clasping her hands against her chest. Eldora Lessing had been a stage actress when Walter Peters met her. Her promising thespian career had ended with her marriage, of course, but the tendency for drama had never quite disappeared.

"To whom?" her father asked, less enchanted.

"Earl Slater."

Eldora went still, then bit her lower lip. Walter rolled his eyes.

"Why would you want to marry a cripple?" he asked.

Alicia had an urge to lash out at his insensitivity, but it wouldn't do any good. "Because I love him, Dad."

Walter laced his fingers across his trim waist. Fastidious dieting, a personal trainer and tennis three times a week ensured he was exceptionally fit for a man of fifty-five. "Very noble, but not very wise."

Her attempts at conciliation always seemed to fail with this man. "I came to ask for your blessing, Dad, not your permission." Her heart throbbed, then pounded when she saw the cold, hard expression on his face.

"Honey," Eldora said, "I think what your father means is that it's not a very good idea to marry someone who can't give you children, whose health is so precarious—"

Walter waved his wife to silence without looking at her. "I doubt you care about my blessing. Why don't you tell me what you really want?"

So much for niceties. "Two things, actually. First, I'd like to know if you're planning to leave me anything in your will?"

"Oh, sweetheart, it all goes to you," Eldora blurted out before her husband had a chance to stop her.

"Then I'd like a portion of it as a wedding present."

"Living on a teacher's salary isn't easy or fun, is it?" he said, not bothering to hide his contempt. "If you'd followed my advice—"

"If I'd followed your advice, my baby would be dead."

Eldora sucked in her breath, while her husband's dark eyes hardened and he silently worked his jaw.

"I want something else, as well," Alicia said, amazed that her voice didn't crack under the strain. Challenging her father was a new experience. "I want you to help Earl and me adopt a baby."

"Darling…" her mother began hesitantly.

"Because of his health I know we don't have a chance of being approved as adoptive parents on our own," Alicia continued, "but you're a very convincing and influential attorney with a lot of powerful connections. I know you can help us overcome the obstacles."

"Why should I?"

She looked him dead in the eye. "Because you owe me."

He stared back, startled by her boldness. A dozen heartbeats passed. "You were the one who spread your legs, young lady."

"Walter, please," Eldora begged.

It took every ounce of self-control for Alicia not to blink, to keep her eyes focused on the man who'd ruled and ruined her young life. She'd come here determined not to cower in his presence. She wouldn't give him that power ever again.

"You're right, Daddy," she said sweetly. "I spread my legs to get back at you for breaking up my perfectly chaste relationship with Earl Slater. You didn't want me associating with a decent, clean-cut guy, so I figured you meant for me to get it on with someone who wasn't so nice. Like your partner's low-life son."

Walter's jaw was set again. "I don't have to listen to this."

"If you'd just left us alone—" her voice had begun to rise; she reined it in before it became shrill "—Earl and I might have broken up on our own, though to be honest, I doubt it. We would have eventually gotten married, and I would have had his children—"

"Who'd be vulnerable to his disease."

"True," she admitted, "but you didn't keep us apart because you were trying to protect me or your unborn grandchildren. So that doesn't really count, does it?"

"He wasn't suitable," Eldora said. "Keeping him away, even after you—"

"Ellie, be quiet," Walter snapped.

A moment passed before the meaning sank in. "After I what?" Alicia asked.

"It doesn't matter," her father said.

*Why didn't you come to me? I would have married you.*

Alicia turned to her mother. "Are you telling me Earl talked to you after I left?"

Frowning, Eldora looked quickly at her husband. Alicia followed her mother's gaze, and saw his menacing scowl. Her mother started to wither under his glare.

"Tell me, Mom."

"It's none of your concern," Walter declared.

"Mom. I have a right to know."

Eldora wrung her hands, flicking her eyes to her daughter, then to her husband and back to Alicia. Straightening her shoulders, she said, "After you and Wayne Armbruster dropped out of school in midsemester, Slater came to see us. He wanted to know where you were. When your father refused to tell him, he asked if you were pregnant, if you'd gone off somewhere to have the baby. He said if

Wayne wouldn't marry you, he would. He was wonderful. He asked us to notify you. I was going—"

"I forbade it," Walter stated firmly.

"Your father offered him money to keep quiet, but he refused to take it. We were afraid he'd talk about your condition."

*My condition. And your social standing.*

Alicia remembered the haunted look on Earl's face. *I would have married you.* She wanted to cry, but she'd save her tears for later.

"Insisting I kill my baby wasn't bad enough," she said to her father. "You even took away the one man who would have made an honest woman of me—"

"Leave the melodramatics to your mother," Walter grumbled.

Eldora's face tightened and Alicia glimpsed something in her eyes she'd never seen there before. More than pain. More than anger. Humiliation that was close to rage.

"What if I don't do what you want?" Walter asked. "You've already disgraced our name. It's a bit late for blackmail."

"That's your style, Father, not mine." She didn't think she could ever call him Dad again. "On second thought, keep your money and your influence. I wouldn't want to pollute my marriage with either." She rose from her chair, just as the maid entered the room pushing a tea cart.

Eldora sprang to her feet. "Don't go."

"There's no point in my staying, Mom," Alicia responded.

Eldora waited until the maid had wheeled the cart to the side and silently fled the room, before turning to her husband. "Walter, do as she asks."

"Ellie, I will not yield to threats."

"Very well." A firmness Alicia had never encountered before seemed to possess her mother. "You've put a good deal of property in my name, Walter, in order to avoid various kinds of investigations. I'll sell it, all of it, and give the money to Alicia. I don't know how much there is, but I imagine it'll be sufficient to establish her and Earl's financial security, as well as hire the best legal counsel in the field of adoption."

"Ellie, don't be ridiculous."

"No, Walter, it's high time I stopped being ridiculous. I don't know why I've put up with you all these years."

"Let's see…" Elbows firmly planted on the desktop, he propped his hands together in front of his chin. "The house, the jewelry, the clothes, the cars, the servants, to name but a few."

She studied him for a few seconds. "I'm ashamed to say you're right, Walter. Come on, Alicia, I'll walk you to your car."

In the hallway, Eldora linked her arm with her daughter's. "Thanks for coming, dear. Thanks for setting me free."

"Mom, I didn't mean… He'll make your life miserable—"

"Only if I let him. And you know what? I won't let him. I'm sorry it's taken me so long to stand up to him, to stand up for you. I hope someday you'll forgive me. I hope, too, you'll invite me to your wedding."

AFTER SEVERAL HANDS of Go Fish with Sasha, Nina opened the bestselling thriller she'd brought along for the endless flight, but her eyes fluttered when she tried to focus on the words. Yet, when she leaned back to get some sleep, her mind went off in different directions.

Jarrod had been close to his mother. He'd returned to Misty Hollow when she got sick and needed his care. Why couldn't he understand that Nina couldn't walk away from her mother's problems, either, especially now that she knew how much she had to make up for? She'd always be grateful to him for giving her this second chance with her mother, but…

No. She shook her head. It wasn't gratitude she felt toward him. She loved Jarrod, loved him as she'd never loved a man, and she loved Sasha. Leaving them was going to be the hardest thing she'd ever done.

But she had no choice, and maybe Russia wouldn't be so bad. It had a vitality now that hadn't been there when she was growing up. Despite the many problems the country faced, she'd found it exciting, filled with a sense of hope, with a positive energy and challenge. Still, after almost half a lifetime away from her birthplace, she found Russia foreign to her. A place to visit, but not to live.

Home wasn't just the United States. Home was a little bungalow half buried in the woods of North Carolina. No. She shook her head. Home was being with Jarrod and Sasha. Home was sitting in the same room with them. Home was making passionate love with Jarrod, then snuggling up against him, listening to his breathing, feeling his heart beating close to hers.

"We're about to land."

"What?"

"You were having quite a dream."

Her heart pounded. "Dream? Did I say anything?"

"You made some sounds and shook your head a few times, as if you were having an argument with someone. I couldn't understand any of it, though. Were you fighting with me?" He wasn't smiling.

*More like pleading.* "I don't remember." She was a coward. Why not tell him she wanted to stay?

"Are we almost home?" Sasha asked from across the aisle.

"Still have a way to go, Son."

"Do you think Laika will remember me?"

"I'm sure she will. Ruff, too."

"It'll be good to get back," Nina said.

"Good to sleep in our own beds," Jarrod added.

She waited for him to whisper that he wanted her in his bed, but he didn't even glance at her.

## CHAPTER FIFTEEN

THEY'D STOPPED OFF at Earl's place to pick up
Laika. To Jarrod's surprise, Sasha had prattled
on to Uncle Earl and Alicia about meeting his
sister, commenting how nice she was, that his
dad was going to send her money for singing
lessons, and that Nina had promised to help
him write letters to her. Apparently his anger
had dissipated—to Jarrod's enormous relief.

There was something different about Earl
and Alicia, too, though Jarrod couldn't quite
put his finger on it. A new comfort level? An
air of serenity that hadn't been there when
they'd left? Whatever it was, he liked the way
being around them made him feel.

Sasha was asleep on his feet by the time
they returned to the house.

"Get into your pj's," he said, "and I'll fix
you some ice cream with chocolate sauce."

"I'll give up ice cream for a year," Sasha
announced, "for being mean to Babushka."

Nina's eyebrows shot up. Sasha's evening dish of vanilla ice cream with chocolate sauce was a ritual that had become sacred.

"A year is too long, son. A month will be enough."

The boy nodded, and Jarrod wrapped an arm around him. "I'm proud of you for accepting responsibility." Sasha didn't say anything, but Jarrod could see the praise pleased him. He kissed him on the top of his son's head. "Now go brush your teeth, and I'll come in and read you a story."

Ten minutes later the boy was sound asleep.

"Are you as tired as I am?" Jarrod asked, when he emerged from his son's room.

"Exhausted."

He touched his lips lightly to hers. "Totally exhausted or just a little exhausted?"

He wanted to make love, and God help her, she did, too. But if they did, would she be able to say goodbye? Was that his plan? Could she take the chance? His kiss deepened and she could resist no longer.

There was desperation in their lovemaking that night, as if they both sensed it was for the last time, that a part of their lives was drawing to an end. When at last they were physically sated, they rested in each other's arms and stared at the dark ceiling.

"Still determined to go back to Russia?"

"My mother needs me, Jarrod, and I need to help her. I have a lot to make up for."

"I love you, Nina."

She'd waited so long to hear those words, to feel them inside her. "I love you, too…" She turned away so he wouldn't see her tears. "But I have to do what I have to do. I wish you could understand that. Look, if the situation were reversed and you had to choose between Sasha and me, you'd pick Sasha— and you should. Your first obligation is to him. That's the position I'm in now. My mother gave me life, then she saved it by giving me up. Now it's my turn to save her. I can't turn my back on her again. I can't walk away."

He wasn't persuaded. She could feel it in his stillness as he lay beside her. "What I have to do is bigger than the two of us," she told him. "If you truly love me, you'll let me go, let me do the honorable thing."

EARL RIFLED THROUGH THE mail Mrs. Burgess had just dropped off. The usual advertisements and mass mailings. He tossed them in the recycle basket. A few bills. He placed them in the corner of his desk for later payment.

The last piece was a legal-size envelope. The return address said the state board of trade. Undoubtedly a notification that they, too, were canceling earlier plans to upgrade their database system due to the uncertainty in the software market following the Supertec collapse. Earl had sent in his bid for the job months ago, making it clear in his proposal that he would be employing state-of-the-art technology. He'd expected it to be Supertec software, though he hadn't mentioned the company by name. He'd included his credentials for doing such work and had had high hopes, but everyone was running scared these days.

He dropped the letter on his workbench, intent on ignoring it, but of course he couldn't. Frowning, he slashed the envelope with a letter opener and unfolded the vellum-quality enclosure.

"After careful and thorough review of all the proposals for the state database upgrade project, you have been selected…"

He must have misread it. He started again, then blinked slowly. They were offering him the job.

Earl leaned back in his chair and took a deep breath. Maybe things weren't so bad, after all. He'd been afraid he'd overbid; apparently he hadn't. This would be the biggest single contract he'd ever received, and would keep him employed for at least two years.

His mind was already working on the problem. The Supertec debacle might slow things down a bit, but his proposal wasn't dependent on their unreleased program. There were other software packages that could be modified to do the job. He'd have to write some new code, of course…

He reread the letter and felt like a kid with a new toy who didn't have anyone to show it to.

On the third reading—or was it the fourth?—his eyes strayed to the upper right-hand corner, where the names of the selection committee were listed. His heart sank. The third name was Walter Peters, Esq., Alicia's father.

Earl's hands curled into fists.

"Dammit to hell." He pounded the arms of his wheelchair. "Dammit it all to hell."

His mood wasn't any lighter when Alicia showed up an hour later.

"I picked up some eggplant," she said as she bent and kissed him on the cheek. "I thought I'd fix it Parmesan style, the way you like it." When he didn't respond, she asked, "Is something wrong?"

"I got a letter from the state board of trade today."

"Another cancellation?" Her voice held sympathy. "I'm so sorry, but don't give up—"

"An acceptance, actually."

"Really?" She was instantly bubbly.

He held the letter out to her.

She read it quickly, and her face lit up. "This is wonderful, Earl. And here you were so worried."

"Did you talk your father into this?"

She stared at him but didn't say anything.

"You did."

"Nobody talks my father into anything. You of all people should know that, Earl."

"What's that supposed to mean?"

"Why didn't you tell me you went to see him and my mother after I left school?"

The question took a moment to sink in. His appeal to Walter Peters had been embarrassing and unsuccessful. What would be the point of mentioning it? She'd thrown him over for someone else, then he'd made a fool of himself by going to her snooty parents and begging them to let him marry her. A man didn't share that kind of humiliation with anyone—not his best friend, not even the woman he loved. Especially the woman he loves.

"It was a long time ago, Allie. It didn't do any good, and I didn't do it behind your back, because you weren't around. But this…"

He held up the letter as the temper he thought he'd corralled began to resurface. "I don't appreciate being patronized, Allie. I leave the Handicapped Minority box on my job applications blank for a good reason. I want people to hire me because I'm the best person for the job, not because I'm in a wheelchair."

"It wasn't like that," she insisted.

He spun around and looked up at her. "Are you telling me you didn't go to see your father?"

She hesitated, and that was all the answer he needed. "How could you, Allie? How could you do this to me?"

She crouched beside him and gripped his arm. "I didn't do anything *to you,* Earl. I went to my father *for us.* And for your information, I was as unsuccessful in getting him to bend as you were. I asked for his help, and he said no."

He glared at her. "Then how do you explain this?" He tossed the paper on the floor.

"I can't, and you can't, either. I didn't

know anything about the job opening when I went to see him. Did it occur to you that you might have been selected because you're the best qualified?"

"It might have if you hadn't betrayed me."

"Betrayed you?" She raised her voice, her eyes darkening. "How did I betray you, Earl?"

"You went behind my back, played the sympathy card."

She shook her head, even as tears glistened. "I love you, you jerk. I don't feel sorry for you."

He blinked. "Then why did you go to your father?"

She snapped a tissue from the container on the corner of his desk, patted her eyes and rubbed her nose. "I told him I wanted to marry you and…and that I wanted his help for us to adopt a baby."

"A baby?" Earl's pulse chugged painfully. He'd tried so hard to accept the fact he'd never be a father, but he'd never quite succeeded. Having a family had always been his dream—until the diagnosis of a disease that didn't kill, but just tormented.

"You know that's not possible, Allie," he said, half in regret, half in anger at having to admit it. "No adoption agency will ever give me a child to raise."

"Never say never. My father has a lot of influence. He could have persuaded people—"

"That I'm a fit parent?"

"You'll make a wonderful daddy."

Earl pulled away and glared at her. "You've lost touch with reality. What you want from me is unreasonable and unrealistic. I can't satisfy you, not the way you want or the way you deserve. I'm sorry."

She studied him for a long moment, the tension between them building until she thought they would both explode. He was fighting her, but more, he was fighting himself. Who won in a battle like that?

"I love you, Earl," she finally said quietly. "I love you. As for satisfying… No one ever can, no one ever will satisfy me the way you do."

His lips parted as if he was trying to catch his breath. He closed his eyes. She would have liked to hear him say, "I love you, too," but she knew he wasn't ready yet. She didn't doubt that he did. Even when she'd run off with Wayne Armbruster, she'd known Earl loved her, and that was the shame of it. That was when she'd betrayed him.

"If it's any consolation, my mission failed," she said. "You don't have to worry about my father helping us or about me going to him for anything ever again. The last thread has been cut. As far as I'm concerned my father is dead."

Earl raised his head and gazed at her. "Allie, I'm sorry."

She laughed. "Don't be. He's never been a real dad. I should have told him to go to hell long ago." She met his eyes. "Do you love me, Earl?"

"You know I do," he said, barely above a whisper. "I've always loved you. There's never been anyone else."

She blew out a pent-up breath. "I guess that leaves us two choices. We can get married or I'll just remain your mistress. Either way, you're stuck with me, because I'm not leaving. Ever."

For a moment he didn't react, then he locked the wheels of his chair and climbed slowly and unsteadily to his feet. Once there he opened his arms and invited her into them. Their kiss was long and passionate.

JARROD HAD NEVER SEEN his friend looking happier. They were sitting in Earl's backyard. Alicia had served wine.

"What's the occasion?" Jarrod asked. He

and Earl occasionally drank a beer before dinner, but this was downright festive.

"Earl got a major contract for software development that'll last at least two years," Alicia said.

Jarrod shook his hand. "Congratulations."

"That's wonderful," Nina agreed.

"By then this Supertec business should have blown over," Earl explained, "and other jobs will be available."

"You're good at what you do," Jarrod stated. "You're not going to have any trouble finding work."

"That's what I told him," Alicia said.

Nina shifted her glance between the two younger people. "Is there something else?"

Earl put out his hand and Alicia took it. "We're getting married," he said.

Nina jumped up and hugged Alicia, then bent down and kissed Earl on the cheek. Jarrod pumped his friend's hand and gave Alicia a hug, as well.

"Congratulations," he said. "That's wonderful news."

"I'd like you to be my best man," Earl told Jarrod, his face glowing.

"I'd be honored. When will this happy event be taking place?"

Earl laughed. "This very minute, if I had my way, but my mother would kill me. Allie and I figure about six weeks. That'll give my family time to make arrangements to get here."

"A big wedding then," Nina observed.

"We want a church ceremony," Alicia said. "We're thinking of taking a cruise for our honeymoon."

"Hmm. Romantic."

"Nina, I'd like you to be my maid of honor."

Nina hesitated. "If I can I'd love to." She shot Jarrod an uncertain glance. She didn't want to put a damper on the party by announcing her imminent departure.

He called Sasha over from playing with the dogs and told him Uncle Earl and Ms. Peters were getting married.

"I'd like you to be the ring bearer, Tiger," Earl told him. "Will you do that for me?"

"What does that mean?"

Jarrod explained.

His son was thrilled at the prospect. "Does that mean you're going to have a baby?" he asked Alicia.

There was a split second's silence, then she laughed. "Maybe. We'll have to wait and see."

It wasn't until after dinner that Nina finally announced that she would be leaving.

"When?" Alicia asked.

"In the morning."

"For how long?" Earl inquired.

Jarrod watched her, hoping she would waver.

"For the foreseeable future." Nina explained about her mother's drinking problem. "I owe her my life in more ways than one."

"So you won't be at our wedding?" Alicia was clearly upset.

"I don't think so," Nina answered.

"You're going away?" Sasha asked, his eyes big.

"Back to Russia to help Babushka get better."

"Will I ever see you again?"

"Of course you will, honey," she exclaimed. "Whenever I come back to America. And if you visit your sister in Russia, you can come and see me and Babushka."

"But you were going to help me write letters to Anna," he said, as tears rolled down his cheeks.

She hadn't forgotten. "I tell you what, you and your dad write the letters in English and send them to me. I'll translate them into Russian and Babushka can take them to your sister, then bring me Anna's letters to you, for translation. Babushka will love doing that, because it'll be like she has another grand-child." Nina patted him on the cheek, her own face damp with tears. "Just like you." She hugged him tightly, feeling as though her heart would break.

On the walk home through the woods, she told Jarrod her plans. "I'll drive to Charlotte in the morning and drop off my car for shipment to Russia. That's expected to take six to eight weeks. I'm booked on a flight through New York to Moscow the following morning."

"Have you told your mother you're coming?"

"I called her late this afternoon. She's really excited."

"I'm sure she is. Where will you be staying?"

"Probably with her while I look for a place big enough for both of us."

"Are you sure she'll want to move? She's invested in her apartment."

"We'll see."

She didn't tell Jarrod that Lydia had been adamant about not wanting to move, offering instead to put Nina at the top of the list for the next available flat in her building.

"Stop by before you leave in the morning," he said. "We'll have coffee together."

He didn't invite her to his bed. She didn't invite him to hers.

The next morning he was there to help her load her car. Finally the last piece of luggage was secured, less of it than when she'd arrived.

"I left a few things inside. I hope you don't mind. Mostly clothes. Would you give them to charity?"

"Sure. Is there anything you want me to send you?"

"I think I have everything."

He held his arms out. She stepped into them as if it was the most natural thing in the world. This was where she wanted to be, where she belonged, but she had a higher obligation.

He nuzzled her hair the way a lover does. She filled her senses with the scent and texture of him, with the sound and feel of his breath along the side of her neck. Her heart was beating with his.

"I'm going to miss you," he whispered in her ear.

"I'll miss you, too."

"Call us when you get there." He stepped back.

She nodded. "And I have your e-mail address."

"Give our best to your mom. I hope everything works out."

Nina bit her lip and nodded again. It was easier than trying to speak past the lump in her throat.

Abruptly he pulled her into his arms once more. "I wish I could find the magic words to make you stay."

Sasha appeared in his pajamas and clung to her hip. "I don't want you to go. Please don't leave."

Jarrod gently drew the boy away.

"Be good," she said, her voice unsteady, "and let me know how you're doing in school."

She climbed into her car, tried without much success to smile through her tears, and drove off. Half a mile down the road, she pulled to the side and sobbed as if she would never stop.

"WHY DID YOU LET her go?" Sasha asked. He'd spent most of the day over at Earl's, throwing sticks to Ruff and Laika or sitting on the back porch lethargically petting the dogs.

"You know her mother is sick. She needs to be with her."

"Why can't Babushka come here? She can live in Nina's house, or she can have my room."

So he, too, had figured out that solution. "Where would you sleep?"

"On the porch with Laika."

Jarrod was moved by his son's willingness to give up his own comfort. This was no ploy, no gambit, but sincere generosity. He opened his arms and gave Sasha a big hug.

"I also wish we could bring Babushka here," he said. "Nina asked her to come but she wants to stay in Russia. That's her home, just as this is your home. Maybe after Nina is there with her for a while she can persuade her mother to move here."

"But I want Nina here now." The boy began to tear up again.

Jarrod wondered if Nina realized how much Sasha loved her.

"Finish your okra, son. There's baked sweet potato for dessert."

"I'm not hungry." The boy pushed his plate away.

He'd only eaten one bowl of cereal that morning, hardly touched his grilled cheese at lunch. Now supper. He'd polished off the mashed potatoes, but just nibbled at his chicken legs. From the looks of his messy plate—the food mostly pushed around—nobody would guess it was one of his favorite meals.

"May I be excused?"

Jarrod nodded. Later, after stacking their plates and silverware in the dishwasher, Jarrod helped Sasha with the summer schoolwork Alicia had recommended. Her aim was for him to skip a grade in a year or two to catch up with his age group. He did the review exercises easily, almost mechanically, a sharp contrast to this time last year. It was hard to realize that less than ten months ago the boy hadn't spoken a word of English. Nina had performed miracles with him.

Jarrod was tempted to offer him a bowl of ice cream as a consolation for Nina's leaving, but that would send the wrong message.

After brushing his teeth and having one of his favorite stories read to him, Sasha fell asleep, and Jarrod wandered out to the guesthouse. In spite of the plastic bags containing her excess clothes, the place felt empty. All the things that had made this tiny cottage *her* house—the magazines and books, her scent—were missing. He'd checked that morning for a letter, a note, a token to remind him she had been there, an acknowledgment that she had been a part of his life.

He'd found nothing.

HE DIDN'T KNOW WHERE the pain originated, or even when. All he knew was that it had taken possession of his chest and was squeezing the life and breath out of him.

So this was what a real heart attack felt like. His next thoughts were for Sasha and Nina: fear for the boy, regret for the woman. He threw his right arm across the bed and grabbed for the bedside lamp. The alarm clock went flying.

His fingers trembled as he jabbed at the top program key on the telephone, starting a ringing sound. One. Two. Then realization slammed him in the gut. He'd hit the button for the cottage. Nina wasn't there. She was gone. From the guesthouse. From his life.

Taking another breath and holding it, he terminated the call and hit the second key. A raspy voice answered.

"My chest—"

"Jarrod?"

"I think…I'm having…a heart attack."

"Have you called 911?"

"Not…yet. I—"

"I'll do it. Be right there."

"Sasha—" he began, but the line was dead.

He fell back against the pillow and thought of his son, who had gone through so much disappointment in his life already, now having to face this new crisis. He was too young, too vulnerable. Jarrod turned on his side and doubled over. What would happen to the boy?

EARL DIALED 911, reported the possible heart attack, gave the address, hung up and threw back the covers. He levered himself onto unsteady legs and waddled to the wheelchair a few feet away. Dressing would take too long. If only Allie were here… Her mother had called late that afternoon. Eldora had left Walter and rented a small apartment in town. She'd asked Alicia to come and spend the night with her. She wanted to talk. Alicia had hesitated, but Earl had urged her to go.

In the bathroom, he pulled on his robe and grabbed a bottle from the medicine cabinet. He reached for his aluminum braces, clamped them between his knees and rolled at top speed, pausing in the kitchen only long enough to snag a bottle of water from the fridge and the key to Jarrod's house. He didn't bother locking his back door.

He drove the short distance to his friend's house. Working his way out of the car, he tried not to think about how much faster he once could have moved. Instead, he focused on getting up the ramp. Laika met him inside the door. The house was dark and silent. He maneuvered down the narrow hall toward the lighted master bedroom.

Jarrod's eyes were squeezed shut.

"Breathe," Earl commanded. "Don't hold your breath. Help's on the way. Have you taken anything?"

Jarrod emitted a ragged moan and shook his head.

Earl reached into his pocket for the bottle. "Take this. Aspirin." He removed the cap on the water bottle.

Jarrod sipped, swallowed. "Sasha."

"Still asleep. As soon as the paramedics get here, I'll wake him."

"I'm sorry…." Earl heard an echo of his own apology when he'd broken his wrist.

"Don't worry about anything. I'll see to it Sasha's taken good care of."

The distant sound of a siren broke the night air.

"HELLO?"

"Allie, Jarrod's had a heart attack. They're taking him to the Misty Hollow Medical Clinic."

"My God." She sprang into a sitting position and reached for the lamp switch. The clock beside it said 2:53. "Where are you?" She was on her feet now, moving toward the bathroom. "What about Sasha?"

"He's here with me. We're still at Jarrod's house. I have to go home and get dressed, then I'm taking him to the clinic with me."

She pulled the nightshirt over her head and tossed it in the corner by the hamper. Alicia recognized the fear in Earl's voice. He hated hospitals. They were symbols of helplessness.

"I'll see you at the clinic as soon as I can get there."

## CHAPTER SIXTEEN

"IS MY DADDY GOING TO DIE?" Sasha asked through his hiccups, his eyes red from crying.

They were in the clinic waiting room. Alicia folded him in her arms, wishing she could assure him that everything would be all right.

"The doctor is doing everything he can to make your daddy better."

She looked over at Earl. He appeared as scared as she'd ever seen him.

"What happened?" she asked.

"He called, said he was having a heart attack. I phoned 911 and went over there in my bathrobe. All I could do was give him an aspirin—"

"That may have saved his life."

Earl shrugged. The medics pulled into the driveway a minute later. The siren woke Sasha, and he came running into Jarrod's bedroom rubbing his eyes. Then saw me and froze. Not only wasn't I supposed to be there, but I was standing over Jarrod's bed. Isn't that right Sasha? He'd never seen me on my feet before."

"Thank God you were there for him. I'm going to try to find Nina."

"Why?" His tone was angry. "If she hadn't walked out on him maybe this wouldn't have happened."

"That's not fair, Earl."

His mouth tightened but he said no more.

She pulled several pieces of paper from her purse. "I called her cell phone number, but all I got was an out-of-area message."

"She probably turned it off. Doesn't want to be bothered."

Alicia ignored his comments. "I stopped long enough to run off a list from the Internet of hotels and motels in the Charlotte area, but there are dozens of them."

"I brought my cell phone." He was still angry as he reached out. "Give me part of the list. I'll start with the major franchises."

Their fingers touched and they both stopped. Their eyes met.

"I love you," he said.

She kissed his cheek.

A sign on the wall emphatically stated that

cell phones must be turned off within the medical facility.

"You stay here with Sasha in case Jarrod asks for him," Alicia said. "I'll go outside and start calling."

Earl nodded. "I'll relieve you when you need a break, or your ear falls off, whichever comes first."

She chuckled, appreciating his willingness to help and his attempt to lighten the moment with humor.

In the parking lot, she sat in her car and began dialing. At each place she received the same response. "There's no Nina Lockhart registered here."

Checking all the hotels and motels in a city of half a million would be a gargantuan task, and time was running out.

A NURSE APPEARED IN THE doorway. "He's asking to see his son. You can go with him, but only for a minute. We've given him something for the pain, so he may not be completely lucid."

Jarrod looked pale, even against the spotless white sheet. An IV was inserted in the left forearm.

"How are you feeling?" Earl asked.

"Better, I think. A bit light-headed right now. Thank you for helping—"

"Daddy, please don't die," Sasha exclaimed. Tears were streaming down his cheeks.

"I'm not fixing to, Son." Jarrod extended his right arm and drew the boy against him.

"I don't want you to die," Sasha sobbed. "I'll be good. I promise."

"Oh, Sasha." He brushed back his uncombed hair. "My getting sick has nothing to do with anything you did. You're the best son a dad could ever ask for." He thumbed away his tears. "I'm very proud of you. I want you to know that. And I love you very much."

"I love you, Daddy."

The best medicine in the world. *I love you, Daddy.*

Releasing the boy, Jarrod motioned Earl to the others side of the bed. "If I don't make it—" Earl started to protest, but Jarrod plowed on "—if anything happens to me, tell your sister I want you and Alicia to take care of him. I had hoped Nina—" he broke off. "Promise me."

"You have my word, but you're not going to need it."

NINA HAD DRIVEN TO Charlotte at a snail's pace and still made the trip in less than two hours. After checking where she would be dropping off her car the next morning, she went to the university library to research WWII small-arms nomenclature for the book she was translating. For intervals of ten and fifteen minutes, she was even able to put out of her mind the sadness on Jarrod's face when they'd parted, and the look of devastation on Sasha's when she'd said goodbye.

She'd never planned on getting that close to either of them, but she had. She'd fallen in love with her employer. A really stupid thing to do after her disastrous affair with Lorenzo in Atlanta. As for Sasha, it was impossible not to love the kid. He'd matured so much in the months she'd known him. Jarrod gave her the credit, but he was the one who'd rescued the boy from an orphanage and provided him a stable home and security. She'd simply been privileged to be a part of it.

The truth was she didn't want to leave either of them, but she had an obligation to fulfill. She also realized after turning off the TV sometime around midnight that she was in danger of resenting her mother almost as much as she had sixteen years ago, when Lydia had sent her away. Then Nina had blamed her mother for rejecting her, which was the furthest thing from the truth. Now it was because she blamed her for being old and lonely and needing help. Which wasn't quite true, either. As Jarrod had pointed out, Lydia wasn't old—not by modern standards—and she seemed to be in good health, in spite of her addiction to alcohol. Most of all, she wasn't completely alone. She had friends who respected and depended on her.

The harsh chirp of the telephone made Nina jump from the doze she'd slipped into.

She reached for the phone, then paused. Who could possibly be calling her at this hour? No one knew she was even here. Probably a wrong number.

"Hello?"

"Nina, thank God I found you."

"Alicia?"

"Nina, Jarrod's had a heart attack."

THE WAITING ROOM WAS JUST inside the wide automatic sliding door from the parking lot. The first thing Nina saw was Sasha stretched out on a wooden bench, his head resting on Alicia's lap.

Looking up, Alicia smiled. "He's out like a light," she said in a whisper.

"Good," Earl said, his back to the entrance.

"The kid didn't get much sleep last night. He's afraid Jarrod's going to die."

"Is he?" Nina asked.

Earl spun his wheelchair around. "Nice of you to show up."

"Earl…" Alicia's voice was horrified.

"I…I'm not—" Nina's heart was pounding with worry about what Earl had just said about Jarrod dying. "I…" She closed her eyes and tried to get control of her emotions. "I came as quickly as I could."

"Maybe if you hadn't left at all, Jarrod wouldn't be stretched out on a gurney with tubes in him."

"Earl, please," Alicia interceded. "That's not fair."

"You blame me for this?" Nina asked, shocked at the accusation. "Why?"

"You knew he's been worried about his heart."

She was incensed now. "What are you talking about?"

Earl closed his eyes, took a deep breath and seemed to deflate. Opening them, he waved her to the seat next to Alicia's bench. "Sit down." It was as much an order as a request.

Her legs were weak, her heart chugging. Rather than argue, she sat.

"Are you telling me you don't know about his family history of heart disease?" Earl asked.

"I know his father died of a massive coronary over thirty years ago, and his mother died of emphysema and congestive heart failure. But they were both heavy smokers."

"Didn't Jarrod tell you about the chest pains he was experiencing in Russia?"

"Chest pains? He never said anything about any chest pains." The antacid tablets. She remembered him popping them several times for indigestion.

Why hadn't he said anything? Because he'd figured it was nothing, or because he'd been afraid it was serious? She mulled it over in her mind, then realized Earl had been speaking and was now staring at her. "What did you say?"

"You're special to him, Nina." The anger and hostility had faded from his tone, and she understood he was terrified at the thought of losing his friend. "He may not have told you that—he's not very good at sharing his feelings—but it's true."

Silence pervaded the room for several minutes.

"What are you going to do?" Alicia asked quietly.

A nurse appeared. "Mr. Morrison's asking about someone named Nina," she said to Earl.

Nina stood up. "That's me. How is he?"

"The doctor has finished running his tests, so we should know pretty soon. You can go in and see him now, if you like."

Nina followed the nurse into a small examining room.

Jarrod's eyes widened and a relieved smile brightened his face. She walked up to him and kissed him.

"Why didn't you tell me you were having chest pains?"

"I didn't want to scare you."

"That wouldn't have been much consolation if you'd dropped dead on me. What was I supposed to do, stand by your grave and say well at least he didn't worry me?"

He smiled at her sarcasm. "How's Sasha?"

"Sound asleep at the moment."

Jarrod nodded. "Good." He let a moment pass. "Have I made a mistake adopting him? Putting him through all this? Giving him false hope? If I die—"

"Shh." She gently touched a finger to his lips. "You told me once that adopting Sasha was the best thing you'd ever done. I agree, and he'll thank you for the rest of his life.

You've shown him love, opened up a whole new world to him, one of promise and hope. That's a lot from a single parent who's been in his life less than a year."

"If I do die—"

"You're not going to die, sweetheart. I think you just pulled this stunt to get me back." She smiled to show she was teasing. Then she became serious. "The truth is you can't live without me any more than I can live without you. I couldn't sleep in Charlotte, away from you. I love you."

With impeccable timing, a technician entered the room. "How are you feeling?" He checked the monitor hooked up to Jarrod's left arm and made a notation on his clipboard. "Any better since that shot?"

"Immensely," Jarrod answered, his eyes never leaving Nina's. "Are the tests complete?"

"The doctor will be in in a minute." He left.

Jarrod winced. "Why can't they ever just answer a question?"

"Relax." She held his hand.

An older man with shaggy, salt-and-pepper hair, wearing a green smock and a pleasant smile, entered the room. "Well, Mr. Morrison, I have good news and bad news."

Jarrod was too busy gazing at Nina to look at him.

"The good news is that you haven't had a heart attack. In fact your heart appears to be in excellent shape. I wish all my patients were as healthy."

"No heart attack?" Jarrod asked, finally giving him his full attention. "You're sure? What's the bad news?"

"Your gall bladder will have to come out."

He blinked slowly, then blinked again. "This pain is from my gall bladder?"

The doctor nodded. "Have you been experiencing indigestion, heartburn—"

Jarrod agreed. "And chest pains."

"All your other tests have come back normal. Enzymes, liver, kidneys, pancreas, but because of your family history of heart disease, I'd like to run a stress test just to make sure nothing's going on there. It won't take long. We can do it chemically, no need for you to get on a treadmill."

"I don't think I could right now anyway," Jarrod said.

"If you pass the stress test, we'll schedule you for surgery."

THE FIRST THING JARROD realized when he woke up was that he was in a strange place. The second was that he wasn't in pain. Not serious pain, anyway. He had what felt like a stitch in his belly. At last the fog cleared and he remembered where he was and why. He reached down and felt his abdomen. A bandage not much bigger than a Band-Aid covered his navel. Arthroscopic surgery. Stick in a needle and suck out a gall bladder. Marvelous.

He let the words rumble around in his head. *Gall bladder. Not a heart attack.* His heart was fine. He'd passed the stress test with flying colors. His cholesterol was well within safe limits. Ditto his blood pressure. According to the cardiologist, he was a model of cardiovascular health. All these months of worry for nothing but a lousy gall bladder. He wanted to laugh, but suspected doing so would hurt.

Nina had told him she loved him. Before he had a chance to explore those words further, a nurse looked down at him. "How are you feeling?"

"Fine, I think. Better than I did, but I'm thirsty."

She offered him water through a straw from a plastic cup.

"We'll have you up and dancing in no time."

He wanted to dance with Nina. To spin and whirl and get that giddy feeling only she could produce.

"My son—"

"He's camped out in your room with your friends. We'll be taking you there in just a few minutes."

HE WAITED UNTIL EVERYONE else had left, Alicia pushing Earl's chair, Sasha, reluctant to leave, holding his uncle's hand. The boy was still worried, even after the doctor assured him his daddy would be going home later today.

Jarrod rose slowly from the vinyl-upholstered chair and extended his hands. Nina's delicate fingers were warm, steady, comforting.

"I should never have left you," she said.

He gazed into her blue eyes, inhaled the scent of her, floral and feminine. "I tried to tell you that."

"Sasha offered to let Babushka have his room and he'd sleep with Laika on the porch."

"He wants you to stay, too."

"I called my mother."

"Is she coming? She can have the guesthouse. I have other sleeping arrangements in mind for you."

She grinned up at him. "She wants to stay there, in Moscow, in her apartment. She promised to get help with the drinking."

"Do you believe her?"

Nina pursed her lips. "Yes, I do. She's already taken the first step by admitting she has a problem." She swung their hands out like schoolkids. "There's something else."

"What's that?"

"She absolutely wants me to stay here. With you. She said if you don't pop the question, I should."

He raised an eyebrow. "A liberated woman. Very progressive."

Nina brushed her lips against his, and he instantly forgot what his next observation was going to be. He savored the taste of her, felt his healthy heart begin to pound, and gloried in the sensations rocketing through his veins.

"I love you, Nina."

For a moment he was afraid she might cry. "Marry me," he murmured. "Be my wife and Sasha's mother."

# EPILOGUE

"HURRY UP, SASHA, we don't want to be late. Your sister will be waiting for us."

"Coming, Dad." He stepped out of the bedroom wearing his new sport jacket and pressed jeans. The tie was a bit wild to Jarrod's eye, but what did he know about kids' fashions?

"Don't you look handsome," Nina commented.

"I wonder what Anna will be wearing."

"Babushka bought her new clothes last week. Speaking of Babushka, we still have to pick her up. Is the car ready?"

"The driver's been downstairs for the last fifteen minutes," Jarrod said impatiently. "Let's go."

Lydia Petrovna was outside her apartment house talking to a group of men and women, probably building tenants. Since the co-op had been established under her management, the front door had been replaced with a more stylish and functional one, both elevators operated full-time—and didn't stop on the fifth floor when nobody was there. Hallways had been updated and a myriad other repairs performed. There was still a lot of work to be done, but things were definitely improving.

*"Dobroye utro,"* she said as Jarrod held the limousine's door for her. *Good morning.* "My, aren't you dashing," she said to Sasha after climbing into the back seat and kissing his cheek. "Your sister is going to be very impressed by these handsome men picking her up. The girls plan to put on a little concert for us when we get there. Anna has a solo."

"Does she sing good?" Sasha asked.

"Sing well," his grandmother corrected him. "She sings beautifully. You'll see."

"Hear," he corrected her.

Lydia laughed. "Smarty. You'll hear what a lovely voice she has."

"How is her English coming along?" Nina asked.

"She's doing fine. She knows a lot of words, but she's still translating everything into Russian in her head."

"I'll help her," Sasha said. "English is easy."

Nina rumpled his flaxen hair. "You didn't think so a couple of years ago."

Annoyed, he finger-combed his hair back into place. "I was much younger then."

She kissed him on the top of his head. "I love you, you know that?"

"Oh, Mom," he said, showing the natural embarrassment of a boy of ten. But there was no doubt her words pleased him, just as she was thrilled every time he addressed her as Mom.

Using her new cell phone, Lydia called ahead to the orphanage and told them precisely when they would be arriving. The chauffeur pulled into the courtyard. Girls were standing on the steps of the main building. After the guests alighted, the music director gave the downbeat and they began singing "Dixie."

Jarrod was all smiles.

At the director's prompt they began another song. Anna stepped forward from the right end of the first row.

"They found music for 'My Old Kentucky Home,' 'Carry Me Back to Old Virginia' and 'Georgia,'" Lydia explained, "but they couldn't find anything about North Carolina."

Anna began to sing "The hills are alive with the sound of music" in a clear alto, mellow and rich.

Jarrod nodded. "An excellent choice."

The last song was in Russian.

"What does it mean?" Jarrod whispered to Nina.

"It's about a coachman driving a troika. The bells on the horses keep them running, and the coachman sings nostalgically of the fields and woods of the home he's left behind."

It seemed a fitting farewell, for Anna was leaving, not in a coach pulled by three horses, but with three people who would be her new family. The same lawyer Alicia's mother had hired to help her daughter and son-in-law adopt a baby girl had persuaded the Russian bureaucracy to allow Anna to be united with her brother. Nina suspected the money she'd sent her mother to grease a few palms probably had more impact than the lawyer's fancy words. Lydia had certainly delighted in her role.

They dined at a fine restaurant in Moscow, an awesome adventure in itself for a sheltered young girl in a new sunshine-yellow dress. Anna relied on her brother to explain things to her. She spoke to him in Russian. He answered mostly in English, not just because he was anxious for her to learn it, but because he was gradually withdrawing from his mother tongue. He rarely spoke to Nina in Russian anymore. Jarrod had become concerned that he would forget the language completely.

"Don't worry about him," Nina said. "It's a form of rebellion. He'll never really lose the language. Whether he uses it will be his choice."

The adults strolled arm in arm through a park, the children running ahead in their own little world.

"Lydia," Jarrod said, "we'd still like you to come to America with us and be part of our family anytime you're ready. I checked with the embassy. We can get you a visa within a matter of days, and once in the States, you can apply for resident status. You can live in our guesthouse as long as you want."

Nina's mother bit her lip and gripped his arm more tightly. "I'm so glad Nina found you. I would very much like to visit America again—" she'd flown to the States to attend the wedding "—and see more of your beautiful country. But deep in my soul I am a Russian, Jarrod. My place is here."

"Mama, are you sure?" Nina asked.

"I'm sure, Ninochka. This is my world. I'm helping build a new Russia, the one your father never lived to see, but that he worked so hard to bring about, a Russia that is better than the old one. I feel close to him here. Besides, the factory will fall apart without me." She laughed. "And so would our apartment building if I'm not around to oversee everything."

Nina tried to smile. Her mother's decision wasn't a surprise, but it still disappointed her.

"Don't be sad, child," Lydia consoled her. "I am so proud of what you have done with your life. Your father would be, too. And now I am blessed with two wonderful grandchildren."

Nina hugged her mother tightly. "I'll miss you."

Lydia stroked her back. "We'll write. We'll talk on the phone, exchange e-mails, and we can still visit each other. The world isn't nearly as big as it was when I was your age."

JARROD AND NINA EXCHANGED happy glances as they watched Sasha lead his sister by the hand through the crowded airport. He was smaller than Anna and younger, but it didn't seem to matter. He'd matured a good deal in the two years since his adoption, and he basked in the role of worldly wise protector-brother. Jarrod smiled when his son occasionally slipped into his first language without apparently realizing he was doing it—so eager was he to please and…well…show off.

His sister seemed equally delighted to let him, but Jarrod wasn't fooled. Every once in a while he glimpsed the intelligence in her eyes as she assessed her little brother and her surroundings. Already her independence was forming.

"She'll be formidable when she comes into her own," Jarrod commented.

"You noticed." Nina chuckled. "I think they're going to be very good for each other, at least between the battles."

He put his arm around her. "And you're very good for me."

She gazed up at him. "I love you."

The PA system blared with the boarding announcement for their flight.

"Time to go home," he said, and kissed her on the lips.

\* \* \* \*

*Watch out for the last instalment of the*
SUDDENLY A PARENT *series.*
Home for Christmas *by Carrie Weaver*
*is available in December.*
*Don't miss it!*

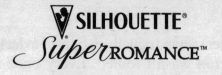

# SILHOUETTE®
# SuperROMANCE™

## THE PROMISE OF CHRISTMAS
### by Tara Taylor Quinn

Shortly before Christmas, Leslie Sanderson finds herself coping with grief, with lingering and fearful memories and with unforeseen motherhood. She also rediscovers a man from her past—a man who could help her to move towards the promise of a new future…

## THE PREGNANCY TEST by Susan Gable
### *9 Months Later*

Sloan Thompson has good reason to worry about his daughter —and that's before she tells him that she's pregnant. Then he discovers his own actions have consequences. This about-to-be grandfather is also going to be a father once again!

## BIG GIRLS DON'T CRY by Brenda Novak

Reenie O'Connell has plenty to cry about when she discovers her husband has betrayed her. Isaac Russell is merely the messenger, but it's hard for Reenie not to blame him. Still, Reenie's initial resentment of Isaac begins to change into admiration and attraction…and maybe something more.

## THE DAUGHTER HE NEVER KNEW
### by Linda Barrett

Guilt and anger made Jason Parker turn his back on his home and family after he lost his twin. Now, after nine years, he's returned to discover that nothing and no one in Pilgrim Cove is the same—and that he's left behind more than he had ever guessed.

### On sale from 20th October 2006

*Available at WHSmith, Tesco, ASDA, Borders, Eason, Sainsbury's and most bookshops*

*www.silhouette.co.uk*

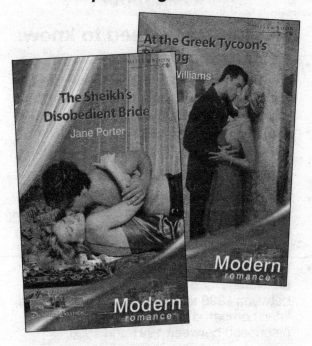

**breast
cancer
CAMPAIGN**

*researching the cure*

# The facts you need to know:

- Breast cancer is the commonest form of cancer in the United Kingdom. **One woman in nine** will develop the disease during her lifetime.

- Each year around **41,000** women and approximately **300** men are diagnosed with breast cancer and around **13,000** women and **90** men will die from the disease.

- 80% of all breast cancers occur in post-menopausal women and approximately 8,200 pre-menopausal women are diagnosed with the disease each year.

- However, survival rates are improving, with on average 77.5% of women diagnosed between 1996 and 1999 still alive five years later, compared to 72.8% for women diagnosed between 1991 and 1996.

**Breast Cancer Campaign is the only charity that specialises in funding independent breast cancer research throughout the UK. It aims to find the cure for breast cancer by funding research which looks at improving diagnosis and treatment of breast cancer, better understanding how it develops and ultimately either curing the disease or preventing it.**

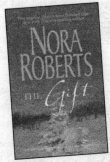

# 2 FREE

## BOOKS AND A SURPRISE GIFT!

We would like to take this opportunity to thank you for reading this Silhouette® book by offering you the chance to take TWO more specially selected titles from the Superromance™ series absolutely FREE! We're also making this offer to introduce you to the benefits of the Mills & Boon® Reader Service™—

- ★ FREE home delivery
- ★ FREE gifts and competitions
- ★ FREE monthly Newsletter
- ★ Exclusive Reader Service offers
- ★ Books available before they're in the shops

Accepting these FREE books and gift places you under no obligation to buy, you may cancel at any time, even after receiving your free shipment. Simply complete your details below and return the entire page to the address below. You don't even need a stamp!

**YES!** Please send me 2 free Superromance books and a surprise gift. I understand that unless you hear from me, I will receive 4 superb new titles every month for just £3.69 each, postage and packing free. I am under no obligation to purchase any books and may cancel my subscription at any time. The free books and gift will be mine to keep in any case.

U6ZED

Ms/Mrs/Miss/Mr ........................................Initials ................................
BLOCK CAPITALS PLEASE

Surname.....................................................................................................

Address .....................................................................................................

..................................................................................................................

..........................................................Postcode.....................................

**Send this whole page to:**
**UK: FREEPOST CN81, Croydon, CR9 3WZ**